SPARTACUS
SWORDS
AND ASHES

J.M. CLEMENTS

SPARTACUS

SWORDS AND ASHES

BASED ON THE STARZ® ORIGINAL SERIES

TITAN BOOKS

SPARTACUS: SWORDS AND ASHES
Print edition ISBN: 9780857681775
E-book edition ISBN: 9780857687289

Published by Titan Books
A division of Titan Publishing Group Ltd
144 Southwark St, London SE1 0UP

First edition January 2012
1 3 5 7 9 10 8 6 4 2

To receive advance information, news, competitions, and exclusive offers online,
please sign up for the Titan newsletter on our website: www.titanbooks.com

A CIP catalogue record for this title is available from the British Library.

Printed and bound in the United States.

DID YOU ENJOY THIS BOOK?
We love to hear from our readers. Please email us at
readerfeedback@titanemail.com or write to us at
Reader Feedback at the above address.

Visit our website: www.titanbooks.com

FOR ANDY WHITFIELD
1972-2011

I

THE IDES OF SEPTEMBER

HE PICKED UP A FRUIT KNIFE AND TAPPED GENTLY ON THE SIDE of
a goblet. The sound barely traveled at all through the noise
around him. Raucous laughter rolled over girlish giggling,
the drums and pipes of the band, and the clash of finger
cymbals from one of the few dancers still standing.

Pelorus climbed unsteadily to his feet, using the table
for support, blocking the diners' view of the two-horned
crest of his house, which hung on the wall behind him.
His fingers clutched at the wine-stained tablecloth,
snagging and dragging several dishes toward him. A
lamp clattered to the floor, bouncing into the shallow
atrium pool, where it joined several floating dishes,
apples, animal bones and a partially submerged, half-
eaten bunch of grapes. The lamp sputtered and died,
leaving a tail of fading smoke and an ever-growing film
of oil on the surface of the pool.

"Friends...! Romans...! I entreat you! Silence for but a
moment or two," Pelorus called, half laughing. Someone

in the shadows told him to fuck off, and there was more merriment all around.

Pelorus wrapped his fingers around the stem of the goblet, forming a crude hammer with which to bang on the table. He brought it down three times with the practiced aim of a man who knew how to smash things up. Red wine dregs shot across the table, adding to the stains.

"Still your tongues! Every one of you!" he shouted.

And then there was something close to silence.

"Gratitude," he began, "for honoring the House of Pelorus with your presence here today, before each of us had consumed too much wine for sense to be made!"

Cheers issued forth from half a dozen diners, and there was polite applause from the women in the room whose hands were not otherwise busy.

"And though wine abounds—" cheers again— "be certain to sample the services of the House of the Winged Cock, flavors sweeter even than what fills cup."

One diner in particular greeted the news with great enthusiasm, half rising to his feet from his couch, tripping and landing on his knees in the shallow pool. Water sloshed over the opposite abutment, while the others laughed and pelted him with grapes.

"Valgus!" Pelorus laughed. "Caius Quinctius Valgus! We shall have to free you from wet attire!" More cheers followed as Valgus's lady companion tugged at his sodden toga, deftly disrobing him in the manner of one well used to such endeavors.

"Welcome, Valgus, old fool," Pelorus said. "Welcome Marcus Porcius, and other dear friends from Pompeii. Welcome, too, guests who have journeyed from Baiae and Puteoli. Welcome good Timarchides, fixer infamous. Your presence here at the table is well deserved and long overdue! I trust you will find the house of Marcus Pelorus most hospitable!"

Pelorus paused, basking in the glow of approbation, watching in the light of the flickering lamps as his guests hollered their thanks. He glowed with their love and then held out his hands in a plea for silence once more.

"We are here for celebration of a day of great fortune for our society of Campanian investors. The noblest among us, Gaius Verres, departs Neapolis in but a few days, to take up a post well deserved as governor... Yes, *governor*! Of all Sicilia!"

Cheers erupted once more.

"To eternal good fortune, and an abundance of coin!"

Pelorus raised his goblet, which had been discreetly refilled, and dropped a stream of wine into the atrium pool. The diners watched in respectful silence as their host invoked the sacred spirits, and offered due homage to the unseen gods.

"I offer this libation in fervent hope of safe travel for our good friend Verres, as he departs Neapolis aboard ship. May his governorship bear fruit of prosperity for his house and for the good people of Sicilia... Those poor, *poor* bastards!"

The loudest cheers of all shook the walls, drifting into the Neapolitan night sky.

"Gentleman, I give you Gaius Verres, our worthy representative in Sicilia!"

The garden erupted with cries of "*VERR-ES! VERR-ES! VERR-ES!*" which soon petered out as heads peered around the gathering.

"Wherever the fuck he has gone!" Pelorus giggled, lifting the tablecloth experimentally, and finding nothing.

"I care not!" Caius Valgus yelled. "Matters of greater

import plead diversion!" And he pointed down in glee at the woman on her knees before him in the atrium pool, her head bobbing enthusiastically between his legs.

Gaius Verres heard people chanting his name, and then the sound of the band striking up once more. The party would have to go on without him as he explored the darker recesses of the house of Pelorus.

Rooms not intended for the celebration were sparsely lit by solitary oil lamps, and many had already sputtered out. The household slaves had other duties, and the party had already far over-run the length of the average taper.

He could hear the woman sneaking up on him, if one could call it sneaking when there were bells on her ankles.

"Verres," she stage-whispered down the hall. "Verres? Do you hide from me?"

He ignored her and lifted his lamp. The room was bare, but for a small shrine to household gods, and a wooden sword hanging from the wall. Verres shook his head and sighed.

"Where lies the adventure, Pelorus, you cock?" he muttered to himself. The ankle-bells tinkled closer with exaggerated steps, and Verres was suddenly enveloped in a sheer scarf of Syrian silk.

"Whose cock?" she asked.

"I was not addressing you," Verres said impatiently.

"Maybe you are not one for conversation," she said, her voice lilting with the hint of a Pompeiian accent.

"I do not desire your company, woman..."

"Successa. I am called Successa."

"As you say." Verres pushed the scarf aside and continued to the next room, fast enough to risk putting out his lamp with the breeze of his passage.

"Successa is my name," she almost sang it, "Successa is my nature."

"I am certain many find that true."

"Why not come close and discover its truth for yourself, Governor Verres?"

"My tastes lie in other achievements."

"But good Pelorus wills it so."

"Leave me and fuck him, then."

With surprising strength, Successa grabbed the governor-designate and pinned him to the wall. Verres dropped the lamp in surprise, dashing its contents into the floor mosaic in a sudden lattice of gentle flames. Successa pressed her hot mouth onto his, her tongue probing, her arms pulling his head closer. She pressed her breasts against him and locked one leg around his calf.

Verres twisted his head away.

"Sample my wares but once, Verres," she insisted, "and your cock will never seek another resting place."

"Leave me be, woman."

Verres pushed her away. His eyes widened as he saw what he was looking for: a staircase down half a floor to the lower level of the house.

"Pelorus's purse is heavy with coin. And I am tasked with lightening both purse and cock," Successa insisted.

She watched in bafflement as Verres gingerly descended the stairs. The former flash of brighter light from the broken lamp was almost fading; the burning oil on the floor already reduced to low simmers of dying blue, the door to the lower level almost entirely hidden in shadow.

"That portal offers path to cells where slaves reside," Successa said disdainfully. "You will discover nothing there of worth."

Verres ignored her and lifted the latch, opening onto a corridor of roughly assembled brick. Torches, not lamps, flickered every ten paces. He snatched up a fresh brand, and lit it from a sputtering stub in a wall-bracket, waiting patiently as the flames licked around the tar-soaked rags until they hissed into fiery life.

Successa pulled the ankle-bells from her feet and followed.

"Gladiators and slaves," she whispered. "Middens and storerooms. Is that what kind of man you are, Verres?"

Verres smiled to himself in the half-light.

"Do you seek the company of women at all?" Successa mused.

Verres snorted.

"Accept, Successa, that my interest simply does not lie with you. My meaning is not to offend."

"Am I too old? Too forward?"

They walked past barred alcoves, each containing one or two dozing male bodies. Some weary heads lifted, only to fall again as Verres passed. Scattered wine flasks in each cell attested to a low-rent copy of the celebrations upstairs.

"I have learned many things," Successa continued. "In Cyprus, the birthplace of the goddess of love. In Egypt, origin of many dark arts of the bedchamber." She frowned at the complete lack of effect she seemed to be having. "In Rome itself, where no true man could resist these thighs…" she added petulantly.

"I simply seek something different," he murmured.

"I can be different."

Verres had stopped outside one of the cells.

"Now that," he said appreciatively. "*That* is different."

The cell was entirely bare, lacking wine or the remains of any supper. Inside was merely a rough covering of sackcloth, drawn over a prone, shapely form. She was already awake, dark eyes glinting in the torchlight.

"Is she a gladiator?" Successa asked.

"Do not be a fool," Verres replied. "Pelorus does not deal solely in gladiators, nor does he tender all coin for spending. This, he locks away as treasure."

The woman in the cage stared back at him impassively, without fear. Verres lifted the slate by the entrance, reading five letters scratched onto it.

"Medea?" he said. "An ill-fated name for such a little mouse."

She clutched the sackcloth against her chest, not carefully enough to hide a shapely breast and pointed nipple. She drew her legs toward her, as if recoiling from the light.

"There is no place to run, little mouse," Verres breathed.

The woman in the cell shook her head in denial, as if willing Verres to disappear, in vain. There was something on her face, like the tendrils of a plant, or matted hair. It was difficult to see in the half-light.

"Suddenly she is coy," Successa observed with a sniff.

"As well she might be," Verres smirked, handing Successa the torch.

"She is nothing," Successa said disdainfully. "Why trouble yourself with earth when you can be grasped by the thighs of the heavens?"

Slowly, ceremoniously, Verres unhooked the lock that lay open in the metal loop, and lifted the bolt that kept the cell door closed. He slid it slowly along its loops with a scraping of dry, old metal.

"Temptation enough for most men," he said to Successa, tugging at his belt. "But one is never closer to the heavens than when one does the taking."

He let his tunic fall to the ground, looking faintly ludicrous in nothing but his sandals. His left hand snaked between his own legs, rubbing gently at his hardening member. His right hand tugged at the heavy cell door, which creaked open on protesting hinges.

"I am a woman valued many times higher than her," Successa protested.

"I do not desire two women," Verres chuckled. "Not this night at least."

"Why do you seek to make your life difficult?" Successa said, scowling. "She will fight you."

"That is my very hope," Verres whispered, moving slowly, deliberately toward the trembling figure.

The woman named as Medea backed further into her corner, her eyes wide with fear, her back meeting unyielding brick.

"You cannot escape from me, little mouse," Verres said. He leaned forward and grabbed her hair in his fist. "So show me what you have to offer."

He dragged her to her feet, the sackcloth falling away to display her naked body. Successa gasped in surprise as she caught sight of a network of regular scarring, at tattoos and swirls, incisions rubbed with colored dirt. The entire left-hand side of the prisoner's body was a work of savage, Scythian artifice, slashed with a thousand knives in careful patterns, or pricked with dyed needles. The woman raised her head in the light, to display a similar pattern across one side of her face—fang-shaped zig-zags across her cheek, and red ochre tendrils reaching across her face and forehead.

"What a work of art you are," Verres breathed admiringly. "A priestess, perhaps. A seer? A valued woman among your tribe, I am sure of it. Highly regarded. Greatly esteemed. And now... here you are. Naked before me."

Successa stared in wonder at the patterns on the woman's body, a world away from the gentle rouges or pinched cheeks of the Roman lady. It was an entire cosmology of symbols and sigils, executed with the barbaric angles and daubs of the primitive peoples of the Euxine Sea. But Verres barely glanced at Medea's decorations. His hands saw no ink. They cupped and caressed the taut, nervous woman's body like any other.

"Rape is the Roman way," Verres said in Medea's ear. "Do you know that, little Medea? We have taken our women this way since before Rome was a city."

Medea's dark eyes stared unblinking into his, unfathomable. Verres felt her breath on his mouth. His hard cock bumped against the soft flesh of her stomach, leaving a gleaming trail like a snail. His free hand caressed her hip, traveling up to the curve of her breast, his fingers circling a hard nipple.

"I see you are excited, little Medea," Verres said with some surprise. "What about me excites you, I wonder...?"

Medea's glance darted to the doorway, where Successa the courtesan stood impatiently.

Successa let out an involuntary sigh of exasperation.

"If your company is paid for, Successa, then remain here and observe!" Verres said. "The idea of an audience amuses me."

"I am at your command, Verres," Successa said, trying in vain to hide a hurt tone.

"Then I command you to witness," Verres said, smiling. "See how a true Roman man imposes his virtue upon the lower races. Watch and lea—"

Verres was cut off mid-sentence as Medea kneed him hard in the groin.

As Verres gasped in pain and surprise, his grip loosed on her hair. He folded on himself, grasping at his bruised gonads, only for his face to come into contact with Medea's knee, forced down onto it by her hands. Verres let out an involuntary yell, keeling over onto the cell floor, but Medea had already forgotten him. Naked, she sprinted straight for the doorway, where Successa watched, frozen in surprise.

Medea grabbed Successa by the throat, her free hand clawing forward at the woman's eyes. They spun through half a turn, until Medea kicked Successa away, back into the cell, simultaneously propelling herself out through the doorway and into the corridor.

Verres was struggling to his feet as Successa landed on top of him, sending both Romans back to the floor in a groaning heap. Successa's dropped torch landed on her expensive, figure-hugging gown, smearing it with viscous, sticky pitch, already burning in multicolored flames.

Medea ran down the corridor, her shadow leaping large on the walls in the light of the newly kindled fires. The shrieks of the burning woman drowned out any other sounds in the enclosed space, but Medea remained focused. She paused momentarily, lost, and then looked at the scuffmarks in the sand left by the feet of her tormentors.

Medea began to sprint along the route they had taken, only to skid to a halt before another cell.

A man spoke to her, in a language she did not know.

She turned to look at him, and he rattled the bars of his cage for effect.

He said something else, but all Medea heard were spits and coughs of Aramaic.

He tried Greek instead, broken Greek, with Latin smeared upon it like dirt.

"Not *slave*! Not *slave*! *Free* Medea *free*?"

Medea smiled with only half her mouth, grabbing the bolt that held the door closed and shoving it aside. She did not even stop to open the door, darting instead to the next cell, and the next, pulling away the opened locks, and slamming their bolts aside.

The occupant of the first cell gleefully shoved open his prison and stumbled into the hallway. The hellish light from Medea's old cell had rapidly diminished, the noise of the woman's shrieks now reduced to whining sobs. The acrid smell of burnt hair drifted into the corridor on a pall of invisible smoke.

"Fucking painted bitch!" roared the voice of the Roman from somewhere within.

Medea peered up at the man she had just freed. He looked back at her expectantly.

"*Vhat?*" he said carefully, his Latin still slurred and unkempt. "Now *vhat?*"

Behind him, several other freed gladiators stumbled into the gloomy corridor, some still bleary-eyed, others alert and ready for action.

Medea gestured toward the staircase up to the atrium.

She chose her words carefully, as best she could.

"*Kill them,*" she said. "*Kill them all.*"

The band was in full sway, the drummer beating a rhythm like that of a galley slave master. Valgus was on top of a woman in the shallow atrium pool, thrusting into her in time to the music. Timarchides lay back on his couch, cradling the head of the girl who fellated him. Marcus

Porcius humped his woman like a dog, grunting and wheezing as he clutched her haunches.

Pelorus lolled smugly on his couch, watching with a contented smile as the Gallic whore ground herself against him. He reached up to tug on her braided red hair, and was faintly disappointed when it came off in his hand. He cast the wig aside with a grumble and concentrated instead on kneading her small breasts.

Medea came out *through* the band, pitching the pipers into the pool, kicking the drummer headfirst onto his drum. The music came to an immediate stop, with only the cymbals playing on, clashing three last times as they bashed into the wall, each other, and then the ground. One spun momentarily like a dropped plate, coming to a swift and silent halt.

The musicians complained loudly, while the partygoers stared in blank amazement at the ferocious naked woman in their midst. The flickering firelight danced on her skin, making her alien pigments seem to writhe in sinuous whirls. The decorations on her face slid into shadows made by the curls of her hair, making it impossible to tell where the hair stopped and the skin began, as the shadows moved like snakes across her skull.

"Do you come to entertain?" Marcus Porcius asked, slapping his woman's behind. Medea punched him in the eye.

Several diners laughed at the sight, but not Pelorus. He shoved his wigless couch-mate to the ground, stumbling to his feet.

"Who allowed her to go free?" he yelled, as the freed slaves began to pour from the same door that had permitted Medea's entry.

"Guards! Guards!" Pelorus called, before Medea leapt

right at him, propelling him to the ground. She snatched up his discarded fruit knife and plunged it into his neck. It caught on something, and Medea wrenched it free with a spray of blood. Pelorus clutched his hand to his throat, desperately trying to staunch the flow, as the gore-soaked Medea upended the nearby dining table into the pond.

Behind her came a platoon of men in loincloths, wielding what meager weapons they had managed to snatch from the house. One held a goblet in each hand. He punched with the metal cups, etching deep red welts into the head of Marcus Porcius. The other freed slaves, armed with fence posts and statuettes, clubbed their way through the dinner party in a scene of terrifying chaos.

Then the slaves came face to face with Timarchides, a towering well-muscled Greek, his skin criss-crossed with the thin white lines of forgotten battles. He stared back at them in shock and surprise, a hurt look on his face, as if they had wounded him more deeply than Pelorus.

For the briefest of moments, the escaped slaves and Timarchides stared into each other's eyes, separated by an insurmountable gulf of liberty. But then the deadlock evaporated in a flurry of limbs, shouts and screams, as the slaves hurled themselves into the fray.

Timarchides dodged a blow from a man swearing at him in Egyptian, who was brandishing a statuette. The snatched deity whisked past Timarchides's head, missing by mere inches. Timarchides leapt forward and grappled with both arms, forcing his assailant backward into the churning waters of the atrium pond. The man's head met the marble poolside with a crack, and Timarchides felt the straining arms relax in his grip.

Dark-clad armored figures poured into the room— the guards from the villa's outer grounds, their numbers increased by members of the nightwatch. With swords and clubs, they swiftly dragged the remaining slaves away from their opponents, cornering them against the far wall of the garden: three bleeding, dishevelled men, and one defiant woman. A guard flung the fifth, unconscious slave at their feet.

Timarchides willed the throbbing in his head to go away. He covered one eye with his hand in an attempt to stop seeing double. But Pelorus lay dead on the floor, surrounded by the wreckage of his last party, his throat torn open like a second mouth, his life's blood swirling into the oily surface of the pond, flowing across the water toward the drain at the far end.

"Dozens of slaves occupy the cells below," Timarchides said, addressing the man from the east as if he were their leader. "And yet, you five alone bring death to them all. "

The man from the east stared back, uncomprehending, at Timarchides.

"Vhat?" he said. "No."

"'*Vhat*' indeed," Timarchides said. "You bray as if a fucking horse. Do you not know what you have done?"

The slave simply stared back at him.

"You repay your master's kindness with the greatest price. His life and your own. And all other slaves in this house."

"Command and I shall strike the blow," the lead guard declared.

"No," Timarchides said. "The death must be answered publicly, as Pelorus must be mourned."

"We can kill them now," insisted the guard, glancing anxiously at his men.

"Lock them all away," Timarchides ordered curtly. "They shall die a slave's death. And all shall see it."

II

JUPITER PLUVIUS

"IT LOOKS LIKE RAIN," GOLDEN-HAIRED VARRO SAID GRIMLY.

Spartacus looked at him and smiled. He shifted his feet experimentally in the sand of the training ground, still damp from the previous day's shower.

"For a change?" he asked.

"Back inside, Rain Bringer," Varro said. "I do not wish to fight in rusty armor."

But Spartacus waited, ready, his wooden training sword and battered shield at the ready. The training space referred to simply as "the square" resounded with the clonks and smacks of wooden swords on wooden shields.

"Look to the heavens," Varro continued. "They will soon break open."

"As will your head," Spartacus responded, "before it has chance to get wet."

Varro turned pleadingly to Oenomaus, the towering African trainer who frowned down upon them like an irritated god.

"Doctore, I beg you," he pleaded.

But the black man shook his head and stood with his arms folded, his whip twitching in his hand.

"A gladiator," Oenomaus said quietly, "has no fear of *water*."

The other fighters laughed uneasily.

"A gladiator," Oenomaus said, his voice rising in volume, his annoyance now more apparent, "does not fear a *little rain*."

Oenomaus addressed not merely the truculent Varro, but the whole gathering of warriors. The few practice fights that had been already underway had swiftly ground to a halt as the assembled fighters took the hint to stop and listen.

Oenomaus stood, his hands on his hips, at the cliff's edge that formed one side of the ludus training ground, a vast open expanse of tantalizing freedom—at least to any man who could imitate Icarus and fashion his own wings. To mere mortals, it was a wall by another name, an empty space above a drop to certain death, and the distant vista of the Campanian hills, wreathed with clouds and glimmers of faraway storms.

"The best arenas have sailcloths drawn across the stands," Oenomaus bellowed, "to protect the noble public from the sun's excesses. If the weather is bad, the awnings will hold the rain from the faces of the crowd. Therefore the editor of the games, who has invested a year's coin in their preparation, need not cancel merely for the sake of some water falling from the sky. The sailcloths do not extend over the arena itself!"

"Doctore," Varro said humbly.

But Oenomaus was not finished.

"A gladiator fights in all weathers. He must be ready

for all conditions, at the editor's whim." Oenomaus allowed his voice its full potential to boom. "If the editor demands that you fight on stilts, you fight on stilts. If the editor elects to clad you in the costumes of gods or heroes, you will wear those costumes and play your parts. If the editor wishes to hold games in winter on a mountainside, you will fight on ice and in snow. Is that understood?"

"Doctore!" the men chorused.

"The editor seeks new thrills and spectacles. He demands weapons and mismatched opponents. The House of Batiatus does not arrange the games. The House of Batiatus rents your flesh to any editor that will pay the price, and prepares you for victory. The gladiator is prepared for all circumstances, because if he is not, he will *die* without honor. Is that understood?"

"Doctore!"

"Then fight!" Oenomaus cracked his whip for emphasis, its leather tip snapping through the air scant inches from Varro's blond curls. The noise of wood clattering on wood recommenced all around them, and Spartacus waited impassively.

Varro snarled and charged toward him. Spartacus waited calmly as the burly Roman advanced.

But then the Thracian charged in another direction, slanting away from the Roman, charging and stabbing at an invisible opponent. His lunge presented his shield arm against the charging Varro; his sword thrust outward at thin air, at the place where an opponent might be.

Varro was unable to veer to the left: such a move would have thrown him straight onto his opponent's sword-point. Instead, he faltered, slamming obliquely into the Thracian's shield as Spartacus wheeled and lifted his arm.

Varro was sent flying, landing heavily on his back, wheezing, the breath knocked out of him.

Spartacus lurched forward, the tip of his sword suspended a thumb's width from Varro's throat. The fight was over before it had even begun.

Laughing, Varro raised two fingers in supplication, and the two men waited for an imaginary signal from an absent audience. They glanced up at the balcony, where a lone figure stood motionless, her robes fluttering in the breeze.

On a better day, Lucretia, wife of Batiatus, might have played along and given the signal for manumission. But although she stared right at the two men, she saw nothing. Her mind was elsewhere.

Lucretia watched from the balcony through eyes reddened by weeping, her expression unreadable. She did not smile at Varro's protestations of Thracian cheating, nor did she stay to watch as the Roman clambered to his feet for a rematch. She turned slowly and walked back inside the house, her ears deaf to the continued din of wooden swords on wooden shields. She swept down a long corridor lined with the busts of former gladiators, stone memories of days past.

"Good news after bad!" Quintus Lentulus Batiatus cried, brandishing a scrap of damp papyrus.

Lucretia did not even acknowledge her husband's excitement, breezing past him into the shrine of the household gods. Too late, she realized there was no other exit. She was cornered.

She turned to meet her husband, straining to smile.

"Word sent that Pelorus does not require us for the Neapolis games," Batiatus continued.

"After such preparations—" Lucretia began.

"For a gubernatorial celebration, yes. Plans have been revised."

"We do not bend to change like Macedonian whores."

"Events beyond the control of good Pelorus."

"What events—?"

"That of death. Death of our good friend Pelorus himself at the hands of his own slaves," Batiatus said with a grin.

For a moment, the house was silent, but for the tinkling of a distant fountain, and the muffled footsteps of a slave going about her duties. Lucretia blinked.

"I can see the loss grieves you," she said eventually.

"My heart breaks," Batiatus smirked, "at the loss of coin."

"The Neapolis games were our last booking this month. And our Prince of Mars lies wounded..."

"And yet I proclaimed good news, as well."

"How can you jest when our best gladiator fights for his life?"

"Crixus?" Batiatus said. "It is Spartacus who is the Champion of—"

"Crixus will soon rise to reclaim what he has lost!" Lucretia shouted, louder than she had expected.

Batiatus shuffled uneasily.

"My heart is touched," he said, "that you are moved to such concern for our business and our *slaves*."

"And where is this good of which you spoke," Lucretia muttered, fussing with some of the smaller statuettes among the Batiatus household gods. She picked up the figure of her late father-in-law and gazed at it, her fingers tracing the face of the small metal token. She then carefully set it back down among the other *imagines*, facing away from its companions, as if lost or addled.

"There will be *funeral* games, Lucretia," Batiatus said. "And the editorship requires gladiators beyond the limits of the town."

"For what reason?"

"The House of Pelorus is finished. Those slaves will suffer execution. And then even the killers will be killed."

"A terrible thing, to be betrayed by ones so trusted," Lucretia said, sucking in air through her teeth.

She stepped from the shrine back to the green-walled atrium, her husband scurrying to keep up with her. She looked around for some sign of her slave Naevia, hoping to busy herself on some ladies' business that Batiatus would find tedious.

"A terrible thing for Pelorus, but a thing of opportunity for us!" Batiatus protested, slapping the papyrus for emphasis. "We only need send a few gladiators, and the very nature of the event assures them all of victory."

"Do you not think this one last insult from Pelorus? To force you to make haste across Campania on some pointless enterprise of maintenance, little better than sweeping up behind horse? Has that man not cost you enough time?"

"We have but time to waste, beloved. All Capua is in mourning for the… *tragic* death of Ovidius. Preventing indulgence in the celebration of our recent victory until nine long days have passed."

"And you would pass day in other town, until our own offers warmer clime?"

"My thought exact. Let Spartacus, Barca and a few promising recruits take to the sun, far from the cloud of Ovidius and the pale of his death."

"All to scrape coin?"

"A much needed infusion. And, of course, the chance to bid proper farewell to good Pelorus."

"And what of it to you, if his funeral passes without remark?"

"I care not a shit for his departure from this world," Batiatus said. "But let us show decorum befitting of this noble house and lend grace to his disgraced house."

"Quintus, must we?"

"We were mutual *hospes*! His threshold was as our own, should we ever have crossed it."

"An opportunity of which we seldom availed ourselves. Nor he with us."

"He shall surely be laid to rest before the calends of October, but three days' hence!"

"Then you had best depart immediately. Lest he be set aflame before you arrive."

"Lucretia, please!"

"He resides in Neapolis, Quintus! Or had you forgotten?"

"Since when do you not care for Neapolis? And the opportunity it allows to part with coin? To say nothing of the sea air," he protested.

"It smells of rotten eggs."

"The friendly local citizens?" Batiatus suggested.

"Quarreling Greek refugees and fishwives."

Something flashed in the sky, like the glint of a sword in the sun. Batiatus paid it no heed, his eyes locked on his wife, entreating Lucretia to offer some iota of spousal support.

"The broad sweep of the bay. Those sparkling waters," he pleaded.

"Muggy in summer. Choppy in winter."

"And here we are, swiftly approaching harvest and

equinox! An auspicious occasion to visit."

Batiatus paused, a broad, winning smile on his face begging his wife to acknowledgment. As if to spite him, there was a distant rumble of thunder on the Capuan hills. A drip of errant drizzle dashed against his cheek, then another.

Lucretia held out her hand inquisitively, craning her head out into the open space of the atrium. She stared up at the low, gray clouds overhead.

"Is that rain?" she mused.

"Impossible," Batiatus replied.

Behind him, the waters of the atrium pond showed dots of activity. Points of water flecked on the previously calm surface, the impact of unseen raindrops. Across the courtyard, Lucretia saw silent flecks of rain dashing against the upper walls, freckling the brown clay plaster into a deeper shade of red.

There was another flash of lightning, and a crackle of thunder almost immediately after it.

Batiatus glanced behind him in annoyance, in time to see the drizzle shift to a downpour, churning the waters of the atrium pond into a rough sea, spattering the green inner walls a murky dark gray. Batiatus shivered involuntarily, and realized that the lower hem of his toga was already drenched.

"Jupiter's cock!" he shouted, snatching his robe from its puddle.

Lucretia turned from the rain's chill, gliding back toward the antechambers of the house.

"Jupiter Pluvius, the divine bringer of rain, himself counsels a roof over your head, Quintus," she called, not looking back at her husband.

"All summer I prayed only for rain," admitted Batiatus. "Now I tire of it."

"Then rest indoors and wait for such storms to pass."

"This storm? It is but trifle," Batiatus declared.

"As is all unwelcome change. Be it by men or gods."

Their upraised voices echoed through the house, but did not travel to the outer gardens. The rain saw to that, pelting onto the Capuan clifftop with increasing volume, until it drowned out all other sounds in a relentless rattle. It pattered on the leaves of the formerly parched trees. It drummed on the cracked ground. It tapped an irritating, unceasing tempo on the waxed tarpaulin of the litter that approached the house of Batiatus.

The four bearers, one shouldering each end of the two carrying poles, struggled with each step to maintain their footing. Feet used to the reliable, measured flagstones of the Appian Way scraped and slipped on treacherous dips and uncleared tree-roots. Three of the slaves did not even look up, crouching their heads beneath their sodden hoods and concentrating merely on putting one foot in front of the other. Only the lead bearer, standing at front-right, exposed his head to the rain, squinting through the storm in case of oncoming traffic.

The litter and its bearers had no other company on the remote track. They plodded on through the rain, their pace picking up as the welcoming lights loomed nearer. The cargo was light, barely noticeable to accomplished porters, such that when the leader called halt, the litter was raised off their shoulders and lowered to the ground with ease.

Within the courtyard of the Batiatus villa, shadowy figures scurried to the portal. The occupant of the litter stirred, placing a foot gingerly on the damp ground. A figure substantially smaller than the vast man's cloak that wrapped it scampered through the storm toward the entrance of the house itself, and the indistinct sound of a couple in the middle of an argument.

"It is inconvenient," Lucretia said.

"Inconvenient!" Batiatus yelled in response.

He inhaled sharply through his teeth, raising his arms up in exasperation at the walls around him. He glared hotly at a wall of painted finches and songbirds, and thought meanly of roasting them on spits.

"It is inconvenient that my prize gladiator lays pierced with hole the size of Rome's Cloaca Maxima, unable to enter the arena any time soon."

"I realize that," Lucretia said carefully. "It grieves me. It grieves me sorely that Crixus is—"

"It is *inconvenient*," Batiatus interrupted, "that this ludus has but one opportunity to secure coin in coming month and it lays forty-five thousand paces from this place, in a miserable, stinking, boy-loving, infestation of Greeks!"

"I thought we liked Neapolis?" Lucretia said with the faintest of smiles.

"I *despise* Neapolis!" Batiatus spat. "A filthy backwater population brimming with smug merchants, pushy beggars, and unruly street urchins, built upon slope toward sea. Every journey a torment of travel uphill, through fucking stone stairways."

"Surely you must travel downhill at least half the time, beloved?"

"And yet, all directions lead uphill."

"Now who defies reason?"

"Pelorus was a dear friend," Batiatus said.

"You loathed each other," Lucretia responded.

"As siblings squabble over pets, we tussled over gladiators. Though given predilections of my Capuan colleagues, my occasional auction-block competition with Pelorus seems now the very pinnacle of amity."

"Still, no reason for *my* involvement in your farewells."

"All of Neapolis society will be there."

"I care not."

"Pelorus shall have in death what he never had in life. Accord as a man of wealth and virtue. Mourners from the patrician class. A funeral fit for a high-ranking Roman citizen."

"I repeat. I care not."

"Pelorus will not be regarded as mere lanista. Important people shall celebrate his life, Lucretia. *Important* people."

"And you?"

"Shall be seen as dear friend to the departed, by his other friends. For which I shall require the presence of *my wife*."

"You will find that Neapolis has plenty that can be hired for service."

There was a shadow in the doorway. A slave had approached, swiftly and silently, as protocol demanded.

"What is it, Naevia?" Lucretia said.

"Apologies, domina, but there is a visitor," the young girl replied, eyes lowered to the floor.

Naevia got no further before the subject of her message caught up with her. A figure appeared behind her, wrapped in a coarse cloak, dripping water on Lucretia's clean flagstones. Underneath the cloak, there was the hint of green Syrian silks, and dainty, pedicured toes.

"Pardon this intrusion," a female voice said, lifting her veil to reveal flaxen blonde tresses, coiled into sodden ropes by the rain. Cheeks usually concealed beneath Tyrian rouge were now flushed with their own glow, with specks of dislodged kohl like ashen tears above an exhilarated smile.

"Ilithyia!" Lucretia exclaimed with exaggerated, mannered delight. "I thought you to be in Rome."

"Such was my hope," Ilithyia said, pushing her wrap into the hands of Batiatus as if he were no more than a cubiculum slave.

"But muddy tracks and tired bearers conspired to find me here," Ilithyia sighed deeply, as if it were the end of the world, "scant steps from your yard and your doors."

"It pains me that we cannot offer you covered walkway," Batiatus said, directing his eyes heavenward, "under which to arrive more comfortably."

"Quite so," Ilithyia said.

"Perhaps decorated in gold," Batiatus continued to Lucretia under his breath, "and with couches every few paces that you might take your rest."

"I thought I might have to walk all the way to Atella to find proper lodging, one closer to civilization," Ilithyia continued, oblivious.

"*Civilization?*" Batiatus muttered.

"We are delighted to receive you," Lucretia said, shooting a sidelong glance at her husband.

"I cannot presume to impose," Ilithyia said. "After all, we are not mutual hospes. I cannot simply turn up at your door—"

"Yet here you are!" Batiatus smiled through gritted teeth.

"Our house is your house," Lucretia interjected

swiftly. "Naevia will see you given proper quarters." She glanced at her slave to ensure that the message was received.

"My bearers shall bring my impediments from the litter," Ilithyia said, following Naevia from the room. "Then, we shall drink and talk of scandalous things!" Ilithyia chuckled conspiratorially, and then was gone.

Batiatus waited, seething, as Ilithyia's footsteps receded. He bundled up her cloak and threw it contemptuously into a corner, before wheeling on his wife to hiss in suppressed rage.

"Even in accepting our hospitality she shits on our name."

"We are lucky to hear her speak it."

"This is our *home*. We were spreading myrrh on our lentils when the Romans were still running around the forests sucking off wolves."

"*Suckling*, Quintus. Ilithyia is giddy with the glory of Rome. She speaks without thought."

"Oh, she thinks. She thinks all too carefully. Every word carefully placed to cut us down. She forces her way into our house—"

"Where she is *very* welcome. She is an emissary of Rome's great and good."

"So she keeps saying."

"She is a doorway to aediles and consuls. She has the ears of men of power."

"For herself. Not for us, as we are not hospes. A point she made certain to make."

"A matter merely of protocol and politesse."

"If you were to knock on her door in Rome, with Deucalion's deluge pouring out of the sky, with Neptune himself *pissing* on your head, she would order the gates slammed shut in your face. We are not fit to be accorded hospitality in her home, yet she thrusts herself upon ours as if tavern in—!" Batiatus suddenly stopped speaking, his eyes wide in surprise.

"What is it?" Lucretia asked, peering behind her, in case her husband had seen a rodent or a spider.

"Atella," Batiatus said. "She journeys to Atella."

"And?"

"It is five hours' march to the south."

"Yes, Quintus. A fact known to all."

"On the road to Neapolis!"

Those gladiators who had shields held them over their heads to keep off the rain. Those who did not did the best they could with the flats of wooden swords, or lifted helmet visors. They stood, intently, watching two lone gladiators who stood waiting in the training ground. The storm pelted every man with rain, but none voiced a word of complaint.

"Now," Oenomaus bellowed over the noise of the downpour, "observe their footing. Barca, the Carthaginian giant, the strongest and heaviest among you, shall fight as murmillo." Oenomaus gestured with his hand, and Pietros the slave darted forward with a sword and heavy shield for the Carthaginian.

"Spartacus," Oenomaus continued, "is fleet of foot, and not the heaviest of our fighters. He shall fight..." Oenomaus glanced over to the weapons store, where Pietros was already fishing out the sword and light shield of the Thracian style.

"...as retiarius," Oenomaus finished. Pietros glanced at him in confusion, as did Spartacus himself.

"I do not fight with net and trident, Doctore," Spartacus noted.

"Indeed you do not, Champion of Capua," Oenomaus said, "and yet you will come to know them intimately in the arena. Hold them in your hands, so you will know how to defeat them."

Pietros scurried over with a fisherman's net and three-pointed spear. Spartacus hefted the trident experimentally, feeling its strange displacement.

"Note the unfamiliar weight of the trident," Oenomaus continued. "Best held either right behind the head or at the far end of the haft. In either mode, an ideal weapon... *for spearing fish!*"

The men laughed as Spartacus looked on grimly. Barca laughed loudest of all, swinging both his sword and shield in great, deadly arcs about him.

"Do I hear a coin bet on Barca, the Beast of Carthage?" Oenomaus called.

"If I had a coin I would wager it so," Varro answered.

Spartacus shot the blond Roman a scowl.

"Apologies, my friend!" Varro laughed. "You are not destined for fishing."

"We shall see," Oenomaus said, lifting his whip and cracking it through the falling rain. "Begin!"

Spartacus clutched the net in his fist like a forgotten towel—he had not even had the chance to spread it out and check its dimensions. Barca had no such doubts, charging directly at his foe.

Spartacus hurled his trident straight at the oncoming Carthaginian.

The gladiators gasped as Barca barely halted the trident—the triple-points pierced right through his hastily raised shield, and stuck fast. The weight of the trident dragged down Barca's shield arm, and the Carthaginian fervently tried to shuck the dead weight as the Thracian launched his second attack.

Spartacus whirled the net around his head, feeling the strong pull of the round lead weights at its edges. He leaned forward and caught Barca's head with the edge of the net, causing the hulking Carthaginian to yell out in pain and surprise. Barca held out his sword to block the net on its next swing, but Spartacus had stepped another two paces closer, causing his net to wrap around Barca's sword. Barca pulled back, in an attempt to drag Spartacus and his net closer to him, only for Spartacus to let go of the net altogether.

Barca's eyes widened in surprise. He lost his footing on the wet sand and mud, pitching backward and landing with a cry of expelled air on the soft sand. He scrambled to get back to his feet, but slipped a second time, while Spartacus grabbed the fallen trident. The Thracian jammed the business end of the trident—Barca's impaled shield still attached—into the Carthaginian's face, temporarily blinding him as Spartacus snatched up Barca's fallen sword and—

"Stop!" Oenomaus' voice rang through the courtyard.

Spartacus froze mid-action, ready to stab the sword down between the ribs of the man who had previously wielded it. The gladiators clapped politely, while Barca disdainfully scraped wet mud and sand off his body.

Barca stared silently, as if willing daggers to fall from the sky and stab Spartacus to death.

"Observe how circumstances can change. Barca fought with his weapons of habit, on ground he thought familiar. Spartacus fought with weapons unfamiliar, and…" even Oenomaus could not resist a smile, "did so in a manner most unorthodox. The change in terrain has served to his advantage."

Oenomaus waited for his words to sink in, as the rain continued to spatter down upon the gathering of men. They stared back at him attentively, squinting as the water ran into their eyes.

"Enough," Oenomaus declared. "To the baths, let oil replace rain."

The gladiators trudged indoors, dawdling only insofar as seemed appropriate, determined to prove that nothing so ineffectual as mere rain could cause them to retreat. Oenomaus was last to leave the square, just as he was habitually the first to arrive there each morning.

"A moment, doctore," Batiatus called, as the towering warrior descended the steps toward the steam room.

"Your will," Oenomaus said. He stood, the water pooling at his feet, and waited for his master's instruction.

"I require five men, in the best condition."

"I will set to purpose," Oenomaus replied. "But the next exhibition is not until—"

"Not for Capuan rabble," Batiatus explained. "Those ungrateful vermin will have to wait their turn. A new audience awaits us, in Neapolis."

"Ah," Oenomaus said. "I have heard speak of the death of Pelorus."

"Word would not travel so fast," Batiatus muttered, "if I were to remove tongues with knife."

"Older voices recalled days spent under roof of this ludus," Oenomaus said. "They meant no malice in its telling."

"No matter," Batiatus said. "The men will be on cart tonight, and bound for Atella by mid-morning, and Neapolis by night."

"Mercury would struggle to sprint such a course," Oenomaus observed guardedly.

"I myself will be spending the next two days in cursed litter," Batiatus scowled. "Find carter to add human cargo for extra coin."

"I shall make preparations for us."

"You will remain."

"But—"

"You will train the men in preparation for exhibition here in Capua. Ashur will handle accounts in my absence."

Oenomaus looked troubled.

"And Domina?"

"Lucretia?" Batiatus laughed. "The woman only wants the wants of her 'friend.' And her friend has business in Neapolis. Trust me, doctore, she makes preparation for departure as we speak!"

III

HOSPES

HE DREAMED OF FORESTS IN SNOW, A SUNSET SHOT THROUGH
with pink and bright orange that lingered on the ground,
and icy trees, making the winter seem warm—until one
touched it. He tramped through the trees in armor bought
at a high price from Greek merchants. He was one of
many Thracian warriors strung out through the forest
like grazing deer, their breath lingering on the air like
phantoms. Each man bore the round shield and crested
helmet of a hoplite, with greaves and spear and leaf-
shaped sword.

The Greeks avoided war in winter. They rarely fought
on mountains. Their battles all so conveniently arranged
when everyone was available to meet on the plains, and
before the weather turned bad. Their armor similarly was
seasonal, and with little thought of the uses to which it
might be put to in cold, forbidding Thrace.

Buskins beneath the greaves kept much of the cold
away from his legs. An animal skin, lashed tightly to

his chest, kept snow at bay with its tawny fur. Only his hands felt the cold—barely able to grip the heavy spear as he advanced, just one warrior in the ragged line of Thracians, picking through the forest.

There was a howling. A distant, mournful howling like that of a wounded wolf. He knew what it was, and that it required hilltops and a strong breeze. He peered through the trees in search of a distant ridge, in time to catch the sight of a dragon's head flashing bronze in the dying sunlight. It appeared above the hill, a long streamer-flag playing out behind it, more and more of its long metal neck becoming visible as its bearer reached the summit of the hill.

Another! There was a second dragon head—it, too, a decorative mounting on a long metal tube, held aloft by one of the bestial standard-bearers of the Getae. The winter wind gusted along the hilltop and into the dragon's mouth, creating the mournful howling, extending the streamers out behind it almost horizontally.

Sura had warned him of a red serpent. Was this what she had meant?

He sniffed, the Thracian cold biting at his nostrils, and squinted at the standards on the hills. His fellow auxiliaries stared along with him, peering into the fading light, searching for archers. But there were only the twin metal standards and their characteristic sound... and a chariot, pulled by two horses.

"The leader of the Getae?" Bronton mused from close by, leaning on his lance.

"No," he said. "See how the tattered dress flaps in the wind. See how the arms are raised in incantation, dripping with charms and bones and bracelets. It is one of their warrior-priestesses."

The wind dipped, lessening the unearthly lament from the horns, affording the briefest of moments when a human voice could carry down from the hill. It was an unearthly, ululating cry, like the call of some mythical carrion bird. The priestess jumped from her chariot and danced on the hilltop, jerking to a music that only she could hear, stamping on the ground and calling down unseen retribution from the multicolored sky.

"Their spells will not save them," Bronton muttered. It was at that moment that the axe hit him.

It clanged into the side of his Greek-made helmet, bouncing harmlessly off into the trees, but heralding a danger closer at hand than a mountain-top sorceress. Getae warriors leapt from behind trees, and out of holes in the ground, throwing off snowy cloaks in a sudden mist of white powder.

He watched as Bronton swung to meet the new assault, screamed a futile negation as Bronton's spear caught on a tree-root, watched in melancholy slow-motion as the hulking warrior struggled, slowly, too slowly, to prepare himself to meet the Getae charge.

The soldier disappeared, engulfed beneath a wave of the animal skins and skull-masks of the wild Getae warriors. The Thracian line was stretched out too far. Its Greek armors were designed for a phalanx — a push-and-shove with locked shields on a notional Boeotian plain, far, too far, removed from this cold, chaotic day on the uneven ground of a winter forest.

But, like Bronton, he would not go down without a fight. He hurled his spear at the onrushing wall of Getae, whipping out his sword and yelling in defiance. His first victim fell screaming, tripping those behind him as they tumbled over his fallen body. He was waiting for them with his sword and shield, the latter shunting foes aside, the former cracking through their fearsome bone masks into the soft flesh beneath.

He heard other Thracians rushing to the point of ambush. He delighted in the wet thuds of spears and swords connecting with Getae bodies. He exulted as their enemies' shrieks of battle-readiness gave way to cries of pain and surprise, as the Thracians converged on his position.

In the distance, he could hear the babbling incantations of the Getae sorceress, but paid her no heed. There was business to attend to closer to hand. His dented shield was torn from his arm. He grabbed a Getae warrior by his topknot and dragged him before him, slitting his enemy's throat, and keeping the body clutched in front of him as a human shield. The man twitched and jerked as Getae spears prodded at his dying form, while fresh blood coursed down his killer's body, bringing welcome warmth to a cold battle.

The snow-covered ground became a clash of pinks and crimsons, darkening with the death of the day, not from the sunset, but from life-blood splashed in torrents. Warm steam rose from the ground, creating an unearthly mist, as if the surviving warriors were surrounded by the departed souls of their fellows.

He fought amid such ominous shades, seeing only the foes in front of him, trusting to his Thracian comrades to shield his flanks from the Getae. Their darting, whirling attacks seemed to slow, as if coming at him through water. His reactions, too, dawdled to a crawl, and, though his mind remained as swift, his body was slow to react, like a plough pulled by tired oxen.

There were flashes of other memories. Of places and times that were far removed.

Sura giggled and splashed water at him, knee deep in the rushes at the bank of the River Istros, in spring.

Their mouths met, their lips entwined, their bodies naked in a warm summer field.

She glowed with pride, as he handed her father the casket containing her bride-price. It had been autumn.

And Sura was at his side in the snow. That was not right. He remembered this battle. He had fought in this battle for real, when he was a younger man. His wife had not been there. He tried to tell the dream that his wife should not be there, but his mouth was too slow to respond.

The dream-Sura danced through the battle in glee, laughing as he fought his way toward her. She ducked swords and spears, and entwined herself around tree trunks, barely clothed.

"Return to me, my husband!" she cried, her arms outstretched as if to embrace him. "Kill the Getae and return, so that we may make more Thracians!" She laughed, musically, as the first arrows whisked past her head.

Even with time slowed, the arrows darted through the forest as swift as wasps, in twos and threes, and then in dozens, their passage marked by low, threatening thrums as their fletchings buzzed in the cold forest air.

He looked back at the hilltop, saw the sorceress, her arms exulting in command before a triple line of archers, preparing for a second salvo. One side of her face seemed decorated with tattoos in swirls and spikes. She raised her arm, her sleeve falling away, revealing similar pigments there. And then her arm dropped in a decisive movement, unleashing a humming, whistling wall of death.

The Greeks had no time for bows and arrows. Archers hunted birds and game—not men. No *real* man brought a bow to war, and so Greek design did not defend against such attacks. Greek-made armor was limited, and designed to thwart strikes from a phalanx of men with spears and swords directly ahead. It was not fashioned to protect the extremities and flanks from cowardly darts from a distance.

As the arrows streamed into the forest, they caught the Thracians unprepared. They broke comically on helmets or caught in crests; they thudded into trees and caromed from shields. But the arrows kept coming, darkening the sky in a swarm, hitting home with the sheer law of averages, plunging into eye sockets, cracks in armor; lodging in upper arms and lower ankles.

He felt the sting of an arrow in his heel, and laughed at it—wounded like Achilles.

For a moment, he felt unfamiliar sunlight dapple on his eyelids, and rocked as if on a moving cart. He heard the clop of horse's hooves on a road and stirred, briefly, in realization. A voice, indistinct and impotent, reminded him that this forest battle had happened long ago.

He need not fear. He would not die.

This was a memory! This was a dream! This was not really happening. He willed himself to wake up, but still fought on, trapped in his invisible cage. Because Sura had not been there when this battle took place, and some part of his dream-self could not let her go unprotected, not even in sleep.

Sura stood, oblivious, in the forest, picking an out-of-season fruit from a dead tree. She held it up toward him, her hand bearing an apple crawling with maggots, as another volley of arrows hummed into the forest.

He shouted at her to get down, to drop to the forest floor, but instead she held out her arms toward the oncoming swarm. He saw her pierced in a hundred places, bloodied in a forest of fletchings as she screamed and called out his name—

"*Spartacus!*" Varro's voice pierced his dream.

"I am not..." he began, groggy. Autumn sunlight scattered through trees that moved overhead. He lay on wood... on a cart, on a moving cart, in chains. The other slaves stared at him in some irritation.

"You dreamed," Varro said. "Loudly, of terrible things."

Spartacus shook his head and wiped his eyes.

"I dreamed," he said, "I was free."

There was little to say. The cart rumbled along the road, its horses steadily dragging it up the gentle undulations of the Appian Way, south toward Neapolis. In its rear were stacked crates of garum—the fish sauce no Roman kitchen could do without—and a huddle of human cargo.

There was little to see. Fields, forests and hills. But no slave farmer cared to greet a passing cart, and no lurkers watched from the woods.

There was little to do. Spartacus sat, silent, lost in thought. The giant Barca's eyes were closed, his eyelids twitching, dreaming of Carthaginian glories. Cycnus, the hairy Galatian, lolled, not asleep but not awake, rolling with the shaking of the cart. Bebryx, of the close-knotted hair and jet-black skin, glared out at the forest. When their cart rumbled past travelers on the road, he stared at them defiantly, as if inviting attack. Varro wore his own chains heavily, unused to manacles but unable to protest to the freeman—a voluntary gladiator was still a voluntary slave, and lacked the freeman's right to better treatment.

Something smelled.

Spartacus sniffed tentatively at the air.

"Perhaps," Varro said, "one of the garum kegs has split?"

Nobody answered him, unless by answer one could mean the endless rambling of their traveling companion, an emaciated old man in rags, his head covered in sores, his arms perilously thin.

"Are you him?" he asked the air. "Are you the one?"

The gladiators did their best to ignore him, as they had done ever since Capua.

"I had a son," he continued. "I think. I had a son. I never saw him. When I was strong, I was taken for breeding. I never saw her face. I never saw her again. But if my seed was true, then she was the mother of my child."

Suddenly, the wasted, bony hand clutched at Spartacus's arm. The milky eyes fixed him with unexpected clarity.

"Do not get old," the man said. "Do not get old."

"I am a gladiator," Spartacus replied. "A state I am not likely to meet."

There was the unmistakeable sound of evacuating bowels.

"By the gods," Varro said, wincing. "It is not the fish sauce. To be sure, it is not the fish sauce."

The old man seemed unaware that he was sitting in his own filth.

"The Gracchi will save us," the old man said. "The brothers Gracchi. Free corn for the masses. Free land for those willing to work. Free games!" He cackled with excitement. "No work! No need to work! Free corn! Free games!"

"Who are the Gracchi?" Spartacus asked.

"Demagogues, long dead," Varro said. "Only after casting spell of promise."

"How long dead?" Spartacus asked.

"He would have been a child," Varro replied, gesturing with his manacled hand at the babbling old man.

"Free games!" the old man declared. "Gladiators and beasts, men fighting men. Criminals thrown to the… to the…" He looked around him, stopped talking and stared at the forest.

The cart came to a gentle halt, the low rumble and clank of its wheels giving way to birdsong and quiet. Their cart stood on the left-hand side of the forest avenue, trees all around, and some branches already entwined overhead. The first errant leaves of autumn made a bid for freedom, whirling downward like falling feathers. A gust of wind shook the branches above them, and caused another dusting of dead leaves to shake free.

They heard the drover clambering down from the front and walking slowly around to the back. He pulled open the rear gate, his nose wrinkling at the stench.

"Old man," he said. "This is your destination."

Spartacus peered into the forest, seeing nothing but the trees.

"I have arrived?" the man mumbled. "I have arrived."

The drover swiftly unlocked the old man's manacles, dragging him by one of his skeletal arms.

"Wait! Wait!" the old man cried, but he was already falling off the cart. He landed on his ankle with a sickening snap, and began whimpering.

"Hold your tongue or I will cut it out!" the drover snapped, dragging the old man to the edge of the road.

"My leg!" the old man shouted. "It hurts!"

"No concern of mine," the drover said, dropping the emaciated body in the gutter, among a mulch of fallen leaves, and wet puddles from the most recent storm.

"Where does he take him?" Spartacus asked, but Varro would not meet his eye.

"What does he mean, 'arrived'?" Spartacus said. "This place is nowhere."

"Do not leave me!" the old man begged, reaching out to the drover, although the man was already walking back to the cart. The old man tried to drag himself toward the cart, moving in agonising increments across the flagstones.

"Leave you?" laughed the drover. "I am not leaving you. I am freeing you!"

The man blinked, uncertain, trembling from the pain in his ankle.

"I... am... free...?"

"For the remainder of your life," the drover said, climbing back into the cart.

Spartacus strained at his manacles. He looked imploringly at his fellow passengers, but none of them would look at him.

"Slaves must work," Varro said sadly. "A slave that cannot work is of no value."

"But he is a *human being*!" Spartacus growled. "Is this what Rome means? Is this your civilization? Is this your hospitality?"

"You Thracian tribesmen care for their elders, I suppose."

"We do!"

"And for your slaves?"

"We hold no slaves."

"No medicus either, I wager," Varro snorted. "Perhaps that is why none of you barbarians lives to see old age."

✦

Their voices receded as the cart rolled on, and soon there was nothing but the sounds of the forest. A broken old man lay sobbing by the side of the road in the dwindling light of day.

A trio of ravens fluttered onto a branch above him and waited. Somewhere within the trees, there was a rustle as something moved toward him. He tried to drag himself up, and the noise from the trees ceased.

The man waited, whimpering, knowing that somewhere in the shadows, some other creature waited with greater patience.

Pelorus's body had been carefully wrapped, his face lightly brushed with pollen, his cheeks pinched with a dash of rouge. Timarchides watched the undertakers labor around the bier.

"The presence of these men makes me nervous," he confided to the man who stood beside him.

"A feeling echoed by any man of sanity," Verres responded. "Undertakers serve to remind all of mortality. A lesser man might see grim-faced men in dark clothes and colored hats. But a thinking Roman sees emissaries of death, and naturally gives them wide berth."

"Slaves, too."

"What of them?"

"They regard such men as ill-starred. You see undertakers, Gaius Verres, when someone dies."

"Er... of course, Timarchides."

"Slaves, however, see them when master requires the extraction of deep-lodged truths. They are despoilers of human flesh. If you wish to ensure that your slave has not stolen from you; if you wish to find out what he has been told by your rivals. If you wish to punish him in a way that leaves no enduring marks, but scars the mind eternally, then it is for the undertakers you will send."

"They are torturers?" Verres looked surprised. "Should I need someone twisted or burned, I order it done. I have little concern with hows and wheres."

"They reside on the outskirts of town," Timarchides said. "Far from neighbours or prying eyes. Far from rescue or disapproving passers-by. Where screams go unheard and smells of burning flesh unnoticed." As he spoke, he let his gaze linger on one undertaker in particular, an aging, fleshless man who stood watching the others. Their eyes met, and the old undertaker looked away, fidgeting.

"Let us hope so," Verres said cryptically. "For now, continue to employ these men in management of this household. A title which, as discussed, I shall see conferred upon you."

"You foresee no obstacle?"

"Pelorus was blessed with no wife, no children. You were treasured companion, as evinced in your recent manumission. Who better to inherit what shall remain of his wealth when justice is done?"

Timarchides glanced to the side to ensure that none could hear them.

"You play a dangerous game," he said quietly.

"You do not desire inheritance from Pelorus?"

"It will amount to little," Timarchides sighed. "But gratitude nonetheless."

"And when this is done, Timarchides, you shall hold advantageous position in my circle. That I promise you.

"One small regard," Verres continued, flicking demonstratively at a scrap of papyrus he held in one hand, newly opened. "There is the matter of the hospes list. Those acquaintances of Pelorus deemed so important as to be *almost like* family members."

"He had none."

"He had two."

"By what name?"

Verres flung his arm around Timarchides in a friendly fashion, and walked him away from the bier. They strode through the house of Pelorus as slaves bustled around them working to make it liveable again. Floors were scrubbed, fragments of glass swept up. Tables were righted or removed for repair by dozens of pairs of hands. Neither man saw the slaves. It was as if the house repaired itself around them.

"Timarchides, now you are a freedman, you must learn to act as one," Verres said. "In Latin, the hospes, it is… like a guest, and a friend. A guest-friend."

"All guests are friends by definition. Surely?"

"It is not such a simple matter. A hospes is a man to whom you must open your doors as if your house is his own. And if you travel to his home, he must do the same for you."

"You are a hospes to Pelorus…?"

"Of course I am. That is why I was staying as honored guest."

"I understand. It is as friendship should be."

"Yet it is, as I said, more than friendship and must be given due care. The friend of a hospes is also your hospes. Make appearance at the door of one such man, and proclaim your friendship for his friend, and he, too, must act as your host."

"Now I see why you cannot bestow such friendship on simply anyone."

"And yet Pelorus seems to have done just that." Verres jabbed his finger at the name on the papyrus. "Who the fuck is this *Batiatus*?"

"The lanista? He provides warriors for the games—that we may ensure that justice is done to all the damned. He held some youthful association with Pelorus, but Pelorus never spoke of days spent in Capua."

"Who would wish to speak of days spent there?" Verres scoffed. "Make no mind, they may treat this residence like a free fucking tavern. To do in this house as he wishes."

"Can we not deposit them in rooms at greater distance than these?"

Their wandering had brought them back to the atrium, causing Verres to lower his voice before the bier. He cared not for the slaves, but spoke softly in the presence of the shell that had once been Pelorus.

"This Batiatus is a hospes, Timarchides!" he hissed. "Has understanding not yet penetrated? As the executor of the will of Pelorus, I am compelled to welcome him. As the inheritor, you are similarly obliged. My sponsorship of your inheritance is dependent on you adhering to Roman law!"

"Are you *my* hospes, Gaius Verres?"

"I would like to think so, Timarchides."

"You reside under my roof, here in Neapolis."

"It is not *your roof* until the estate is conferred upon you. An estate which it lies in my power to withhold."

A curtain of silence rose up between the two men, each struggling to control the urge to truly speak his mind. They breathed, and waited for the passions to pass, while the undertakers fussed around the body of Pelorus like sombre nurses.

"How does one get to become a hospes?" Timarchides said, eventually.

"Only by being deeply, indivisibly, connected to an associate."

"Can Batiatus bring trouble to our door?"

"His arrival must not be permitted to interfere with our plan."

"*Your* plan, Verres. Your plan."

"I simply forge pleasant results from unpleasant situation."

"One created by your hands!" Timarchides said, anger flashing in his eyes.

"Did I drive in the knife?" Verres snapped back. "Did Gaius Verres murder your master? The gods may have smiled upon us, but they failed to do so upon good Pelorus."

"Very well," Timarchides said, resignation in his voice. "You shall have it your way."

"Then we are in agreement. Play the host to this Batiatus until time comes that we can be rid of him. You shall handle the funeral games and an end to the slaves."

"I have done so. Most of the gladiators can be dispensed through—"

"I care not, Timarchides. Just do it, and I shall applaud from the balcony and give you true acclaim. Do any other surprises await around the corner?"

"I have but one question. Though it is probably of no great import."

"'*The Greeks have left a big wooden horse behind. It is probably not of import*,'" Verres laughed.

"Not a line from *The Iliad* of which I was aware," Timarchides said.

"My version is the more amusing."

"I positively shake with mirth," Timarchides said, without the trace of a smile. "A matter of the schedule."

"For the games? Were you not charged with the arrangements?"

"*During* the games. Pelorus expects to be visited by a quaestor."

"An investigator? With what intention?"

"Perhaps none of concern."

"And if this proves worthy of concern?"

"Then let us hope no *misfortune* befalls him."

The bearers took their rest at the next hilltop, before the descent into the valley taxed different muscles in their legs. Ilithyia slid daintily from the litter, supporting herself without a word upon the proffered shoulder of one of the bearers.

"Oh, this is... *tiresome!*" she breathed, flapping her fan. The sweat-drenched slaves who had borne her thus far knew better than to say anything. She stretched provocatively, uncaring that her breasts strained against her sweat-dampened silks in full view of the slaves.

Sighing with the effort of being carried for several hours, Ilithyia walked to the edge of the cliff, to gaze down at the long, undulating land that slid away toward the mist in the distant southeast.

"Can you see the sea?" Lucretia asked, as she too stepped away from the litter.

"I am not sure," Ilithyia replied. "The distant land fades into cloud, as the clouds fade into the horizon."

Just for a moment, the sun peeked through, glinting on something in the distance.

"A spark on waters?" Ilithyia said. "The bay of Neapolis lies before us."

"Yet some hours of walking, I fear," Lucretia said.

"Then let us tarry a while. We are plainly ahead of your husband's litter."

"I see no reason why not," Lucretia agreed, flapping one of the panels of her gown in an attempt to dispel the muggy heat. "We may as well enjoy the open air before the rain's inevitable return."

Ilithyia stretched again.

"I shall come to enjoy this road, I hope," she mused.

"Are you planning on making this journey often?"

"Perhaps," Ilithyia replied. "There is talk of a new dawn in the fortunes of Neapolis."

"I have always found it a ghastly place."

"And yet you accompany me, fearful your own counsel might be mistaken? Rumour has a hundred eyes and a hundred ears. I must see for myself and decide whether to broach the subject further with my husband."

"You would really consider a move to Neapolis? Your household and slaves? Your life and impediments?"

"Rome may be the eternal city, but one cannot live there eternally."

Lucretia bit her lip, and thought of the countless citizens who boasted of their connections to Rome, and yet still yearned to see it.

"Does Capua not offer enough diversions for you?" Lucretia enquired with half her mouth.

"It boasts certain *primitive* charm, of course. Though one mired in heat and dust. Do you not tire of it?"

"The Batiatus family has dwelt in Capua for three generations."

"Mobility is a virtue."

"Says one dragged from eternal City of the Seven Hills, her fingernails clawing at the stones of the Appian Way! Perhaps I shall just make us mutual hospes, and then appear at your doorstep whenever I have the urge for sea air."

"But if my husband were to be made consul..." Ilithyia said.

"An honor that lies yet before him."

"A course to which he is eminently capable!"

"Of course, Ilithyia."

"And he shall have some divine aid set to his purpose."

"Sacrifices? Games in his honor?"

"My husband struggles to find favor with the senate. The foreign wars go badly, and he is shunted aside on the course of military commands. He seeks possible avenues elsewhere."

"Politics? The gods?"

"The conditions are as changeable as this autumnal weather. Sunny one moment. Tinkling with rain the next."

"And no man can predict the weather."

Ilithyia giggled and took Lucretia's hand.

"No one man." she whispered. "But perhaps ten *special* men."

Lucretia frowned.

"There are men in Rome, a select group of men to be sure, but a group that falls open to newcomers when death claims a new member. Men who consult the books of prophecies past to divine future course."

"And your husband has a guide to posterities yet unknown?"

"He may yet gain one, should he be well considered."

"What books?"

"There are books, in Rome. Kept by the priests of

the Capitoline, collating oracles and predictions from all over the known world, all to the greater good of Rome. Catalogues of prophecy."

"I have heard of them," Lucretia said.

"Then you must know only few may consult them."

Lucretia laughed, feeling the weight of her journey lifted by such humor.

"If the priests of the Capitoline Hill truly had books foretelling futures, would we not already know what tomorrow holds?"

"We are citizens of Rome, the greatest Republic that the world has ever seen!"

"But it would still be a blessing to know if the day yet holds rain."

IV

IMAGINES

THE HILLSIDE WAS CLOAKED WITH CYPRESS TREES, OLD AND young, reaching to the sky like tall, green fingers. Below, the streets and houses of Neapolis stretched toward the distant sea. Above, the slopes continued ever higher, as the hill became the dark, ashen mountain that loomed above Neapolis like a permanent shadow.

The scent of pine wafted. As the trees bowed in the wind, they sometimes revealed the bright white of stone memorials, glimpsed for the briefest of moments before the limbs sprung back into place.

Slaves placed cypress branches against the stack of dry wood, while others carefully slipped rolls of cinnamon or cassia wood into the gaps between the logs and straw. They set final, greener branches against the sides, putting the workmanlike bonfire kindling out of sight, creating the impression of a green, growing altar in the middle of the hillside forest. With each gust of wind, the branches shifted slightly, making it seem as if the altar could breathe.

The slaves turned to other activities. They swept the ground clear of pebbles. They fiddled with the line of lit torches, deliberately incongruous in the daylight, that stretched toward the road into Neapolis. And they studiously ignored the men who were picking through a pile of outsized, burnished armor.

"We are to be attired as warriors of the north, it seems. Cimbri, perhaps, or Teutones," Varro said.

"And these warriors from the north, they wear helmets such as these?" Spartacus mused.

"I believe so."

"Believe? No wonder the gods did not favor them."

"Your meaning?" Varro asked.

Without warning, Spartacus leapt at the tall Roman, grabbing his newly donned helmet by one of its prominent horns. Varro stumbled backward in surprise, but Spartacus had him in a firm grip, dragging his helmeted head down into the dust as if he were wrestling an ox.

Varro hit the ground with a whoosh of air, and did not even attempt to struggle from the hold, instead raising the two fingers of submission.

The slaves with brushes and torches looked up momentarily from their labors, and then returned to work as if the fight had never happened.

"The horns serve no purpose," Spartacus said coldly. "There is no way for you to employ them in combat, and even if you did, they are blunt to the point of futility. But to an opponent, they offer secure purchase. Absent the defence of your sword-arm from the front, these horns offer your foe a handle by which to drag you down."

"Very well!" Varro protested in an anguished growl. "Your point is made. Let me go."

Spartacus climbed nimbly to his feet, holding out a hand to help up his friend.

"The costumes are chosen for us," Varro said. "I cannot choose my armor."

"Indeed," Spartacus agreed. "But you can choose how to wear it."

He drew his sword from its scabbard and carefully began sawing through the leather chin strap.

"Have you lost mind?" Varro asked, scraping the worst of the black Neapolitan dirt from his frame.

"I do not wish to enter battle unprotected," Spartacus said calmly. "But I can aid its removal if pulled with sufficient force."

He held it up for Varro to see. A neat nick in the chinstrap left it only half as wide as it once was.

"I suggest you do the same," Spartacus continued.

Varro nodded, unsmiling, with the calculation of a man in search of any advantage.

"You are cunning, Thracian," he said. "No ordinary man would think to win victory by losing that which is to protect him."

"My only thought, to stay alive," Spartacus said.

Their fellow slaves from House Batiatus, the swarthy Galatian Cycnus and the jet-black Numidian Bebryx, watched their chatter sullenly.

"You would do well to listen to the Champion of Capua," Varro said to them quietly. "Or die with closed ears."

Bebryx sucked thoughtfully on his teeth, peeling them back from his lips with a contemptuous smack. Cycnus also said nothing, fussing instead with the straps of his armor.

"Please yourselves," Varro said with a shrug. "But mark well our opponents."

He jerked his head across the clearing toward a second group of gladiators, picking through a pile of antique Roman swords and shields. The others followed his direction.

"Why are there but three of them and four of us?" Cycnus asked.

"Their fourth marches in the procession itself," Varro explained. "The freedman Timarchides, friend to the deceased."

"Does this mark advantage?" Spartacus asked.

"A freedman will not seek true danger. He has too much to lose."

"Strike him with flat of sword and see honor restored?" Cycnus suggested with a grin.

Bebryx sucked on his teeth again, and looked away at the trees warily, as if expecting the wood itself to come for him.

"But he is a freedman," Spartacus said, "in a house of gladiators."

"What is your meaning, Thracian?" Varro asked.

"He is not a weak-willed patrician, thinking of wine and the next banquet," Spartacus said. "He is a gladiator so proficient that he received the wooden sword. We fight a man skilled enough to *fight* his way to freedom."

"Oh," Varro said quietly. "Fuck."

Batiatus wore black. The unfamiliar color kept taking him by surprise, as if there were a fly on his arm or a mosquito at his neck. He looked around him at the Neapolitan villa, so oddly like the one he had left behind in Capua, as if its architect had hoped to imitate every aspect of House Batiatus.

The floors had been cleaned, scrubbed and washed, but there were still telltale stains. To a lanista's accustomed eye, a benign pink patch on the marble was no mere discoloration, but evidence of the recent removal of a pool of dried blood. There were chips and nicks in the friezes, suggesting swords and metal objects had been swung in an enclosed space in some recent frenzy.

Pelorus ran a house of warriors, but there was no cause for there to be war in his dwelling. Slaves had cleared away the worst of the debris, but Batiatus still sensed the echoes of that last, bloody dinner party.

Marcus Pelorus was laid out on a long bier in what had once been his atrium. The pool was drained, the furniture removed. Many of the side doors were firmly shut. The house was conspicuously, ominously, silent.

Batiatus approached the bier, glancing down the side aisles in the vain hope of seeing other mourners. Much to his surprise, he appeared to be alone.

"Well," he said grimly to the corpse. "Present moment holds just you and me, you old bastard."

Pelorus said nothing, for Pelorus was dead. His face had an odd yellow pallor, dusted with pollen to present the illusion of life, but dusted too much, it seemed the pollinctores had been over-zealous. Batiatus reached out, and then decided against it. He looked around, saw nobody was coming, and reached out once again to poke Pelorus tauntingly on the chin.

Batiatus's touch inadvertently dislodged the shroud that covered Pelorus's neck, revealing a gaping throat wound. His lip curled in revulsion as he carefully tucked the folds of cloth back into place. They had been poorly tied, and he shook his head at the low quality of Neapolitan craftsmanship.

"Good Pelorus, at last you find end," he said to the body. "An end that proves its worth I hope."

"And what worth is that?" said a loud voice from behind him. Batiatus started. He turned to see a thin, handsome man with carefully tousled hair, wearing a patrician toga with practiced ease.

"Apologies," Batiatus said. "I thought myself alone."

"I am Gaius Verres, hospes of the deceased," Verres said.

"Quintus Lentulus Batiatus, likewise."

"I do not recall him mentioning that name. Was your friendship close?"

Batiatus's eyes widened.

"My name never crossed his lips?" he asked, carefully.

"Never," Verres said, smiling apologetically. "But perhaps he never spoke of Gaius Verres to your ears, either."

"The years have found us infrequent companions, save haggling over matters of human cargo."

Batiatus made as if to say something more, then thought better of it.

"The friend of my friend…" he said hopefully, holding out his arm.

"Indeed so," Verres responded, clasping it firmly with his own. "You have journeyed far?"

"From Capua!" Batiatus said.

"His former home," Verres said nodding, "though I think his preference was to be by the sea in Neapolis."

"And you?"

"From Rome," Verres said quietly. "I was traveling to Sicilia, and resting here with my hospes good Pelorus, before my journey's resumption. My expectation was not that this would also be our last farewell."

"You are on business Republican?"

"I am to be Sicilia's governor!"

Batiatus gasped.

"I was innocent of the elevated circles in which my old friend good Pelorus moved," he said.

"He was a contributor of great generosity to my campaign," Verres said. "A wondrous benefactor for a Roman on the course of honors. I am in debt to him for my position, in some ways. And you?"

"Many years ago," Batiatus said, "the good Marcus Pelorus saved the life of my father."

"A deed that deserves recurrent voice." He shook his head and stared appreciatively at the body on the bier. "May the gods bring you reward in the afterlife," he said to the corpse.

"I have exchanged messages with a man called Timarchides," Batiatus said. "I am to receive my payment from him."

"Payment for what?"

"I bring gladiators for the funeral and celebratory games."

"Then you are in my employ. I am editor of the games!"

"I have brought many fine gladiators from Capua. Although I confess to finding such a request strange."

"Why?"

"You are aware, good Verres, that in the house of a murdered master…"

"…all slaves must die. Of course."

"And since the ludus must be considered part of House Pelorus, and prize gladiators played their part in the revolt, there can be no debate upon the subject. They too, must perish."

"A sad state of affairs," Verres agreed.

"My fine gladiators fight in these games as executioners more than warriors," Batiatus pointed out. "Why bring in such men from Capua? Pelorus was not the only lanista in Neapolis. Why not seek such executioners closer to hand?"

"Perhaps good Timarchides knew of your past association with Pelorus, and felt the coin best spent on friends?" Verres said expansively.

Batiatus sighed. "The bitter death of Pelorus, sweetened by last gesture of friendship."

From outside came a dreadful cacophony of flat horns and discordant flutes.

"Curse them," Verres muttered. "This cloud leaves no sun for the dial, making it a task near impossible to tell when the procession should start."

"It holds the sound of starting now," Batiatus said.

"I must don my mourning robes," Verres scowled, dashing toward the bedchambers.

"I shall see what weight I can add to its slowing."

"Do not trouble yourself," Verres called behind him. "They would not start without me."

Clad in dark, heavy clothes a world away from her habitual lightweight silks, Ilithyia watched the distant sea from the colonnade that circled the house of Pelorus. She heard footsteps approaching, and the rustle of rough cloth.

"You should attend to your husband, Lucretia," she said, without turning around. "I think he is still sulking after the journey."

"I expect the solitude pleased him."

"You are cruel!"

"I know my husband. Besides, I do not wish to enter the house while the body is still laid out within. Let him take on the bad fortune!"

Ilithyia smiled to herself.

"Your mourning weeds become you," Lucretia said.

"Gratitude," Ilithyia said. "It was kind of you to provide them."

"Anything for a dear friend."

"I have none of my own, not even in Rome. One is supposed to wear rags to funerals, and all of my clothing is too fine!"

Lucretia smiled with clenched teeth.

"It is to your good fortune that my clothing should be so poor," she said.

"The great and the good of Rome are building their holiday villas here," Ilithyia continued.

"For all that is sacred, why?"

"The views across the bay. The sea air."

"But the journey here is miserable. As our own experience can attest."

"Not with the right companion," Ilithyia said, pointedly. "One does not have to trudge through the hilly backwaters of Capua, you know. You can ignore the Appian Way and take the road along the coast from Rome."

"Ilithyia, you tease me. That way lays Cumae and the Fiery Fields."

"The fiery what?"

"Have you not seen them? This whole region is shot through with doorways to death itself. Molten rocks like Vulcan's very furnace. Hot waters gushing from cracks in the earth."

"You make that sound as though it were a bad thing."

"The dust! The rock turns powdery as ash, and

throws up clouds of gray dust upon everything."

"Merely a matter of perspective," Ilithyia said touching Lucretia's arm condescendingly. "Look past the rude bricks toward the marble that will come with further prosperity."

"Do you suggest Pelorus had wisdom and forethought?"

"Where you see gateways to Hades, some see cleansing hot springs. Why commandeer armies of slaves to heat water when nature will do it for you? Think of the coast around Neapolis strewn with villas for the wealthiest and noblest of Romans. Land costs little."

"Because the former owners met their deaths in a generation of war!" Lucretia said with exasperation.

"And there is so much *history* to be found. The cave of the Sibyl at Cumae. The old Greek colonies. You can sail north to Ostia from Neapolis, or take the Appian Way through Capua across land. Roads lead to the south, or if your business takes you further afield, you can sail straight from Neapolis to Sicilia, or onward to the east."

"Perhaps you would like to stay here forever," Lucretia said icily.

"Perhaps," Ilithyia replied, ignoring her companion's tone. "When there are more residents of suitable rank to welcome me! Have the other mourners yet arrived? I want to put this parade behind me. The wake will see the wine cellar plucked dry."

Batiatus knelt in the Neapolitan dirt, a choking dust more like black talcum or the ashes of hell. He scooped up a fistful in several careful sweeps, and dumped it on his head, taking care to run his fingers across his face.

At his side, the gladiator Barca loomed in watchful guardianship, clad in a dark tunic.

Gaius Verres approached, his eyes on the towering bodyguard, as if awaiting permission to come closer. Barca made no indication either way, but kept his gaze on the approaching Roman.

"You do him suitable honor," Gaius Verres addressed Batiatus. Verres was now correctly attired for the occasion, his bright, clean toga replaced by a tunic and cowl in black and dark gray. He, too, knelt in the dirt in search of suitable ash, carefully dragging his fingers down across his face to create a cage of dark bars on his cheeks.

"I would say good morning, Gaius Verres," Batiatus said solemnly, "but such a morning cannot be in such conditions."

"Death comes to us all," Verres mused. "Let us bid farewell to good Pelorus as best we can."

"His friends, where might they be?" Batiatus asked. He glanced around, checking to see if Verres led a new set of arrivals, but saw only the hired help as before.

"Us two I believe in number," Verres replied, patting Batiatus's arm.

"Yet Pelorus met death at a banquet among dozens of guests. Was their friendship so fleeting?"

Batiatus stared in apprehension at the other six bearers, every one of them a dour-faced undertaker. None met his eye. As he watched, they donned white masks bearing the *imagines* of deities. He shook his head in sorrow that Pelorus had no family *imagines* to walk in his procession, but remembered he had been the newest of New Men.

Nearby Lucretia and Ilithyia lurked, their necks craning as they peered down the road, searching in vain for any other arrivals. Close to the women stood a small gaggle of slaves, and servants. They, too, donned masks that bore the images of gods and heroes. Batiatus saw a Hercules and a Theseus, a Jason and an Achilles, a Hector and an Ajax—warriors all. Absent *imagines* for their faces, Lucretia and Ilithyia fastened their veils, drawing them down from their headdresses to render their faces all but invisible.

Batiatus caught sight of a wide-hipped, shapely woman in a veil and mourning robes, but no other candidates for friends or relations.

"I see pipes and drums, trumpets and horns," Batiatus muttered to Verres. "I see professional mourners and undertakers, slaves to clear the way. I see my wife and her irritating friend, and another woman whose visage is unfamiliar. And you. And me. And that is all. That is all!"

He scowled at the six men standing impassively nearby, each in the dark, long-sleeved tunic and brightly colored hat that marked them out as undertakers.

"Tradition often allows a dying master to free some slaves in his service, that his funeral procession might have some grateful associates walking freely amongst it," Verres commented.

Batiatus snorted scornfully.

"Such a plan has little to recommend it when the slaves attempt to free themselves, and slay the master in the process," he said dryly.

"It is an honor to be one of the pallbearers," Verres said. "And you and I, Batiatus, we are in the frontmost position, rated the most high among all the men of Pelorus's acquaintance."

"By whom are we rated such?" Batiatus murmured. "There are none here to observe it. I am honored before an audience of no one."

Verres chuckled wryly, leaning down with the others to grab a purchase on the bier.

"The gods, Batiatus," he whispered. "The gods see your actions and note them."

"Fuck the gods," Batiatus snapped in retort. "Once again they conspire to fuck me."

"Ah," Verres said. "Timarchides arrives. We are ready."

Batiatus followed Verres's gaze, to see a man he knew only from correspondence moving toward them. He was a towering, burly Greek, his hair in tight black curls against his head, his deep tan marked in places by thin white scar lines. He was clad in a dark toga edged incongruously with a white border, as if in defiant reversal of everyday wear. In his belt he wore a rudely fashioned wooden sword. Batiatus squinted at the flat of the blade, making out enough letters scratched in it to know the name it bore was Timarchides's own.

"And a freed gladiator," Batiatus muttered, acidly. "All the great and good are present."

With careful deliberation, Timarchides raised a mask to his head, strapping it in place. He turned to look at Batiatus, his face a golden parody of Pelorus himself.

"Surely the best of all the *imagines*," Verres said. "That is based on Pelorus's own death mask. Set in wax upon his face and painted by the swiftest and most diligent of craftsman."

"So Pelorus may walk among us, even in his own funeral procession," Batiatus said.

"Indeed so. And he will walk among us as a giant of a man."

"Larger in death than he was in life—" Batiatus began, only to gasp at the sight of another figure, suddenly raised above the bier. Looming above the whole procession was a giant winged creature in black, a cowl covering a face that was featureless and shadowed. Standing twice as tall as a man, the imposing being was held up on a frame by an unseen slave, creating the impression that a Titan walked among the lesser mortals of the procession.

"Nemesis," Batiatus breathed.

"A goddess of some importance to Pelorus, I believe," Verres said.

Batiatus nodded.

"Vengeance herself?" he said.

Verres gazed up admiringly at the figure of the goddess.

"I thought it particularly fitting," he said, "in consideration of the manner of Pelorus's passing. And my intentions for the games that celebrate him."

The band struck up their music, a discordant clash of cymbals, limned by moaning pipes. The horns blew a grave fanfare, announcing to the world ahead that a dead man was on his last journey, and Verres signaled to the other bearers.

Barca gestured for Batiatus to stand aside, seeing a burden to be shouldered, but Batiatus shooed him away.

"Barca," he said. "Ever my protector. Today shall be some small Saturnalia, when you walk unencumbered and your master bears a slave's burden."

"As you wish, dominus," Barca said.

As one, the eight men lifted their load, causing Batiatus to struggle for a moment, but only for balance. Distributed among eight sturdy men, the dead form of Pelorus weighed little.

Batiatus chuckled, despite himself.

"You are amused, good Batiatus?" Verres asked, his voice slightly muffled on the other side of the bier.

Keeping time with the slow drum, the bearers began to advance.

"The weight of man is not so momentous," Batiatus said, keeping his eyes focused ahead. "Litter bearers never make mention of that."

"I do not follow."

"This job is not so difficult. The slaves should silence tongue."

Two women in black began to screech and wail, stumbling ahead of the coffin in exaggerated pantomimes of desolation. They tore at their hair, and yelled defiant, confrontational questions at the sky. *Why did he have to go? Why him? Why have the gods treated us so?*

Lucretia sighed, and turned to say something to Ilithyia, but the Roman woman was still sulking to herself. True to noble tradition, Lucretia maintained a stoic, unmoved disposition and walked on calmly, letting the professional mourners do the official grieving.

Red-faced with effort, the two mourners screamed and sobbed, entreating the gods to be merciful upon the dead man in the afterlife.

"Be merciful," they cried, "on our dear *Plorus*. Witness us, in our grief for the dear departed *Pilorux*."

Batiatus tutted, despite himself.

"Something is wrong, Batiatus?" Verres asked. "Your load is not so easy to shoulder as you imagine?"

"I carry this dead weight with ease," Batiatus replied. "I merely wish someone had informed those ignorant whores as to the pronunciation of the name Pelorus!"

Verres chuckled.

"Workers of worth are a challenge to procure," he agreed. Batiatus smiled weakly to himself, and plodded on toward the cemetery.

There was no great crowd assembled for the funeral of Pelorus. No Neapolitans gathered by the roadside to bow and bid a fond farewell. Pelorus the great New Man of Neapolis was already a forgotten figure, an unidentified corpse borne by eight men on a slow journey out of the city, accompanied by mourners bearing lit torches at midday. The horns of the musicians were intended to clear the way, but Batiatus had always imagined them doing so through a crowd of well-wishers. Instead, the horns announced the approach of ill omen. Batiatus heard doors slamming up ahead, and shutters clattering fast. Through the keening music of the band, he heard the occasional scuffle of sandaled feet on the road as mothers herded their children indoors. In the yards they passed that were open to the street, he caught momentary sight of recent occupation—well-water left sloshing in its pail, or unattended spinning wheels grinding slowly to a halt.

"Careful now," Verres said. "Presently we begin to move uphill."

"Of course we fucking do," Batiatus muttered in resignation, glaring upward at the threatening black mountain that dominated the landward side of Neapolis, looming above the city like Nemesis herself.

They continued on their way, past villas and houses that seemed recently deserted, as if the ashen hills had suddenly been stripped of all human life, leaving only the buildings. Once, Batiatus felt a positive thrill of relief at the sight of farmers working in the fields, but as the procession drew near, he realized that they were slaves, ordered to remain at their posts, and hence unable to flee the bad fortune that approached them.

Lucretia walked beside a statuesque, shapely woman whose robes clung tightly to broad sinuous hips and an impressive bust, her face hidden beneath a black silk veil.

"Lucretia, of the House of Batiatus," she introduced herself, with a sad smile fashioned to suit the occasion. "United with you in mourning and grief."

The woman turned to look at her. The wind tugged momentarily at her veil, revealing a red mass of puckered flesh and scar tissue, as if she only had half a face.

"Successa," the woman replied in a small voice. "My name is Successa, of no house."

"Were you well acquainted with Pelorus?" Lucretia began, already regretting her attempt to socialize.

"I was present in House Pelorus, the night he met his death," Successa said. "I was offered a rich purse to ensure his guests were adequately entertained. I believed it good coin!"

She spoke as if in jest, but Lucretia knew not to laugh. The pause that followed the woman's statement stretched into a silence, and Lucretia found herself deeply relieved at the sight of Ilithyia drawing near.

"Ilithyia," she stated. "Wife to Gaius Claudius Glaber. United with you in mourning and grief."

Successa turned to meet Ilithyia's gaze, allowing her veil to blow fully aside.

"Oh sweet gods!" Ilithyia exclaimed.

"The lady Successa was present the night of the incident," Lucretia said hastily.

"Oh, I see," Ilithyia said frostily. "My... condolences."

She turned to face forward, as if Successa had suddenly disappeared.

Successa did not wait around for further insult, but graciously modified her pace so that the two women moved ahead of her.

"We have been lured to this place under pretences, I can only describe as false," Ilithyia muttered.

"What is your meaning?" Lucretia asked.

"You promised a gathering of the great and the good."

"Well, *you* are here, Ilithyia."

"Indeed I am, a companion to disfigured whores and masked slaves."

"One of the pallbearers is the new governor of Sicilia!"

"I should never have come."

"An invitation upon your insistence!"

Ilithyia pouted and marched on with heavy steps.

The funeral procession wound along the road, the doleful music silencing birds in the trees, the wails of the professional mourners putting everyone on edge. Batiatus felt the ground start to level out.

"We approach the summit...?" he wondered aloud.

"Of this mountain, not at all," Verres answered. "We merely wander in its foothills. This smoking peak stretches far above us, into the mists and beyond."

"I cannot imagine Pelorus desiring such a lofty funeral?"

"We approach our destination," Verres said calmly from the other side of the bier. "The cemetery is not at the summit."

Batiatus was surprised to see that despite the empty roads, the procession was growing in size. Small boys wielded saplings like staffs, alongside grubby men with unkempt hair, old women with hungry eyes, and bony, pock-marked girls who had already seen better days.

"More professional mourners?" Batiatus whispered.

Verres shook his head.

"Beggars and souvenir hunters. Pay them no heed."

"From where did they come?"

"Do not let it trouble mind. They are nothing."

"They appear as if from an amphitheater's dirty crowd," Batiatus mused.

"Then Pelorus will be cremated among friends," Verres laughed.

"But why would they come here…?" Batiatus said.

"For the same reason they will surely flock to the arena," Verres replied. "The violence and bloodshed of the fight."

V

BUSTUARII

DUSTY FROM THEIR JOURNEY, AND ASHEN FROM THEIR CARE-
fully applied dirt, the funeral party rounded a bend in the
road. An ancient, Oscan altar and a partly fallen archway
marked the entrance to the cemetery.

The crowd now numbered almost a hundred.
Batiatus could smell them over his own sweat. Striding
by his master's side, Barca was obliged to rudely shove
some of the new arrivals out of the way, lest they come
too close. Some pushed at the edges of the bier, while
others dogged its rear like curious hounds. Still more,
particularly the children, ran on ahead, pushing past the
musicians with shoves that sent their notes into unlikely
syncopations, kicking up dust and stones as they ran
into the cemetery proper, screaming with incongruous
glee at the prospect of what was to come. They hurtled
among the monuments, playing tag and leapfrog, in
search of what they knew to be lurking somewhere
in the grounds—a group of men, suiting up in armor,
preparing to do battle.

"Bustuarii! Bustuarii!" they cried, calling out the name of gladiators of old, those men who would fight in honor of a departed dignitary, shedding their own warm blood in memory of one whose blood was already cold. The children, unimpeded by their exertions, as if they could run and jump forever, were first to find the greenwood altar, rushing ahead of the procession to secure the best places to sit.

The priests came behind them, jingling their bells to dispel evil spirits, chanting in a Latin so old that its meaning eluded many of the attendees. Their faces were hooded, their rituals occluded, such that their meaning seemed to only carry weight to the priests themselves. They reached the greenwood altar, turning to face the assembled gladiators, and then moved on, on a course of their own.

Timarchides took off the mask of Pelorus, reverently laying it atop the bier. He then grabbed at a box by the altar, swiftly pulling on the armor of an earlier generation, a battered old set of the kind of soldier's garb that had been commonplace when Batiatus was a boy. He and his three fellows stood with shields and swords, eyeing their opponents with the calm, assessing gaze of men who knew that the battle had already begun. They watched their stances, looked for limps and tan-marks where bandages might have recently been removed. They studied practice swings for telltale over- or under-extensions, and brooded all the while on how to bring their opponents down.

Batiatus and his fellow bearers made the last ascent, lifting the bier high above their shoulders in order to place it atop the pyre. There was a final strain, a last farcical panic that the bier might tumble and take its load with it, and then Pelorus was placed firmly on top of the pile of wood and incense.

Verres draped a cloth over his head, in the manner of a priest reading the auspices. He glanced across at Spartacus, who gave him a discreet nod of readiness. Verres turned to Timarchides, and received an identical, discreet signal.

"The name of Marcus Pelorus has been declaimed from his death bed," Verres shouted over the hum of the crowd. "His house purged of spirits of malicious intent. Now it but remains for us, his friends and associates, to see him on his journey to the afterlife, so that we may feast in his memory."

While Verres spoke, Timarchides carefully ascended a ladder that was propped against the bier. He held a burning torch in his hand, and the nearby cypress branches bent gently beneath the leaning weight, until he reached the top. There, he reached out and tenderly opened each of the corpse's eyes.

"The eyes are open," Verres intoned solemnly. "And our friend prepares for the hereafter."

As the priests shook their bells, intoning grim portents of the afterlife, Verres nodded at the freedman, and Timarchides set the torch to the stacks of wood.

There was a brief, tense movement as the woodpile gave off only the twisting smoke of wettened branches. But then, something caught within the stacks, causing red and yellow flames to flicker deep within. There was soon the hiss and pop of oils released from jars, and the crack of breaking glass.

Timarchides descended the ladder as solemnly as he could, but with the slightest hint of agitation at the growing heat. When he reached the bottom, he took his helmet from the waiting gladiators, and began to tie it fast upon his head.

"It is fitting that Timarchides, the man who was so dear to Pelorus in life, should appear here at his graveside as we lay him to rest," Verres said.

The jingling of the priest's bells faded into the distance as they began their customary journey around the edges of the cemetery. Nobody paid them any heed.

"Timarchides wears the accoutrements of a gladiator one final time," Verres continued, "to honor his former master, and lifelong *dearest* friend."

Batiatus exchanged a confused glance with Lucretia, who now stood beside him.

"Were they *lovers*?" he whispered.

"A thought known to them alone," Lucretia responded with a shrug.

"One not shared with me in our days together," Batiatus hissed into her ear.

"There have been many since, spent here in Neapolis."

Up on the dais, Verres continued to praise dear, dear Pelorus, the lanista made good, the supporter of local businesses and politicians. He thanked him for his generosity in life and lamented his untimely death.

Batiatus maintained a civil countenance, but scowled nonetheless at the tales of a man who was a stranger to him. There was no talk here of Pelorus the rowdy young man; Pelorus the dutiful student of swordsmanship, who once boasted that he would grow up to train warriors himself; Pelorus, the beloved friend of House Batiatus, whose greatest deed was to save the life of Titus Lentulus Batiatus, the paterfamilias. Pelorus, who was rewarded for this action with that most precious of treasures: freedom itself—of this there was no mention.

Batiatus chewed sulkily on the inside of his cheek, wondering if any man in Neapolis even knew that Pelorus had once been a slave. He turned to his wife to whisper another unhappy criticism of the eulogy, but was stopped in his tracks by Verres's next words.

"...and so," Verres was saying, "the time approaches for us to bid final farewell to our dear friend Pelorus. A man who departed this world leaving no family nor any heir, but who with his dying breath entrusted to me the honored role of familiae emptor, disburser of his estate. A role I vow to fulfil swiftly and without prejudice." As he spoke, Verres nodded at the solemn Timarchides, and Batiatus caught the faintest of acknowledgments in return.

It was as if a sun had burst within the chest of Batiatus. He looked around him in frustration, unable to speak out of turn, unable to run from his position. Rooted to the spot amid the other mourners, he dared not leave his position. He looked at Lucretia, but was unable to attract her attention.

Red faced and shaking, Batiatus glared across the cemetery at his two gladiators, his eyes wide, willing one of them to meet his gaze.

"Batiatus looks not himself," Spartacus mumbled out of the side of his mouth.

Varro glanced over at their master, in time to see the lanista's hand emerging from beneath the long sleeves of his mourning robe. His thumb jerked in a gesture that no gladiator could mistake.

"Does he not signal the delivery of the death blow, before battle is even joined?" Varro asked.

Spartacus met his master's stare, and watched as

Batiatus's eyes grew comically wider, rolling repeatedly in the direction of the unsuspecting Timarchides.

"He is a most unclear oracle," Spartacus said, implacably. "Perhaps he is transforming into a frog."

Varro stifled a chuckle.

Batiatus scratched at his neck, his gaze still locked on Spartacus. As the Thracian watched, Batiatus carefully drew his finger across his throat and then turned away, to stare directly at Timarchides.

"He wants the Greek dead," Spartacus whispered.

"This is a fight for exhibition," Varro hissed back. "Nobody is supposed to die today."

"He would have it otherwise," Spartacus replied.

The funeral pyre was now in full effect, the flames leaping high above it, the body of Pelorus already invisible beneath them. Rolling clouds of smoke issued forth from the lowermost levels, where the wood remained wet. Hissing could be heard from within, as cypress wood gave up its resin, imparting a pine aroma to the proceedings.

A gust of wind shoved a pall of smoke closer to the crowd, who backed away, protesting.

All eyes were locked on the two squads of four men who stood ready to fight.

Nobody gave the word. But the fight began.

They advanced. The "Romans" locked their shields, forming a small imitation of a legion's front line.

Spartacus launched himself at the line before they could get their spears in place, smacking into the shields with the spear-points safely behind him. The force of his charge immediately broke his opponents into two pairs, the men staggering back.

Ignoring one couple, Spartacus flailed against Timarchides himself and his surprised lieutenant. At his back, he heard the clang and clatter as Varro and his fellow gladiators pressed against the other two—and a sudden scream.

Spartacus glanced behind, and caught a fleeting glimpse of Bebryx reeling with a spear in his shoulder his face contorted with pain, before he turned back to face his chosen foe.

Lucretia shot a concerned look at Batiatus.

"I know your thoughts," he muttered. "Your expectation cannot be for me to intervene."

Bebryx, the spear protruding from his shoulder, let go of his sword. He dropped to his knees, clutching at the spear. Its haft smacked into the ground, levering the point deep into the wound and causing Bebryx to scream in agony again.

Varro backed away so that he stood between his opponents and the wounded gladiator. He flung the pointless round shield at the "Romans," and grabbed the hilt of his own sword with both hands, swinging it straight for their heads.

Cycnus grappled his opponent, the two men shoving together, grunting with effort. Cycnus drew back his sword arm, repositioning the blade ready to stab, when, suddenly, his opponent grabbed one of the horns on his helmet, and tugged downwards.

Spartacus caught a look in Cycnus's eyes, a momentary spark of realization, as the gladiator was dragged headfirst. He tried to struggle to his feet, but his opponent had a tight wrestling hold on both his head and his torso. Cycnus roared in frustration, his free hand flailing, trying to punch a soft spot in his assailant. Instead, his knuckles scraped on unyielding armor. The man in soldier's armor raised his sword to stab into Cycnus's pinned neck, and a snarling Cycnus raised the two fingers of surrender.

The soldier did not even halt, but plunged his sword into Cycnus's throat. Silencing his angry growls in an instant, the blade pierced straight through the throat and the bones of the neck.

A cry escaped Lucretia's lips, her mouth agape in surprise at the unexpected death. A fountain of blood sprayed across the killing ground, spattering in hissing droplets on the ever-growing fire, tainting the air with the sudden tang of copper.

Batiatus sank onto his haunches, one hand held despairingly over his left eye, as if he could barely endure the sight.

"We cannot afford such losses as these!" Lucretia said.

Batiatus sat meekly by the sidelines. Lucretia yelled at Timarchides to call an end to the bloodshed, but her voice was drowned out by the crackle of the fire, the continued dirge of the musicians, the clash of blades, and the shouts of the crowd.

The killer of Cycnus tugged brutally at his blade, pulling off his victim's head, and holding it aloft by one of the helmet horns, the head still held in place by its strong leather chin strap. A drizzle of blood fell from the severed neck and spattered the killer's arms.

The victorious gladiator laughed as he brandished the grisly trophy, and then spun to cast it upon the flames.

Spartacus and Varro stood back to back, the two of them still facing four opponents. At their feet, Bebryx moaned in pain, his hands grasping the blood-wet spear in his shoulder.

"The odds fall out of favor," Varro muttered.

Spartacus said nothing for a few moments. He glared in turn at each of the men who faced him as he and Varro spun in small circles.

"I have won victory against worse," Spartacus muttered.

Cackling, Cycnus's killer drew close to Spartacus, his sword arm outstretched, his other hand held far away from his body.

"Mark the others," Spartacus said to Varro. "I am for this one."

The man stopped laughing, but still drew near, his eyes staring deep into Spartacus's own, his arms held wide, presenting a tantalizing target.

Spartacus feinted, watching his opponent's left arm twitch in response to an attack that never came.

Spartacus smiled to himself, and lunged for real.

The man darted to the side, his left arm coming up to grab at the horn of Spartacus's helmet, tugging savagely down as he had done to the luckless Cycnus. But the helmet came off clean in his hand, throwing him off balance, sending him tumbling back onto the grass, his arms crossed protectively over his body, warding against a blow that never came.

For Spartacus had immediately wheeled and plunged

his sword into the neck of one of the other attackers, a man who had been too busy watching the scuffle to parry an unexpected blow. The crowd roared.

While Varro railed against the remaining two, keeping them at bay, Spartacus turned back to the fallen man, who was struggling to his feet.

Spartacus kicked away his sword arm, dropping to his knees on the man's bicep, cracking the bone even as he lifted his sword to strike downward.

His victim tried to ward off the blow, shoving the stolen helmet in front of him. Spartacus's sword glanced off its curves, missing the man's face, but plunging deep into his chest.

The sword was stuck fast. Spartacus wasted no time wrenching it free, instead he snatched up his victim's Roman sword—and that of the other fallen opponent.

Now it was two against two. His paired new swords threshing in an unstoppable onslaught, Spartacus cut and slashed against his remaining opponent, pushing him back under a hail of blows, forcing him perilously close to the mounting flames. The man stumbled against the edges of the pyre, pushing up a cloud of red embers that danced in the smoke around the fighters like angry flies. There were choking coughs from among the crowd of onlookers, but few dared to give up their place. Ilithyia retreated, one hand over her mouth, another clutching at her hair, but among the rest of the crowd, there was barely a rustle.

Varro was face to face with Timarchides. The two men shifted, each sizing up the other. Timarchides made to thrust with his sword, revealing it as a feint only at the last moment, as the edge of his shield shoved up toward Varro's face. Varro darted to the side, spinning so as to wheel upon the Greek with the full force of his sword, wielded with two hands.

Beside the pyre, the heat of the flames stung Spartacus's flesh. He saw his adversary struggle and shift as the warmth infested his armor plates. Sweat poured from their bodies as the two men labored against the heat like blacksmiths in a furnace. Spartacus's opponent flinched, and the Thracian saw his moment, driving forward with both swords, shoving the other man back into the flames. Parallel, his twin swords rammed through the gaps in his rival's shoulder armor into the vulnerable flesh, traveling straight through his body and sticking fast in the burning logs.

The flames leapt up, crackling along the hairs on Spartacus's arms. He let go his grip on the two hilts, stumbling back from the shimmering heat as his opponent began to scream. Pinned to the heart of the fire, the man struggled to pull at the blades, even as the flames caught on his hair and in the padding beneath his armor.

"SET ME FREE!" the trapped gladiator yelled. "FREE ME!"

Backing away, his eyes still on his victim as though he was hypnotized by the grim sight, Spartacus tripped into a sitting position. He stared open-mouthed at the other gladiator's dreadful torment. The man screamed for mercy, pleaded in vain for the gods to save him even as Vulcan claimed him.

"Finish him!" Verres shouted angrily.

Spartacus looked back at Verres, and saw him animatedly giving the signal for execution, even as the doomed man shrieked for merciful death.

"This is misery without end," Lucretia muttered.

"An end made worse by burning fool, pulling down the pyre with his struggles," Batiatus wailed, casting about him as though the roaring crowd could provide a solution. Even as he spoke, the struggling human torch tried to drag himself from the flames. He brought the impaling swords with him, pulling one of the flaming logs dangerously out of alignment as he moved. From within the pyre there came the noise of clattering wood and the *whump* of pine needles exploding in the heat. Atop the bonfire, Pelorus's bier teetered threateningly.

Varro did not see it. He pounded with his blade on Timarchides's shield, the distant red flames wreathed behind his head.

Spartacus scrabbled around in search of a weapon. His own purloined swords were jammed fast within the doomed man, their blades already poker-hot within the flames. His former blade was still stuck in the chest of his earlier victim, while Varro had need of his own as he railed against the retreating Timarchides.

Then, Spartacus spied the crawling form of the injured Bebryx, the spear still lodged in him. The wounded gladiator inched in an agonised slither away from the killing ground, toward the crowd. Striding over to him, Spartacus kicked the protesting Bebryx onto his back, and grabbed at the haft of the spear with both hands.

Bebryx cries truncated with a scream as Spartacus wrenched the spear free from his shoulder. As Bebryx collapsed to the ground, whimpering, Spartacus flung the spear toward the burning man, pinning him to the fire one more time, but now in sudden silence.

Varro's sword rang on Timarchides's shield, their combat the sole noise now but for the roar of the fire.

There was a lull, barely noticeable in the rain of blows, in which Timarchides shoved back, punching with the hand that held his sword, slamming into the side of the blond gladiator's unprotected head. As Varro fell, his grip loosened on his sword, and he grabbed instead at Timarchides's wrists, dragging the Greek down with him to the earth.

Varro and Timarchides grunted and strained on the ground. Too close for sword thrusts, each grappled with the other's hands, their weapons dropped, and Timarchides's shield dangling forgotten from his armor. Timarchides seemed to gain the upper hand, clambering on top of the other man, only to roll head over heels, Varro's legs propelling him up and over. Their hands locked in a violent parody of a lovers' embrace, they rolled back to face one another, wrestling to a stalemate, their legs locked, their arms immobile.

"Spartacus!" Batiatus yelled from the crowd. "Finish him!"

Spartacus roused himself, searching around for another fallen weapon, as the other two gladiators wheezed and puffed, each straining against an impossible hold.

Lucretia tutted angrily.

"A ludus error," she scowled at Batiatus. "The crowd sees nothing. There is no victor."

"Spartacus shall play Nemesis," Batiatus said hopefully his gaze fixed on his men as the Thracian gladiator snatched up a fallen shield, staggering across the killing ground toward the grappling pair, his arms upraised, ready to use it as an improvised club.

"To what?" Lucretia spat. "Your gladiators shame you!"

Timarchides managed to roll on top of Varro once more. But, seeing Spartacus's approach, he rolled again, dragging his opponent on top of him as a human shield. Spartacus frowned in confusion, looking for a place to club his enemy. Varro struggled against Timarchides, trying to force him to roll again—

"ENOUGH!"

Verres's voice cut through the melee.

Varro and Timarchides looked into one another's eyes, as if each were daring the other to slacken his hold first.

"Enough! Heed my words!" Verres shouted.

As if in agreement from beyond the grave, there was a tortured crackle from the burning pyre, as Pelorus's flaming bier collapsed in on itself, creating a brief flurry of yellow flames amid the deep reds.

"Noble bustuarii, your battle is done," Verres called. "Release your opponents and stand before your audience."

Exhausted but still tense and wary, the three surviving gladiators formed a ragged line. Spartacus helped the wincing Bebryx to his feet to make four, as the crowd applauded.

"A sight fit for a lanista's funeral!" Verres cried. "Four sent to the afterlife as his guardians in a fight to the death!"

The crowd yelled further approvals. Timarchides nodded curtly at Spartacus and Varro, seeming to offer a grudging respect. Amid the cheers, none but his wife heard Quintus Lentulus Batiatus shouting irate epithets about the genitals of gods.

Wiping the funereal grime from his face with the sleeve of his robe, Batiatus stomped away from the pyre and its attendants, kicking at any Neapolitan pebbles that were unfortunate enough to get in his way.

Lucretia stumbled after him, one piece of her gown draped over her arm to aid her swifter passage along the uneven path.

"Quintus, break open head and share thoughts!" she demanded.

Batiatus grabbed her arm and dragged her off the path behind one of the more imposing cypress trees.

"A plan, hatched in the moment, unhappily subject to unexpected setbacks," he muttered, leaning one arm on the tree trunk and glowering back at the figures silhouetted around the pyre.

"Bebryx will surely not fight again this month. Two of our gladiators out of action before the games even commence," Lucretia hissed. "Of what 'plan' do you speak?"

"Realization only dawned during the eulogy, as Verres was speaking," Batiatus replied.

"Realization of *what*?" She batted his hand away, nursing a forearm that still bore his eager fingermarks.

"No written will exists. These games in 'honor' of Pelorus are mere showmanship for Verres and his eternal desire for greatness." Batiatus stumbled over his words, gulping extra breaths in excitement, like a man who had run twice up a hill.

"Are you unwell, Quintus?" Lucretia asked.

"We are better today than we have been for many years."

"How so?"

"If Pelorus died intestate, Roman law is clear as water. Our departed friend was a freedman, and if a freedman is without an heir, his estate defaults to his former owner."

Lucretia frowned in thought.

"Your father? But he is—"

"Dead! Yes, the old bastard is dead, leaving all of his worldly goods, both material and notional, in the hands of...?"

"You!"

"His grieving son! His noble heir!"

Batiatus grasped Lucretia's hands, trembling with joy.

"It is ours! His house! His ludus! The gladiators within! It all belongs to us!"

Lucretia's eyes narrowed.

"At the very least, we can sell it all off. Our Capuan debts paid."

"Or see our house extended to the shores of Neapolis!"

"So what is the problem?" Lucretia asked.

Batiatus peered around the tree at the imposing form of the freedman Timarchides, who stood watching the flames.

"Him," he replied.

VI

CENA LIBERA

HE STOOD AT THE EDGE OF THE THRACIAN PLAIN, WHERE THE first of a series of rocky outcrops marked the beginning of the foothills. The sky was shot through with the rusty marblings of sunset, though the clouds scudded past at an unearthly pace. Gentle winds tugged at his long hair, while round pebbles poked at the soles of his feet through sheepskin buskins.

He saw figures far away. Thracian shepherds stood as still as statues, surrounded by their flocks. He glanced around him in search of his own animals, but there was nothing there.

Nothing except Sura.

"My husband," she said, in a language he had not heard for more than a year. "My husband has returned."

Her lips were wet and red, like the fruits she picked on the hillsides. Her black hair swirled, the color of tar. He reached out to her but she floated beyond his grasp, seemingly not realizing the ache she caused within him.

"Thrace lives on without us," she said, her voice

echoing, her arm gesturing at the plains below as lightning arced and struck a distant tree.

The clouds scudded faster, and he saw the armies of Mithradates and Rome clashing on the plain below. He looked for the flocks of sheep, and thought for a moment that he saw sheep among the soldiers, but when he looked again, he could only see other warriors: the Getae with their skull-masks and painted warrior-priestesses, Mithradates himself, standing fearless amid flashes of lightning.

Sura kicked her legs behind her, floating in front of him as if swimming in the air, coiling about him, her dark hair puffing behind her as if held in invisible waters. Her tattered clothes drifted apart in a similar fashion, showing him the curve of her breasts and the shadows of her thighs. She reached out her arms to him, beckoning him to take to the sky with her.

"Come with me, my husband," she said. "Be free once more."

He reached out to her, but his fingers could not quite stretch to hers. He leaned over the edge of the rocky outcrop, straining to reach her, but never quite managing to touch. Flames sprang up in the folds of her dress, small at first, then gaining in strength, swiftly rising to engulf her. He recalled the screams of the man fixed to the funeral pyre, who begged for freedom but asked for death.

She looked sorrowful, but not in pain.

"Touch me," she pleaded. "Touch me and we shall be together."

The clouds whipped past her head, as red tears of blood began to trace lines down her cheeks.

"Sura!" he called. "Come back to me!"

Red rain pelted from the sky, drenching them both,

dousing the flames on her body with hisses of red mist. It was blood, blood that covered his arms as they stretched out to her.

"Are you still my husband?" she asked, her voice growing smaller, her form drifting away. "Can you remember who you are…?"

"I will never forget!" he shouted, his words drowned beneath the wind. "My name is—!"

"Spartacus!" Varro said, shaking him. He was awake instantly, his arms up to ward off an attack that never came. He was wet, but with sweat, not blood. There was rain, but it came down outside their cell. He was not in Thrace. He was not free. He was not with her.

"You snatch slumber wherever you can," Varro muttered. "Is this the secret of the Champion of Capua?"

"Unlikely," Barca sneered from the corner of the cell. "He prattles all his secrets while he sleeps."

"My love for my wife is no secret," Spartacus said, rubbing his eyes.

There had been an apocalypse of pigs. Several of the animals had been slaughtered and roasted, their rich meats baked to flaky perfection. Crisp skin and succulent interiors, just the right relic of soft, silky fat. An old slave with a sharp knife carved haunches and hams for those guests who did not simply reach across the table and tear off a chunk for themselves.

Already, the band was playing. Already, there was laughter among the guests. Timarchides and Verres mingled with a crowd that had been too busy to attend the funeral, but all too willing to come to the cena libera— the dinner that marked the eve of a gladiatorial event.

"And why not?" Verres said, laughing diplomatically. "The day was a time to mourn. The night is a time to dance, celebrate, and anticipate the delights of the arena. To the arena!"

He shoved his goblet forward in a gesture of celebration, and was met with enthusiastic echoes from other diners. Timarchides raised his own goblet half-heartedly, and flicked a pinch of wine at the floor.

"To Pelorus," he mumbled, before lifting his head and smiling once more.

Noting Timarchides's mood, Verres turned away from the crowd, and flung an arm around the Greek in earnest camaraderie.

"His shade pours a libation to you in return, my friend. I am sure of it," he said smiling.

Timarchides took a breath, looking around the atrium.

"It was but scant days past," he said, "that we fought for our lives within these very walls."

"A fight well remembered." Verres said. "And honored with vengeance."

"Quaestor or not."

"The quaestor arrives tomorrow for sure?"

"As surely as wind and waves allow. Marcus Tullius something. Strange name."

"An unfortunate interruption during these sad times."

"He is intended to reside with Pelorus."

Verres leaned wearily on the wall.

"Quaestors investigate all things. Legal cases, tax, disputes marital…"

"My release from slavery?"

"Let us hope so."

"Pelorus expected him at the harbor tomorrow."

"Then I shall perform that duty, and divert him

with games and wine. Did Pelorus not have a slave to remember his appointments, and details thereof?"

"The nomenclator? I sought his aid, and he was most uncooperative."

"Why?" Verres asked.

"He is sentenced to die tomorrow," Timarchides replied.

"He should still do his duty."

"This I explained, through the bars of his cell, but his answer was... colorful."

"Would that we yet had some friendly undertakers, who might wring information from him with pliers and tongs."

"It is too late for that. The slaves of House Pelorus are now beyond our reach, locked in the arena under armed guard to prevent them from committing harm to themselves and ruining the spectacle."

"A necessity most inconvenient."

"None of the slaves here tonight belonged to Pelorus. They are rented from our neighbour, the lady Successa."

Verres looked at the anonymous figures that walked among the dignitaries. Their clothes were neat enough for servants at a party, their faces as blank and expressionless as all slaves' faces inevitably became. He did not recognize any of them.

"I am not accustomed to paying attention to the furniture. Are we safe?" Verres asked, inclining his head at the old slave with the butcher knife.

"From him?" Timarchides said. "I am surprised he has not wounded himself. Fear him not. But watch anyone else with a knife!"

"Even I feel wary in the presence of gladiators tonight," Verres admitted.

"We are only exhibiting stock from House Batiatus," Timarchides said. "They are sure to be docile."

"Particularly after the whipping you dealt them this morning," Verres laughed.

"After viewing of the gladiators, other delights will entertain," Timarchides added, ignoring Verres's last words.

Verres shrugged.

"Whatever pleases the guests. Let us begin the viewing."

He glanced around him.

"Where *is* Batiatus? The responsibility lays with him."

Timarchides peered around the atrium in his turn but saw only the table piled high with meats and fruits, and the revelers clustered like fussing bees around the slaves with flagons of wine. Then he spied two figures hunched in the shadows. Timarchides squinted in the half-light, thinking perhaps he bore witness to a lovers' tryst. But the heads jerked and gestures twitched with the animation of harsh words. *Not lovers*, he mused, *a married couple*.

"Patience, Lucretia," Batiatus hissed. "Put it from mind, all will be well."

"Will you buy and train new gladiators before tomorrow's games?"

"That will not be necessary."

"Will you raise Cycnus from the dead? Will you brand your mark upon our porters and see them elevated? Will you heal Bebryx with powerful herbs?"

"Lucretia, calm yourself. Think of the *imagines*!"

"From the funeral? Have the gods deprived you of your senses?"

"A mask changes identity. We command as many gladiators as there are masks."

Lucretia stared at her husband with eyes sharper than a sword.

"They need only be bare-headed in the primus," Batiatus said hastily. "When they chase lions on horseback, their helmets will serve to conceal their identity!"

"And what of their strength?"

"Was such a question asked of the three hundred Spartans? Was it asked of Alexander? Of Horatius? These men are warriors. They can fight all day and all night if I command it."

"I see no problem then," Lucretia said, flatly.

As was her habit, she declared the conversation over by walking away from it—though Batiatus had other ideas.

"Admittedly, beloved," he protested, scampering to keep up with her, "the situation is far from being ideal. But we must work within the possible."

Lucretia stopped suddenly and turned to address her husband.

"You stand at the edge of a precipice," she hissed. "You gamble with our livelihood. Is it not enough that Crixus lies bleeding back in Capua?"

"Spartacus is up to the task."

"Let us hope, Quintus."

They strode into the light of the party, the gathering illuminated by multiple torches in front of burnished bronze mirrors.

"There you are," Verres said to them, beaming. "It is time for you to unleash your beasts!"

Caged in another part of the house, the "beasts" sat around a small fire in a brazier.

Bebryx gulped from a flask of wine, found it empty, and cast it across the room, all one-handed—his other arm was in a sling. He reached for another wine from the dwindling pile.

"You drink beyond your own entitlement," Varro said.

"And you not of yours at all," Bebryx pointed out sourly.

"I am not drinking of it *yet*," Varro replied calmly.

"Varro does not wish to be caught off-guard," Spartacus explained. "Unexpected action may be demanded of us at the cena libera."

"Not my concern," Bebryx said with a shrug, nursing the bandages on his shoulder.

"Indeed," Barca put in. "You have already been caught off-guard today!"

The other gladiators chuckled. Bebryx glared at them with a look that said he willed them all to be struck by lightning.

"To Cycnus," the injured gladiator mumbled eventually, raising a flask that was surely Varro's. Varro made as if to get up, but Spartacus stayed his friend.

"Let him have mine," he said.

"I see not fight avoided," Varro grumbled, "but fight postponed."

Bebryx smacked his lips and smirked.

"The day you cannot take a one-armed man," Barca said, "there will be no more fighting for you." He speared a sausage onto a stick, and held it carefully above the glowing embers. Varro and Spartacus followed suit. The ever drunker Bebryx looked at them and shook his head in revulsion.

"You Romans—" he began.

"I am not a Roman," Spartacus and Barca chorused.

"You Romans and you Roman slaves," Bebryx continued, ignoring their protest. "Look at you."

The other three exchanged baffled glances.

"Roasting your masters' table-scraps over the fire."

Varro laughed.

"You look upon sausage, Bebryx," he said. "What grievance can you have with sausage?"

"Lips and offal, skin and organs," Bebryx replied. "Minced and forced into intestines."

"I know what a sausage is," Varro said. "A rare luxury for a slave."

"Where I come from," Bebryx muttered, "the warriors receive the best cuts. The hunters take the haunches and the steaks. Such relics are the dishes of women and dogs."

"*Victorious* warriors?" Varro asked innocently, glancing at Bebryx's bandage.

"An animal!" Bebryx slurred, bellicose. "A beast of burden flayed, and slain, and shoved up its own ass."

"More for us, if you do not want your share," Barca said.

"I had more distasteful food as a freeman," Varro agreed.

"Better to starve free," Bebryx sneered, "than bend to a master's will."

The sausages began to spit and whine in the heat, their outer skins popping and scorching. Sloshing wine from his purloined flask, Bebryx caught his fingers in some of his elaborate braids, accidentally unraveling part of them. Beads dropped and scattered on the straw-strewn floor. Bebryx cursed in the language of Numidia, using a term close enough to Carthaginian for Barca to smile in recognition.

"Too much trouble," Varro said.

"What?" Bebryx mumbled, not quite focusing on the golden-haired Roman.

"Your hair is too much trouble," Varro continued. "A gladiator should not fuss over his looks like a preening woman."

"You know nothing," Bebryx said. "I suppose you would have me close-cropped and anonymous like the Thracian." He pointed vaguely in the direction of Spartacus, who said nothing, munching slowly on his food. "Or shave my head entirely?" the drunken gladiator added.

"There is a middle ground," Barca said, his mouth full.

"A shaven head is the mark of a prisoner of war," Varro said in agreement. "Unkempt hair, the mark of a barbarian. A gladiator must find some middle ground. He must decide if he wishes to look like a presentable, neatly trimmed, Roman."

"Such as you!" Bebryx snorted.

"Or find some form of hair that marks him out to the crowd from a distance," Barca said.

"Barca's size marks him alone," Spartacus said.

"And what of those who lack Barca's stature?" Varro said. "They need the crowd to remember them. Particularly if," and here, there was the slightest, briefest glance in Bebryx's direction, "their honor in the arena is wanting."

"Honor is what the crowd remembers," Spartacus said with a shrug. "Honor and victory."

"That is easy for you to say, Champion of Capua," Varro said. "What of we mere minnows in the sea of swords?"

"You are easy to see," Barca scoffed, "with your ridiculous golden hair."

"And what of those poor unfortunates who lack the height of Barca or the jet-black skin of Bebryx?"

Spartacus asked. "What then?"

"Perhaps," Varro said thoughtfully, "the crowd might note the hair. They might call for the 'Plaited One' or the 'Braided One'? Will women swoon at the sight of some lizard-like crest down the middle of his head? Will the crowd remember a distinctive mustache or knotted beard?"

"I doubt it," Barca said, belching.

"You talk too much," Bebryx added.

"Ask yourself these questions, and mark them well," Varro continued. "Plaits or braids or knots can serve as additional cushioning, too. Beneath a helmet, they might soften an enemy's blow."

"You talk absent thought," Spartacus said. "What if the crowd uses hair to call for death? Death to the Plaited One! What then, if the Plaited One is *you*?"

"Come," Batiatus said, appearing behind the guard. The shadows in the room lurched sideways as a lantern threw new light through the bars. "It is time to show you off to the crowd. Save Bebryx, and his wounded shoulder."

They marched down the corridor in silence.

"My arm tires with this lantern," Batiatus said after a few moments. "Here, Barca, lead the way."

And as the expressionless Carthaginian lifted the lantern and strode ahead, Batiatus moved to walk beside Spartacus.

"You fought well, Thracian," he said.

"Gratitude, dominus."

"You saw my signal to take on Timarchides."

"Apologies that we did not succeed."

"He is a foe of unexpected prowess. But rest assured that, should another occasion arise to *accidentally* press upon him with deadly force, your dominus approves."

Batiatus scurried ahead to announce his fighters' arrival, while Varro and Spartacus exchanged a cynical glance.

"Fellows all," bellowed the voice of Verres, "the shade of Pelorus welcomes you to this banquet."

The gladiators reached a curtain, where Batiatus was standing. He signaled them to wait.

A few ragged cheers erupted, but most of the crowd stayed respectfully silent.

"And as you surely know, tomorrow, Pelorus, the greatest lanista in Neapolis, will be celebrated in games." The voice of Verres continued with a practiced air of moment and importance. It was the speech of a man used to making others believe that what he had to say mattered.

"When I call your name," Batiatus hissed to his gladiators, "enter as if you are walking into the arena itself."

"Dominus," they chorused in response.

"And for the gods' sake, look *gladiatorial*."

"Dominus."

In front of the curtain, Verres's voice rose to a crescendo, intoning a cue for Batiatus, the lanista of the hour.

Batiatus ducked through the curtain as Verres introduced him.

"Citizens of Neapolis," Batiatus called, voice full of warmth. "united in mourning and in grief, but also in expectations! The surviving slaves of my good friend Pelorus will die tomorrow *ad gladium*, in rightful recognition of their crimes. But tomorrow will also see the finest that another town has to offer. Yes! Prime gladiators from the Campanian hills, the greatest warriors from that nest of Mars—Capua!" Batiatus finished with a flourish and waited, expecting at least a fraction of the cheers that had greeted Pelorus. But, instead, he was greeted with stony silence.

"Capua!" Batiatus cried again pointedly this time. Verres applauded solo, and was eventually joined by a few desultory echoes from among the crowd.

The gladiators lurked behind the curtain, waiting in the dull shadows while their fame was declaimed by Batiatus.

"I give you, Varro!"

Shooting his fellow gladiators a pained look, Varro strode through the curtains, arms raised as if in victory. He was greeted by a series of ragged cheers.

"The Beast of Carthage... Barca!"

Barca swept the curtains aside and roared at the crowd, whose applause rose considerably.

"And the prize of our ludus. The Bringer of Rain. The man who slew the Shadow of Death. The Champion of Capua... Spartacus!"

Spartacus grabbed the curtain and wrenched it from its hooks, staring into the sea of expectant faces. They were low in his line of sight, clustered before the stage. To the crowd in the atrium, the gladiators would seem to tower above them, like statues of the gods.

He walked in to complete silence, peering into the watching crowd in search of—

Women stared up at him hungrily, their gazes dwelling lazily on his chest and thighs. Men stared at him in appreciation or envy... and there, there in the front row, he saw the faintest hint of a sneer. On the face of a Roman youth in his twenties Spartacus saw the contemptuous gleam of a man who thought no gladiator was worth such praise.

He strode tantalizingly close to the audience, within reach of the women's fingertips should they reach out toward him. He walked slowly, deliberately, round to the place where he had sensed a challenge.

His quarry was not expecting it. The man had already forgotten him, and was picking absently at a tray of sweetmeats. It was only as Spartacus drew near that he noticed he had caught the gladiator's attention. The young man looked up, his eyes now wide and fearful, as Spartacus stepped to the edge of the stage, his oiled muscles firm in the brazen light. The gladiator looked down at the man who had glared daggers at him.

Their eyes met, and Spartacus stared deep into fear, into the mind of a foe who only now realized that there were no safe barriers between him and the wild arena animal. Had he bragged to his friends that gladiators were mere clowns? Had he boasted of the prowess of a Roman freeman versus a mere slave? There was no evidence, no facts to lean on, nothing but the simple, naked fear in his eyes as he stared back into the soul of the arena, and realized that he had nowhere to run.

"Spar-ta-cus!" the man said, tremulously. "Spar-ta-cus!" he said again, punching the air. His chant was joined by others, first in hesitant echoes, then in a more powerful voice, as the Champion of Capua basked in the glow of their approval.

At last, he looked away from his antagonist, and gazed out into the crowd at a hundred voices raised up, calling that name by which the Romans knew him. It was praise for another. It was praise for an ideal, not a man. But Spartacus drank it in, all the same.

From the corner of his eye, he caught Varro chanting along with the freemen, while Barca waited in solemn silence.

Batiatus grinned at the crowd's reaction, and twirled his finger in a signal for his gladiators. Spartacus, Varro and Barca marched to the edge of the stage, and began a slow walk around the colonnade, now within touching distance of the crowd. Women giggled excitedly at the sight of their near-naked forms. Men shrugged in approval or masked envy. As they walked, Batiatus addressed the crowd, meanwhile the musicians clambered back onto the stage.

"Such fine specimens of Mars," he cried. "Such deadly creatures in the arena. Tomorrow they will draw blood in memory of Pelorus. Tomorrow they shall fight in the primus, to avenge his death!"

Amid further cheers, Batiatus signaled the band, and the music began once more. As Spartacus and his fellow gladiators left the stage, the dancing girls arrived, tinkling with bells and cymbals, sparkling in the bronze light, their skins bearing the starry sparkle of mica rubbed into oil.

The men in the crowd cheered even louder than they had cheered for the gladiators, pushing toward the stage, while Batiatus detected a distinct rush of soft silks toward food and drink as the women found other diversions.

Seeing no sign of Lucretia or Ilithyia, Batiatus turned instead to watch the stage, as the girls writhed in time to the music. He ignored their pert breasts and glittering skin, and did not dwell on the shadows of their thighs or the curves of their bottoms. Instead, he looked at their faces with the practiced eye of a slaver. The girls jutted their hips in time with the music, curling their hands in gestures of erotic symbolism, but Batiatus watched instead for the look in their eyes.

This one had the sullen, dead stare of a beast of burden.

That one curled her lip as if her every moment on stage was distasteful to her. Perhaps it was, but that was of no concern to Batiatus. Another kept her lips pressed grimly together, concentrating on her movements as if her life depended on it. Perhaps it did—Batiatus saw the telltale welts of a corrective whip on her shoulders, and suspected that her dancing skills came at a price. The fourth, however, the fourth had it all. Long blonde braids fell below her waist. Bright blue eyes, the mark of a northern savage, glittered in the light from bronze mirrors. Her skin was milky white, in stark contrast to the dusky, tanned flesh of most of the other slave women present. She weaved sinuously on the stage, a bright smile upon her lips, her eyes shining beneath her tiara. She saw Batiatus watching her and tongued suggestively at her upper lip. Their eyes met momentarily, before the next turn of her dance took her away from his line of sight.

"She favors you," Timarchides said, who had appeared, unnoticed, by his side.

"As she will any man for a price," Batiatus laughed. "Even you!"

Timarchides said nothing, and Batiatus laughed too long, in an attempt to make it clear it was a joke.

"Cheer yourself," Batiatus said. "Soon you must purchase slaves of your own."

"Indeed," the freedman conceded. "But I shall be sure to buy local stock. *My* house shall be staffed exclusively with *Roman* slaves."

"Local slaves with heads rammed right up their own asses, like other eunuchs in this crowd," Batiatus commented.

"Their response gave surprise?" he asked.

"Capua was once the greatest city in Italia."

"Remind me again why it cannot still make that claim," Timarchides said, his eyes fixed on the gyrating dancers. One half-heartedly held out her arms to him, as if entreating him to embrace her, but he met her gaze without expression, and she turned away with the next phrase of the music.

"Were it not for Rome..."

"Or *Carthage*. The people of Neapolis have heard many tales of the famous war against Hannibal that almost brought Rome to its knees. When the Carthaginians marched across the Alps with their war elephants, and crushed the Roman army at the battle of Cannae. The people of Capua *welcomed* their new Carthaginian overlords on bended knee, with cheeks spread, reaching out hands to stroke Carthaginian cock."

"You twist events long past."

"I merely repeat facts."

"Some have died for repeating less as fact."

"Capua boasts of its champions, but it is nothing but a city of sheep. Its heroes ignorant of true conflict, with knowledge only of the staged victories of the arena. The road to redemption is one fraught with difficulties for citizens of Capua. Though one supposes even the most craven cowards might better themselves in time, with enough luck and virtue."

"I see," Batiatus said stiffly.

"And what do you see?"

"You speak with tongue wet with only days of freedom. Merely because your freedom permits you to speak without being whipped for your insolence, Timarchides, does not mean that you should spit out any bile that springs to mind." His gaze darted around in search of Barca, who could always be trusted to protect him in times of trouble, but Barca was already gone, assuredly already marching back to his cell. "The clarity of the language you speak. Your very ability to complain with such concision is a benefit to you from the Latin world. As is your freedom to whimper like a pup without being slapped like one."

The music and merriment thrummed around them as they stared expectantly, each at the other. Batiatus tensed, wondering how long he would have to ward off any blows before someone came to his aid. His heart pounded, his fists trembled.

And then Timarchides laughed.

"You must forgive me, good Batiatus," he said. "I am, as you so bluntly observed, only recently liberated, and not yet used to the chains of manners that still constrict the free."

"There is time," Batiatus replied, somewhat confused at the sudden change in tone from his companion. He patted Timarchides on the arm in an attempt at camaraderie, and turned away in search of friendlier conversation.

VII

ROMA AETERNA

BEBRYX SNORED FITFULLY IN THE CORNER, HIS BREATHING labored, one hand clutched protectively at the seeping bandage on his shoulder. Empty wine flasks were scattered all around him.

Varro shook one experimentally, then hurled it at the wall. It bounced, noisily, but Bebryx did not stir.

"Bebryx has been defeated by wine," Varro mused. "It has laid him lower than this morning's combat."

Barca ignored him and stretched out by the dwindling fire. Varro hunched sulkily by the embers, and watched as Spartacus lay back on a bundle of straw.

"Fine living can wound a man as easily as hunger," Spartacus observed. "As deadly as a spear."

Varro smirked, and poked at the fire.

"Perhaps," he said.

"And perhaps," Spartacus asserted, "Rome will be brought down from the inside. Not by barbarian threats, but by honey and cured meats."

"You know nothing, my Thracian friend," Varro

said smiling. "Such luxuries are the rewards for Roman virtue. They do no harm in moderation, for the residents of Roma Aeterna, the eternal city."

"Nothing is eternal. Not even Rome," Spartacus said. "There will come a time, some day, when Rome is a distant memory, like the Egyptian Thebes or Barca's Carthage." Barca scowled at him, but listened. "Some day they will wonder at the 'glory' that was once Rome."

"Then glory, too, is eternal," Varro protested. "They will see our roads and aqueducts, our statues and our temples, and they will see a republic grander than any other."

"You see bricks and marble, and Republican finery. But I see the brick-maker, the stone-carver, the weavers and water-carriers. Rome does not rest on victorious laurels or noble sentiments. It rests upon millions of slaves."

"So speaks the ant as he carries a leaf back to the nest. Sure of his importance."

"A great nation can fall. Ask Barca what became of Carthage. What is Carthage now but barren ruins in Africa?"

"Carthage had no divine destiny," Varro insisted.

"And Rome does?"

"Assuredly."

"So speaks the sacrificial bull, nurtured and pampered throughout its life—unaware of its ultimate fate."

Barca chuckled at the Thracian's deft reversal of Varro's argument, but soon grew solemn again.

"Do you not think that the Carthaginians said something similar around their campfires?" Spartacus said. "Right up until the moment they were sold into slavery."

Across the fire, Barca glowered silently.

"Carthage was fated to fall," Varro stated carefully, with an apologetic nod at Barca. "Rome is fated to rise."

"On whose authority? On that of the gods that have shown you such ill favor?"

"Of course."

"Show me their words. Show me their assurances."

Varro chuckled.

"What you ask for is not beyond the reach of men."

The fire crackled between them, as if daring each of them to speak.

"We have no other entertainment," Spartacus said. "Tell us."

"You do not wish to hear this," Varro said. "It will make you seem yet more foolish."

"Really?" Barca interjected suddenly. "Spartacus will look foolish? What better entertainment than that?"

There was muted laughter all around.

"You surely know this story?" Varro said. "It is told to Roman children in their cradles."

"I am a Thracian," Spartacus said.

"I am the last of the true Carthage," Barca said.

Bebryx snorted in his sleep, and then turned over, still dozing.

Varro sighed.

"Then I shall tell you," he said. "I shall tell you a story that you would have done well to know *before* your peoples thought to oppose the might of Rome. It is a tale that dates back to the age of kings, before Rome became a Republic. A story of the last of our kings, the feckless Tarquin the Proud."

"Are you allowed to call a Roman nobleman 'feckless'?" Barca mused. "We would be whipped."

"*I* can call him that," Varro replied. "For I am a

Roman, myself. Those were the days when Greek culture had impact much greater on Italia, when Greek customs and beliefs held great sway with the people. You might even say that Italia was not the center of the world. Instead, it was regarded as a land of distant Greek colonies, 'Greater Greece.'

"Not far from here, in Cumae, there was a prophetess, a strange woman from the east, who dwelt in a cave on the slopes of the citadel. Some say her name was Amalthea, some Herophile, others Demophile. The Romans simply call her Sibyl. And this Sibyl came to King Tarquin with the strangest of offers. She offered him nine books, for a costly sum."

"What was in nine books that was worth so much?" Spartacus wondered.

"Ah!" Varro said. "What indeed?"

He glanced round at the expectant listeners, enjoying their anticipation.

"What could possibly be worth a hundred lifetimes' wealth? I can see you thinking on that very question, as did King Tarquin when he returned to his hearth. What madness was this? What did the witch know? Moreover, what knowledge did she possess when, in full view of Tarquin, she threw three of the books upon the fire?"

He kicked the embers before him for effect, throwing out a cloud of sparks and glowing ash.

"Tarquin watched as the papyrus curled and burned, as the wooden covers darkened and smouldered. Through the flames, he caught sight of ancient letters, scrawled in fading inks, succumbing to the flames! But still he did nothing. And the witch turned to him, brandishing the six remaining books, and asked him if he wanted to buy them at *double the price*!"

Spartacus laughed. Barca muttered something about the foolishness and melodrama of women, particularly hypothetical prophetesses.

"If nine books cost a hundred lifetimes' labor," Varro continued, "how could six be worth twice as much? King Tarquin laughed at the crazy Sibyl, this addled crone from the smoking fields of Cumae. He scorned her offer and told her to leave him in peace, and she looked at him with pleading, tearful eyes. Once more, she begged him to take the books for the sum she demanded, and once more Tarquin turned away in disgust.

"And so, the Sibyl held up three more books, half the remaining total, and weeping this time, as if she were murdering her own child, she cast them also onto the fire!"

Varro kicked at the hearth again, sending up another flurry of sparks.

"Tarquin stared into the flames, and watched three more books burn into cinders, while the witch wept silently. She looked mournfully at the three remaining books, and spoke through her sobs. 'King Tarquin,' she said. 'These last three are all that remain, and they are yours for ten times the original asking price!'

"Ten times, my friends! A thousand lives' labors, for a mere fragment of the original!"

"But what in the books was of such value?" Spartacus pressed.

"Tarquin wondered that himself. He saw something in the witch's eyes that told him this was his final chance. He sensed something in her inverted, perverse means of bargaining, that struck fear into his heart. And so, angry at himself, rage boiling up in his breast, he ordered his slaves to bring him the fortune the witch desired. She went away with a thousand lifetimes' wealth, and left him with nothing but the three books. And Tarquin opened up the books, and looked at their strange lettering, a form of Greek so ancient as to be barely intelligible to the educated Roman. He read verse after verse of arcane oracles, and began to understand the enormity of what he had done. Only now, as he sat in the fading firelight, unrolling these delicate, brittle scrolls, did Tarquin start to realize his monstrous crime. And Tarquin sat by his hearth and wept."

"What was in the books?" Barca demanded, seemingly ready to punch the answer out of the storyteller.

"You tell me! What could it be that was worth *more*, the less there was of it? What text could there be, that would cause a ruler to weep as he read through to its premature end?"

"The… the history of Rome…?" Spartacus asked.

"*THE HISTORY OF ROME!* From the first time the word was uttered on the banks of the Tiber, to the fall of the kings and the foundation of the Republic. Our tribulations against Carthage and the crisis of Hannibal's invasion. The Social Wars, and our campaigns in Greece and Hispania. You and me, here at this very moment! All our victories and our loves. Our children yet unborn, and our children's children! Slaves and nobles, farmers and soldiers, wives and mothers. Everything we are and will be. The people we meet and the enemies we fight; the women we love and the places we settle; the seas we cross and the mountains we climb! Anything and everything that Rome has been or ever will be, was *in those books*!"

"And Tarquin watched six of them burn…"

"So he did."

"Fool," Spartacus murmured.

"Maybe so."

"Rome's history is Rome's history. I shall not be part of it."

"Oh, but Spartacus, you already are. Whether you desire it or not."

"All books must end," Spartacus said, thoughtfully.

The bolt rattled in the door to the cell, and the men looked round to see a guard fumbling at the lock.

"Varro. You are summoned," the guard grunted.

The three gladiators looked at each other in surprise.

"Spartacus is the Champion of Capua," Varro said, carefully.

"Varro. Varro alone."

"Are you sure they do not want the Beast of Carthage?"

"You, Varro. Now."

Lucretia sat up with a start.

"I see you found quiet room, far from moving lips," Ilithyia said.

"A taxing day," Lucretia said, "of great cost."

"A torment," Ilithyia agreed. "You would think Timarchides would arrange enough couches and benches."

"In death," Lucretia mused, "Pelorus has attracted considerably more friends than he had in life."

Ilithyia's eyes widened in excitement.

"We are over-run!"

"Who is to say who is a friend of Pelorus, and who a chancing passer-by? There is no man, free or slave, at the door."

"The nobler Roman would have a nomenclator to remember the names," Ilithyia added, as if Lucretia could not possibly have known this. "My husband has a fine one who is always on hand with appointments, and reminders, and the like. No face comes to our door without the nomenclator whispering: '*Master, it is so-and-so of such-and-such a place. His wife's name is Calpurnia and he is secretly fucking his body slave.*'"

Lucretia raised an eyebrow.

"We are the sum of those that know us," she said. "I was barely acquainted with Pelorus, but I carry fragments of him in my mind. Things my husband has said. Things my late father-in-law mentioned. I carry pieces of his life at one remove. It is all that will be left of him."

"Nonsense," Ilithyia said. "He has a whole day of games to honor him tomorrow."

"Who troubles their mind to remember who gives the games?" Lucretia said.

"Great games stay in the memory for years!" Ilithyia protested. "And it surprises me to hear you, a lanista's wife, claim otherwise!"

"When I die, I would prefer temple offered to gods in place of games."

"I want *games*. I want the best of men, a primus of primuses. I want the finest muscles straining against death in my honor. I want a crowd to see men pierced by blades, screaming in pain in my name!"

"It will be of little solace to you."

"I want to hear them in the afterlife. I want to hear their grunts and moans. I want them to celebrate their victories with an orgy of ludiae, and when they spend their seed inside their whores, I want them to say: 'This I do for Ilithyia.'" Ilithyia gave a little gasp of ecstatic satisfaction, and laughed at her own arrangements.

"Take it from me," Lucretia said with a yawn, "gladiators are not the sort of creatures to dwell much on such things."

"They live for their editors, *and* for those whose honors they enact." Ilithyia pouted at her friend. "You shatter all my illusions," she said. "The more I know of the workings of the arena, the less I crave its delights!"

"Apologies," Lucretia said. "Today's fight leaves me truculent and uncharitable."

"And me parched and coughing!" Ilithyia declared. "And yet Pelorus would have been proud of the House of Batiatus, for providing such a fine show at his last exit."

"I do not think pride was much of a consideration," Lucretia said, setting down her goblet. She looked around her at the shadowy corners, listening for the faint noises of merriment in the main rooms. Outside, she heard footsteps approaching, unhurriedly.

"What do you mean?" Ilithyia asked. "I thought the House of Batiatus was the very core of Pelorus's existence."

Lucretia snorted.

"He never spoke to Verres of the House of Batiatus," she said.

"Indeed he did not," Verres's voice said. The two women looked round to see the subject of their gossip in the doorway, bearing two flagons of wine.

"Apologies, my intention is not to intrude," Verres said. "But I heard the music of your laughter from the hall and wondered if these wines would buy me audience to its notes."

Ilithyia proffered her empty cup with a cascade of giggles.

"We are at your command, Governor Verres," she said, gazing at him from behind her eyelashes. Lucretia managed a pained smile to match, and Verres approached with his purloined wine.

"Is it Gaulish?" Lucretia asked, noting the strange shape of its jar.

"Indeed it is," he said. "Suffused with the flavor of barbarism!" He sloshed some of the red liquid into both their cups, while the women carefully held the drape of their sleeves out of harm's way.

"I fear I have already had enough!" Ilithyia said.

"Ilithyia," Verres breathed. "If you were not already taken by so noble a husband, I would be unable to resist."

"I am sure she would not put up much of a fight, either," Lucretia said dryly.

Ilithyia shot her a dirty look.

"If she were not married, of course," Lucretia added hastily.

"When I have a wife," Verres said brightly, "I shall have a wife." He settled himself on the floor cushions that were scattered at the foot of the couch.

"No woman has laid claim to you?" Ilithyia said, her voice full of disbelief.

"It is true, I have no wife. But there are many women that can be taken to wife—even temporarily. My lesson from a young age was that the Roman way is not one of love, or even lust. But of *power*. Ever since the Sabines. Ever since our men of legend. The Roman way has been one of the exercise of force, if you understand my meaning?" he added, nudging Ilithyia suggestively.

She laughed in peals of glee... and then said, "No."

"I was but a boy when I discovered what it meant to truly *own* a woman," Verres continued. "She was a household kitchen slave, which kept her out of the way for most of the time. But I would see her carrying and chopping, and heading out to market.

"She would wash in the atrium when she thought

herself alone. And she treasured a small, rude-fashioned pot of rouge. When she went to market she would dab the slightest dash of it upon her cheeks. Perhaps there was a grocer she hoped to impress. I never asked."

The two Roman ladies listened in rapt attention. Ilithyia with one hand held to her chest as if to still her beating heart.

"I ordered her to follow me. She made as if to protest but... *sssh*... I reminded her that I was the master in the absence of my parents. Master of the house, and master of her. So she followed me into the bedchamber, and stood there, waiting, nervously."

Verres gazed into two pairs of wide eyes, and smiled inwardly that two women should take such pleasure in the tale of the ruin of another of their sex.

"To have her trembling like a little bird in a snare. That is the joy of being a Roman man, to know that Roman virtue has woven an invisible cage around such women."

"What a thought," Ilithyia said. "Lost to women of our position."

"Why should it be?" Verres asked. "You promise in marriage to give yourself to no other man but your husband. But a free woman cannot give herself to a slave—a slave is not equipped to *take* anything."

"You mean legally...?" Lucretia asked.

"Legally," Verres confirmed with a smirk. "If a slave were to seize you, his life would be forfeit. But if you seized a slave... what harm would there be?"

Ilithyia seized Lucretia's arms excitedly, like a little girl with a new dress.

"Did you hear that, Lucretia?"

"I did," Lucretia said, peeling her friend's hands away. She took a deep drink of her wine and said no more.

"I am sure you do not begrudge your husbands the occasional... *need*, absent the delights of your good selves. Surely they should not begrudge you, either? What matters it to them if you feel a slave's tongue between your legs every now and then?"

Verres flicked his own tongue over his teeth suggestively. Ilithyia slapped him playfully, hooting with excitement. Her face was flushed and her breathing quick.

He stood up as if to leave, only for Ilithyia to jump up and snatch hungrily at his sleeve.

"Do not leave us on the edge!" she cried. "Tell us more."

"I cannot share *all* my secrets with you, lady," he said in mock affront. "It would be like sharing the Eleusinian Mysteries or gazing upon the Sibylline Books. Such matters are secrets for a reason."

"We promise not to tell," Ilithyia said.

Verres glanced about him, as if checking for eavesdropping enemies.

"Be seated," he said, patting the cushion beside him, "and I shall tell you of the delights of the free. Not of slaves merely used, but of loves freely given."

Ilithyia sat, gracefully, a respectful distance from him.

"You too, lady Lucretia," Verres said.

"There is not room enough," Lucretia protested from her couch. "I can attend perfectly well from here—"

"Lucretia, imagine we are at the races and there is but one seat beside me," he insisted. "Though we might accidentally touch! You might tread on my foot. I might..."

Verres suddenly reached out and picked a speck of fluff from Lucretia's gown, his wrist brushing lightly against the top of her breast.

Lucretia gently slapped his hand away.

"My lady, I was merely picking away a scrap of lint from your dress!" Verres protested. "It was marring your otherwise flawless beauty!"

Lucretia laughed in spite of herself.

"And she *smiles*!" Verres cried in victory, while Ilithyia applauded. "The icy demeanour melts before my onslaught. And suddenly we are talking."

"This is also not unusual," Lucretia pointed out. "Men and women have conversation all the time!"

"But we were strangers, and now we are not. I have already crossed the hardest of seas. I am almost in the harbor." Verres raised an eyebrow suggestively.

Lucretia blushed.

"What next? What next?" Ilithyia demanded, bringing the attention back to herself.

"Since we are imagining we are at the races," Verres mused. "Perhaps we should place a bet. I let her go before me, of course, for that is also gallant, but I mark well what horse or chariot she favors, and I wager my coin on the very same. We return to our seats, close to the object of my affections, and *the race begins*!"

He leapt to his feet excitedly, staring across the room at an imaginary racetrack, dragging his two lady companions up by their arms until they were standing at his side.

"The chariots thunder around the circus!" he declared, gesturing wildly. "Every person in the crowd screams the name of their chosen sportsman! And, by the gods, how can this be? We two are yelling for the same rider! We share in his victory! We commiserate in his defeat! If he is victorious, we meet again at the bookmakers. If our chariot falls, in unison we tear up our tickets and lament the cruelties of fate. Whatever the outcome, we have an experience that is most definitely shared!"

"It is almost as if you were *fated* to meet!" Ilithyia breathed, clutching closely at Verres's arm, her crinkled nose nudging at his ear.

"And as the day wears on, we spend more time in each other's company!" Verres continued. "Perhaps the gods are smiling upon us after all. Perhaps, as you say, it is fate indeed. And if it is fate, perhaps we should help it along by conceiving another encounter."

"In the alleys behind the circus?" Ilithyia suggested. "Against the empty barrels?"

"Ilithyia!" Lucretia scolded, aghast.

"At the temple!" Verres responded, with almost as much vehemence himself. "I suggest that we meet the next day at the sanctuary of Venus or at the festival of Mercury. Whatever seems most favorable to bring her back to me."

"Do such stratagems work for you often, Gaius Verres?" Lucretia asked.

"Now, that would be telling," Verres said with a smile. He reached out behind Ilithyia's ear, adjusting an imaginary hair out of place, caressing her ear as he did so. She shivered involuntarily with excitement, and they both laughed.

The guard ushered Varro into a darkened chamber. The shutters had been closed against the night air. Candles and lamps illuminated little, in half a dozen weak glows dotted about the room. In the half-light, Varro saw plush cushions and boxed possessions, as if the occupant were partway through moving in, or moving out.

It was only as the door shut behind the departing guard, that Varro realized the room's occupant was already present.

"You fought well today," said a voice.

"Timarchides?"

"My name, to you, is dominus. Mark it well."

"Apologies, dominus."

"You tried to master me on the field of battle. You and your fellow gladiators seemed intent on bringing death to your foes."

"Apologies, again, dominus."

"You should not apologize for that. A little… eager perhaps for an exhibition fight, but fighting is what gladiators do, after all. Fighting and dying."

Timarchides drew close to Varro.

"You gave me a taste, Varro," he said, "a dim memory reawakened of my days as a gladiator. For a moment, I forgot the dreary security of freedom, and felt the visceral, vital surge of a life lived by the sword."

"You fought well, dominus," Varro said, carefully.

"Of course I fought well!" Timarchides declared, momentarily piqued. "I fought as I fought for my freedom. And won it, too. But you, Varro… you, I hear, gave your freedom up."

"I did, dominus."

"To pay a debt. Your last act as a freeman was to submit to a new master. Where slaves are usually torn from their liberty, resisting, you gave yourself of your own free will."

"I had no choice, dominus. I needed coin for—"

"I care not. I care only that you are a Roman, who has lost his will."

"Dominus?"

"Take it off."

"Dominus?"

"Remove your loincloth."

Varro exhaled and did as he was told. He stood, naked in the dim firelight.

"Excellent," Timarchides said. "You are a fine Roman specimen."

Varro said nothing.

"The cock's a little small," Timarchides said. He reached out to touch it. Varro flinched.

"Such a big man," Timarchides said, caressing Varro's shoulder admiringly. "And yet between his legs, there is nothing but a little finger."

Varro twitched, but said nothing.

"There is something on your mind, slave?"

"There is not, dominus."

"Oh, but there is. You find my words to be an assault on your manhood."

"No, dominus."

"I am sure you would build a tower tall enough with the right incentive. But it is no matter. It only adds to your attraction. In Greece, we are not particularly keen on large cocks anyway. Small is beautiful, for our purposes."

Varro swallowed nervously. Timarchides continued to run his hands slowly over Varro's body, a feather-light touch on the hard curves of his muscles.

"I was a slave myself," Timarchides whispered. "Not by choice."

"Nobody is a slave through choice, dominus," Varro said.

"Oh, but *you* are," Timarchides laughed. "Not I. I was raised in captivity. I was bought and sold like cattle. I was passed from master to master, I fetched and carried, I worked in the fields. I tramped grapes day after day. I was a handsome boy, Varro. Do you know what that means?"

"I do not, dominus."

"Do you know what it means to be a handsome boy, when everything you are can be bought and sold?"

Varro said nothing, for there was nothing to say. Behind him, he heard the sound of something wet and viscous.

"I got accustomed to the sound of fingers dipping in olive oil," Timarchides said. "I got accustomed to the cold touch of oil between my thighs." Varro flinched again as Timarchides's wet fingers pressed between his legs.

"Now, bend over," Timarchides hissed.

"Dominus… I…"

"Bend over. Or should I call your fellow slaves in here to hold you down and witness your humiliation?"

"Dominus!"

"Dominus I am. And slave you are, Varro. And how delicious to imagine there was a time not long ago when our roles could have been reversed. You, the master, and I, the slave who must bend to your will. You cannot resist, Varro. Grapple with me in games, and we are gladiators well matched. But here, in this bedchamber, your very life is forfeit if you do not obey me. Obey me now."

Knowing he had no choice, Varro bent over, resting his hands on the table. He felt Timarchides's hard cock pressing between his thighs, nudging against his testicles. He gritted his teeth.

"Oh it feels so good," Timarchides breathed. "See, it is not so bad to have another man's cock between your thighs. This is how the accomplished seducer acquires all his conquests. First the cock rubs here, in the crux of the legs. Finely plucked, too, Varro, like the best of youths, my congratulations. This must have been how my thighs felt to my seducers, when I was but a young slave."

Varro looked across the room at the flickering lamps and the curtain across the bare window opening. He tried not to think of the man behind him, far too close, whispering in his ear in a manner that no man had ever done before.

"But it is never enough for the man who can have everything," Timarchides continued, his tongue flicking playfully into Varro's ear. "For if I have come this far, why not further?" His hands seized Varro's buttocks, gently but firmly, prising them apart.

"So tense, Roman?" Timarchides said. "There is no point in resisting. What use was there in resisting when the Roman armies came to Greece? Why stand and fight like Philip and Antiochus, Perseus and Andriscus?"

"I do not know of whom you speak…" Varro pleaded.

"Why should you know?" Timarchides responded. "They are forgotten Greek heroes, who fought for nothing."

The tip of his penis nudged against Varro's anus, the olive oil now warm and liquefied, melting the men together.

"My ancestors gave up the fight soon enough, in favor of roads and taxes, prefects and praetors. And what did we give you in return? Answer me, Varro. What has Greece given Rome?"

Varro cleared his throat nervously.

"Philosophy?" he ventured. "The playwrights, Sophocles and—"

Timarchides shoved his cock roughly inside Varro, his hands seizing Varro's waist, refusing to permit any struggle in any direction.

"Culture!" Timarchides shouted. "Greek culture! How does it feel inside you, Roman?"

Varro gasped, his hands clutching at the edge of the table, his eyes screwed tightly shut.

"It is what I tell myself," Timarchides laughed, thrusting repeatedly. "Every… time… I… fuck… a Roman…!"

Varro thought of Rome, eternal and ever greater. His mind dwelt on the unstoppable, ever-widening growth of the everlasting city, as her sons forged ever further, bringing the light of civilization to the world. He thought, proudly, of his birth as a citizen of no mean city, and put from his mind all considerations of his fall from grace. He thought not of his loss of freedom, or the course it set him on. A course that brought him here, bent over a table, in a dark, unforgiving room, while a sweating stranger ground against him, causing waves of sharp pain in his bowels, as spurts of hot liquid forced their way inside him.

VIII

VENATIO

IT WAS BEST TO ARRIVE WITH THE OTHERS. BEST TO BE ONE with the crowd, a surging, teeming mass of humanity. Farmers and blacksmiths, wives and daughters, temple maidens and priests, all came to the arena. But most of all there was the rabble—the crowds of men and women who had no true profession. Freed slaves and unemployed laborers, inured to a generation of grain dole and handouts from politicians, drones happy to suck on the teat of Mother Rome, while other, nobler men fought the wars and brought in the wealth.

Successa was one of them now, she imagined. Who would want a disfigured whore, after all? She might find clients in the darkness. She might make an occasional trade at masked orgies. But what long-term client could she ever hope to cultivate? What man would retain her if she removed her mask to show her seething, weeping welts and scars?

Successa smiled all the same, clutching her veil close to her face as she sauntered through the crowd. She passed fruit sellers and sausage sellers, wine merchants and barbecues. She breezed past the sizzle of chicken and mice, and only briefly glanced at the morning doxies. A woman leaning on the wall by one of the staircases pulled down her gown to reveal full, veiny breasts. The man passing by smacked his lips approvingly, but did not reach into his pouch for coins. Nor was he likely to. Not before the first blood of the day was shed; not before the crowd felt their own blood quicken at the sight of blood on the sands.

The early arrivals thronged toward the front. Successa squinted at the welcome sun, and climbed toward the upper seats, which she knew would be in shadow by midday. And if it rained, the awnings, those great protective sails, were overhead. Seeing the musicians and trumpeters setting up on their dais, she carefully paced a few dozen steps away for the sake of protecting her ears. Eventually, she found the perfect seat, not too far from the killing ground, not too close to the band. It afforded her, too, a view of the balcony, a place where she had once been fondled by a shipbuilder from Puteoli. She looked hungrily at its marble benches and soft cushions, and tables whose coverlets fluttered in the gentle breeze. The balcony was a world away from Successa, now, and as desolate as her heart.

And then, she watched as the dignitaries began to arrive.

"Apologies, apologies," Batiatus laughed, his hands held high in supplication. The sudden rush from the shadows to the sunlight caused his eyes to tighten against the glare. Shading them with his hand, he squinted around the balcony, and found it empty.

"The pulvinus yet stands empty?" Lucretia asked beside him.

Ilithyia glared at them both, as if this was somehow their fault.

Cushioned chairs were placed in prime position, with small tables set ready for refreshments. But there was not even a single slave standing ready to serve. Batiatus leapt back nervously, not wishing the crowd to take him for someone of importance.

"Do we arrive at appointed time?" Lucretia asked.

"Once again this town conspires to fuck me." Batiatus spat in exasperation. "Apologies," he muttered. He smiled cautiously at Ilithyia and Lucretia, and glanced at the position of the sun.

"The time is right for the games to begin," he mused. "The crowd arrives in all its questionable glory. We are mere moments away from the venatio: the great hunt itself. Who would miss the sight of beasts locked in battle? Where are the dignitaries? Why does the sacred chair of honors, the pulvinus itself, sit absent noble ass?"

He leaned, baffled, on the balustrade and scanned the crowd below. A woman in a veil seemed to be staring up at him, but turned away to gaze at the empty sands.

A gust of wind puffed a scrap of dirt into Batiatus's eye, and he flinched, cursing.

Lucretia looked about for a slave to come to his aid. Seeing none, she shook her head in resignation and prepared to dab at her husband's eye with a corner of her gown.

"This is most unwelcome," Ilithyia said sourly. "The sun shines, and I fear I shall have to fan *myself*."

✦

Sailors called it the Afer Ventus, the wind out of Africa. Sometimes it brought warm rain out of the sky as it spent itself against the coast of Italia. Sometimes, it brought reddish dust, mingled with a storm as if the sky were bleeding. Sometimes it brought ships.

Household slaves cursed it for the scum it left on marble floors. Sailors blessed it for the ease with which it filled the sails of ships out of Sicilia. Tack a sail before the Afer Ventus, and there was a clear line straight to the western Latin ports—Ostia or Puteoli or Neapolis.

The ship had been a dot on the horizon, but steadily it grew in size, her sails appearing redder as the distance through the mist decreased. Soon, they were the color of wet terracotta or whipped skin, straining with the full force of the southwesterly wind. The dockside slave masters watched her with half an eye as she grew nearer. There was no need to take to the water in man-powered cutters too soon, no point in rowing out to meet a vessel that was already powering toward port under full sail. Instead, they waited until they saw small, crawling dots, like tenacious beetles, clambering up the masts to furl the sails.

Despite the pitching sea, the distant sailors clung on and drew in the vast sailcloths. To observers on the harbor watchtower, she did not visibly halt, although she stayed in place on the gently rolling waves, neither growing nor diminishing in size.

Now there were shouts from the crews of the cutters— three thin boats packed tightly with heavily muscled oarsmen, heaving against the waves and out toward the waiting vessel. Drenched already by the spray and spume, the cutter crews made swift work of the distance between the harbor and the newly arrived ship.

Sailors aboard the ship threw strong ropes to the cutters, who wound them swiftly about sturdy stern posts. Then, the rowers heaved once more back to shore, towing the sea-going vessel behind them, guiding it into port without the unpredictable winds. It helped that the ship rode with the tide, past the stone abutments of the outer sea wall of Neapolis, and into its calmer inner harbor.

He stood at the prow, lost in thought, watching as the quayside drew ever nearer. His eyes stared but somehow did not see the cluster of toga-wearing men who stood out in stark white contrast to the hempen clothes of the dock laborers. One of the dignitaries waved at him, but he did not acknowledge it, not even with a smile or grimace. It was as if he did not believe the attention of the crowd was directed at him.

He was not the first to descend. That honor lay with the several sailors who swung from ropes onto the harbor side, or who darted along the gangplank to check its purchase and safety. But he was the first of the passengers to touch the stones of the harbor, a tall man in his late thirties, his hair already receded and thinning, his lips pressed together in a grim stoicism.

He was well-fed but not fat, but for the merest beginnings of jowls at his jawline. His prominent nose had a shallow cleft in its tip, like the indentation in a chickpea. He was clad in a simple tunic, more suitable for shipboard life than an unwieldy toga. His left arm, however, jutted prominently from his side as if from force of habit, as if he were used to carrying cloth draped over it—this was a man fit for the Forum, a magistrate and civil servant. His youthful slave walked behind him, at a respectful distance.

The new arrival stared with some degree of suspicion

at the committee on the quay, then looked away and began to walk toward the center of town. He only, truly, acknowledged their existence when a man bodily blocked his path, his arm raised half in hail, and half in entreaty.

"Marcus Tullius Cicero," the man said. "You do us honor with your presence here in Neapolis."

"An unexpected welcoming party," Cicero replied. "If you wait expecting news from Rome, you will be much disappointed." He paused, as if in thought, staring intently as if trying to remember something.

"Gaius Verres, sir," the man introduced himself. "I am on my way to Sicilia to serve as its governor."

"Verres, of course! I hope that in my own small way I have left part of the province all the more efficient, and ready to accept your rule."

"I hope you have kept everyone honest."

"Certainly, I have done my best."

"Well then, I trust you have not tried too hard, or there will not be sufficient sums for me to make, eh!" With that, Verres nudged Cicero hard and laughed. Cicero did his best to smile, but only managed to stretch his lips along a thin and disapproving line.

"To what do I owe this... parade?" Cicero asked, glancing with thinly veiled disapproval at the well-draped dignitaries on the dockside. "My journey is of no great import."

"Oh, but good Cicero, you hide the light of your lamp!" Gaius Verres said. "Your mission is surely of prime importance to the Republic, and we would have you rested."

Cicero appeared decidedly unhappy to hear this, looking about him with some urgency.

"Are there no soldiers here to greet me?" he mused.

"Come," Verres said reassuringly. "The House of Pelorus awaits. My slaves will bear your impediments to your quarters."

"My presence is due elsewhere?" Cicero asked, in some confusion.

"The games commence," Verres responded. "Let us move with haste."

Cicero shrugged, noncommittally.

"The balcony offers prime view! The pulvinus yet reserved for you," Verres said.

"Well then," Cicero said, barely masking his lack of interest. "Fortune smiles upon us."

Varro had been quiet all morning. Spartacus had not pressed the matter, and did not much care. But now he needed assistance, and the hulking blond Roman was the only candidate.

"The grating is level with the arena and faces the killing ground," he said, standing on his tiptoes, peering at a scene that showed him little but the assembling crowd on the terraces.

"Then it is a shame that you are not the height of a Titan," Varro said with a frown.

"I am not, Varro. But two of us may be if we stand together."

"And who, I wonder, do you expect to stand the lower?"

"You are by far the stronger, my friend."

"Stand on Barca's shoulders. He is the tallest."

"He awaits the primus in another cell. So it falls to you."

"Very well," Varro sighed in resignation. He climbed

wearily to his feet, lacing his hands together to form an impromptu step.

Spartacus grasped Varro's shoulders and hefted himself up so he was standing upon them in two swift steps. He grabbed onto the iron grille for purchase. Varro planted his feet firmly in the ground, snaking his own arms to steady Spartacus's calves.

His eyes level with the floor of the arena, Spartacus gazed at a broad expanse of dust and sand. It was like any other arena, except for the center, which was occupied by a small cluster of what appeared to be grassy turf, festooned with fresh cabbages.

"Of what do you see?" Varro asked.

"I can see... a patch of vegetables," Spartacus replied in bemusement.

"I want information of note, not more of your Thracian fever-dreams."

"I speak only truth," Spartacus insisted. "The center of the arena is occupied by a stand of greenery several paces wide."

Four slaves entered the arena bearing a litter shaped like a long, square coffin. Each man was attired in a Greek huntsman's tunic of little more than sackcloth, underdressed for a cool autumn day.

The crowd grew silent as the mystery procession marched solemnly toward the patch of greenery. The men halted a dozen paces from the center, setting their cargo down gently.

Spartacus leaned forward intently, straining to get a glimpse of the strange events.

"What is it?" Varro demanded. "What do you see?"

The whole arena was quiet, the hush broken only by the flapping of the overhead awnings in the capricious wind. All eyes rested on the four slaves as they walked slowly toward the center of the killing ground.

Among the spectators on the north side, someone belched loudly, and there were scattered titters from nearby patrons. Then silence returned once more.

Slowly, deliberately, with a ritual, theatrical quality, the lead slave lifted one corner of the strange box. He reached inside, took hold of something, and leapt to his feet, brandishing a small white object at the surrounding crowd.

The sight was met with an enthusiastic roar of approval, shaking the rafters and spiking into the gladiators' ears. The slave turned slowly, relishing his moment, holding up his small burden for all the crowd to see.

"Now," Spartacus mused, "I truly have seen *everything*." He described the spectacle to Varro.

In the slave's hand was a white rabbit, as pure and clean as a sacrificial temple animal, held by the ears, its hind legs kicking nervously and fruitlessly against its captivity.

The slave knelt on the ground and released the rabbit, which darted immediately for the shadows around the rim, only to stop, raise its head, and dart in another direction. The crowd screamed and jeered, assailing the animal with a wall of noise, from which it retreated in the only direction that would make sense to a woodland creature. After several abortive runs, it turned and pelted to the furthest point from the walls of the arena—the dead center of the killing ground, amid the artificially placed greenery.

"It runs for the center," Spartacus reported, still unsure of the reason for such an arrival. As he watched, the slaves removed the entire lid of the long box, upending dozens of similar white rabbits into the sand.

Many went through similar motions to those of the first arrival, stumbling in confusion in the face of the fearsome din, before turning and bounding for the central green patch. Others sat dumbly on the arena ground, frozen in terror or indifference.

There was the sound of clashing cymbals from below ground—a signal to slaves on both sides of the arena to heave open the doors at either side. A dozen other slaves, similarly attired as huntsmen, struggled into the arena, each holding a snarling, straining dog by a thick leather collar.

"Really," Cicero said. "My preference would have been to walk."

Their litter swayed and jerked as the bearers negotiated their way through the streets of Neapolis. The traffic all seemed to be of one mind, all litters and carts heading in the same direction. Cicero saw nothing but the backs of heads and headdresses, as the litter picked its way through the throng like an interloper in a school of fish. All climbing toward the same destination: the flag-bedecked, sail-topped arena.

"I entreat you," Verres said, "trust my word, you would not care to climb the hill. The long, winding, gentle slope would occupy you far too long, or the several steep stairs that run direct, would leave you wet with perspiration before the commencement of the games."

"Games that *mourn* Pelorus?"

"Indeed. It grieves me to impart sad news, but Pelorus is dead. As executor of his estate, I discovered details of your arrival, and hence came to ease your journey."

The litter suddenly rose and dropped an entire foot, as

the bearers briefly dodged a cart by clambering up onto the kerb. Cicero and Verres smiled.

"Ease my journey?" Cicero laughed. "My passage was calmer at sea! Still, if you hold the estate of Pelorus, my dealings can proceed with you."

"Later. Our journey is near its end," Verres assured him. "The arena and its delights are but moments away."

Cicero winced.

"Delights not sought by me, good Verres."

"You speak not as a Roman!" Verres chuckled.

"I think we may disagree on what makes a Roman," Cicero replied with a shrug. "For me, it is not this... oddly barbaric custom."

"Barbaric? Noble games make us Romans! A tradition most cherished!"

"Truly it is not, good Verres."

"I must disagree! The arena is our proud symbol of military virtue! Our manifest destiny!"

Cicero snorted.

"Of swords and ashes," he said, flatly. "Of death and oblivion. Of ill will and joy in others' pain."

Verres spluttered, unable to form words.

"A quaestor says this! An emissary of Rome says this? Good Cicero, your boldness is Roman even if your words are not. I fear this litter may be struck down by an angry Jupiter."

"Jupiter cares not for games. Nor does any prime god."

"Now, good Cicero, I must protest."

"Then I shall mount my *apologia*. Which deity rules the arena?" Cicero smiled indulgently, signaling that he still regarded their conversation as a game, and not an argument.

"What?" Verres shook his head, unsure of why he was being asked such an obvious question.

"Which divinity rules the blood and sand? You shall have three guesses."

"Mars, of course."

"Not so! Mars rules soldiers and men of war. Presiding over men who fight for just cause. Mars is a god of Rome and Romans, not any rabble that takes up arms."

"I confess surprise," Verres said.

"I thought you would."

"Apollo, then?"

"That lyre-playing peacock? Whatever for?"

"He shines like the sun, he struts around the arena inviting adulation of girls and envy of men. Surely Apollo must be the true god of the arena?"

"You think gladiators fight for vanity's sake?" Cicero said. "They might take care with their appearance, and bask in the love of the crowd, but their minds are occupied with more than merely what eyes hold."

"You have me at loss. You speak of a deity? Perhaps gladiators claim patronage from some famous warrior of legend. Hercules, perhaps? Or Achilles?"

"I said *three* guesses! Already you have had four!"

"Very well. I concede defeat. Who is the true god of the arena?"

"Nemesis!"

"But she is a *goddess*!"

"The daughter of Night! The queen of rough justice! The goddess of vengeance!"

"I believe you not!" Verres said, but even as he spoke, he recalled the fixtures in the House of Pelorus.

"Then become a quaestor of your own doubts," Cicero suggested. "Wander within the warriors' quarters and you shall see their cells adorned with rude statuettes and medallions. You shall see them laying coin for temple sacrifices and whispering her name as they walk onto the sands. It is Nemesis to whom they pray. Nemesis! The architect of spite!"

Curious, Ilithyia peered over the balcony.

"Rabbits!" she cried, clapping her hands excitedly. "Delightful!"

Batiatus looked to Lucretia for support.

"Do I alone find this to be time used to foolish end?" he bellowed.

"I adore the rabbits!" Ilithyia declared, ignoring him.

"I have never seen the like," Lucretia said.

"We have not seen a ludus coniculus in Rome for years," Ilithyia said. "But I suppose it has yet to exhaust its novelty in the provinces."

Batiatus snorted in disbelief as the bewildered rabbits sat, unmoving, in the middle of the arena.

"What now?" he asked. "Do we wager on where they shit?"

"Just wait! Now they shall let loose the hounds!"

Trumpeters on the orchestra dais burst into a brief fanfare. The crowd fell silent, until a final flourish from the musicians. Then, in unison, the dog-handlers released their hold on their animals, and barking with excitement the hounds charged at full speed toward the rabbits.

Ilithyia screamed in peals of glee as the rabbits scattered.

"See how they run!" she yelled. "Is it not marvelous?"

Lucretia did her best to smile in mute agreement.

"You can see a dog chase a rabbit anywhere beneath the sky," Batiatus spat in disgust.

"Perhaps in your rural retreat, close to the land as you are," Ilithyia laughed. "But cultured Romans never get to see such *rustic* pursuits. And from above, too! A bird's eye view indeed!"

"You *live* in Capua," Lucretia said to her friend through gritted teeth.

"We have a Capuan residence, true," Ilithyia said, her eyes not leaving the scene below. "But I think Capua a backwater. I shall be advising my husband to look for a new residence around the bay of Neapolis. It is so *vibrant* here, is it not?"

She giggled again, applauding as one of the dogs pounced on a fleeing rabbit, its jaws closing in a deathly vice on the back of the creature's neck. The dog skidded to a halt in the sands, viciously snapping its head back and forth, tossing its dying prey in a cruel game, whipping the broken body against its own flanks.

"If a simple view from on high is *entertainment*," Batiatus said. "Give me a moment and I shall descend to the arena to take a piss. You can watch from above with heavenly perspective!"

"Tell me the truth or you shall lose your giant's purchase," Varro said, glowering up at Spartacus who still stood upon his shoulders.

"Upon my life," Spartacus replied. "There are dogs chasing rabbits."

His eyes widened at the sight of one of the rabbits dashing directly toward the grille, a pair of panting hounds close behind it.

"That one will make it!" Ilithyia trilled, pointing. "See it run for the edge!"

In spite of himself, Batiatus leaned over the balcony, and watched the chase, the dogs gaining.

"A denarius on the dogs," he said, folding his arms.

"Ten on the rabbit!" Ilithyia cried, striking him playfully.

"Run, little one!" Lucretia shouted, entering the spirit of the game despite herself.

The pursuing dogs jostled for position, each shunting the other, their jaws snapping. Their contest for mastery was to their prey's advantage, the rabbit pulling ever so slightly ahead.

"Bite the little cunt!" Batiatus shouted at the dogs, a sentiment echoed by thousands all around the arena.

One of the dogs tripped, rolling and yelping, leaving its companion to leap ahead in a new burst of speed. The rabbit charged for the hole in the wall, seeing only shadows and darkness and the promise of refuge from the fanged beast that was even now panting its hot, covetous breath against its hindquarters as—

Instinctively, Spartacus jerked back his head as the rabbit plunged through the grille and into the chamber. It tumbled past him onto a surprised Varro. The dog smashed, yelping, into the grille itself, spattering Spartacus with saliva and blood, before stumbling back, its whimpers drowned out by the screaming crowd.

Varro grunted in surprise as the falling rabbit bounced off his head and into their cell. He lost his purchase on Spartacus's calves, and stumbled, falling. Spartacus was left dangling, supporting his own weight wholly on the grille, as Varro fell to the floor laughing.

"Varro!" Spartacus called in annoyance. When it became clear that the blond giant was not coming to his aid, he dropped nimbly to the floor.

"If this spectacle is what the people of Neapolis call a day at the arena," he mused, "our fighting abilities shall hardly be taxed."

He sat back down, leaning against the wall, and listened to the distant chatter of the crowd. Outside, he heard the sound of the guards herding a new group of unfortunates toward a nearby cell.

"Fresh warriors?" Varro mused, his laughter almost subsided.

"Perhaps," Spartacus said. "Or perhaps they demand we fight on the sands against ants and mice."

Partly illuminated by a shaft of light from the arena outside, the broken body of a dying rabbit shuddered, breathing its last before an audience of none.

IX

MERIDIANUM SPECTACULUM

"WHAT FOLLOWS, QUINTUS?"

"The usual midday spectacles. The old and the infirm, the weak and the inconsequential—all set alight."

"How dull. What has been provided for our midday repast?" Lucretia poked the trays of food, and largely ignored the action below, as the newly arrived Timarchides raised his hands for silence, and then bellowed out the coming agenda.

"These games celebrate the life of Marcus Pelorus, honored resident of this town."

A few half-hearted cheers issued from the stands. Batiatus plainly heard some comedian in the stalls grunt "Who?" to cackles from his cronies.

As Timarchides spoke, guards led chained figures out to a series of wooden posts—a dozen in a circle dotted around the middle of the arena.

"It is fitting the first blood of the day should be shed in his honor, and in the attainment of justice for his demise. Those you see before you are slaves of the Household of Pelorus, sentenced to death, as is our custom for all slaves beneath the roof of a murdered master."

"They do not look particularly deadly," Ilithyia observed, chewing on a walnut. "That one looks too old to carry a sword. And *those* are all but children."

"They did not actually murder Pelorus," Batiatus said. "There is yet another fate reserved for *them*."

"You are the expert on gladiators, Batiatus," Ilithyia laughed. "But their appearance seems to lack a warlike quality."

"They are not the gladiators of House Pelorus," Lucretia said. "*Their* sentence is 'to the sword,' which the arena will assuredly take care of in the next few games."

"Then who are *they*?" Ilithyia asked.

"Mere bystanders," Lucretia explained. "In the house of a murdered master, all slaves must die."

"Seems a little unfair on the cook," Ilithyia said with a shrug.

"Then he should have made intervention to prevent the tragedy!" Batiatus said.

"What of the stable boys, and chamber maids?" Ilithyia added. "Simply because some escaped bitch pulls a knife on her master."

"It serves as deterrent," Lucretia suggested. "These slaves cannot be saved, but they can serve as example."

"That is one view, I suppose," Ilithyia mused. "Imagine yourself a slave accused of small crime or indiscretion. If certain death awaits, then what do you have to lose? The thought terrifies."

Outside they heard the cheers of excitement from the crowd, and the shrieks of agony from the burning slaves.

It was nothing unusual for the midday spectacles, and Spartacus and Varro ignored it, as if it were background music in a tavern, or the sound of children playing outside.

A group of half a dozen slaves, marked with the thin welts of castigatory whips, huddled in the next cell. They were five men and a woman. Spartacus found himself unable to take his eyes away from the tattoos and swirls visible on those parts of the woman's flesh that were bare. She saw him looking.

"Have we met before this day?" she asked, as if no bars separated them, and no cage encircled them.

"Perhaps," Spartacus replied, "in the winter forests by the Istros. In the throes of battle."

"A warrior of Thrace," she mused.

"A witch of the Getae," he observed.

"How goes the war, Thracian?" she asked, leaning on the bars. "Have your Roman allies proved to be invaluable?"

"As useful as your Getae witchcraft, it seems," he said, and she laughed.

"Our tribes were friends *before*," she said. "Let us not be enemies now."

Varro snorted in derision.

"You can start your own society," he said. "Savages Together."

"What have you done?" she asked Spartacus, ignoring Varro.

"Done?" Spartacus replied, baffled. "I have yet to do anything."

"Spartacus and I pursue the wild animals in the arena," Varro said, quicker to ascertain her meaning. "We are the catervarii."

"The hunters of beasts…?" she said, sadly.

"It will be a sight to behold," Varro said, his eyebrows

raised conspiratorially. "Our gleaming armor, our flashing spears!"

"It is a sadness that I will not be there to see it," the woman sighed.

Now it was Varro's turn to be baffled.

"Brother," Spartacus said delicately, "they are in the cell before ours. They enter the arena first."

Varro inclined his head.

"But," he ventured, "no gladiators enter before us. Only—"

Varro stopped short, not meeting the woman's gaze.

"Apologies," he said. "I did not understand."

"Only the convicted criminals," the woman said, "only those about to die. Nameless and forgotten. Remembered only for our crime."

"Of what crime do you speak?" Spartacus asked, curious in spite of the situation.

"I killed a Roman," the woman replied with a deadly smile.

Varro sniffed and walked away. He sat on the bench and tightened the straps on his boots, as if the other cage and its occupants had disappeared.

Spartacus, however, grabbed the bars and leaned in closer.

"Whom did you kill?" he asked.

"Marcus Pelorus," she replied, enjoying the surprise in his eyes.

"By all the gods," Spartacus whispered. "*You* killed Marcus Pelorus?"

"I slashed his throat with a table knife. I watched him drown in his own blood."

"Why did you do it?"

"For a moment, I was free," she said.

"How far did you get?"

"We gained but the top of the steps." She shrugged.

Spartacus stared at the dusty floor.

"You will be next," he said after a time. "When human torches burn out, the executions by beast follow."

"What will it be?"

"Lions," Spartacus said.

"You seem sure of it."

"I have been told."

She nodded, thoughtfully.

"Is there any hope?" she asked.

"None," Spartacus said.

"You are honest."

"This is no time for deception."

"You speak true. But they will remember me anyway. If you show me how to fight."

Varro snorted contemptuously in the corner.

"Me?" Spartacus said. "I should offer advice to a woman of the Getae?"

"I am already dead," she said. "Show me how to take a Roman lion with me, purely for spite."

Spartacus recalled the many lessons of Oenomaus, and spoke as his trainer would have done.

"You are not unarmed," he said. "You have your chains. You have the sun and the folly of your opponents. You have the sand and dust of the arena floor."

As he spoke, he realized that his audience had grown. The woman's fellow convicts now stood attentively before the bars that divided them, listening to his every word.

"Any small thing can be used as a weapon. The arena is kept clear of stones, but look for what may have been left by those that came before you. Bones. Nails. Splinters."

She nodded.

"Understand, too," Spartacus continued, "that you are going to die. Nothing will change that."

The slaves grimly met his gaze.

"We knew," she said. "Inside ourselves, we knew that we would never make it far. But it was better to be free, if only for those moments."

"Then you will be free again," Spartacus said. "You will be free for the time it takes for the lions to eat you."

"We will fight," she said.

"Fortuna be with you," Spartacus replied.

The heavy door to the arena swung open, and several armored guards came in. They unbolted the door to the neighbouring cell, prodding at the chained slaves, herding them toward the light.

The woman looked at Spartacus as she was ushered from the cell, calling out to him as she and her fellow convicts were taken on their last journey.

"Remember me," she said. "Remember I was free for a few moments."

"Who are you?" he called after her.

"I am Medea!" she called. "What is your name, *doctore*?"

"My name is…" he began, but the great door had slammed shut.

"She killed a Roman," Varro said quietly. "A Roman like me."

"I have killed many," Spartacus responded with a shrug. "As have you!"

"All the same," Varro said. "My opponents volunteered or paid for crimes past. Hers did not."

✦

The wind drew the stench swiftly over to the balcony. There was none of the modest cedar wood and Asian spices of the recent funeral. Instead, Lucretia's nose caught a whiff of seared flesh and singed hair, with the distinctive tang of cheap lamp oil.

The novelty had worn off for the crowd. In the first throes of the burning, there were cheers at the screams and pleadings, and gasps of excitement as certain articles of clothing seemed more flammable than others. There were jeers and mock gasps at the most colorful of curses yelled at the watching Romans by some of the older slaves, but as the fires rendered them first inarticulate, and the fumes rendered them unconscious, there was nothing to see but a series of burning carcasses.

"You would think this rabble would crave the sight of justice done," Batiatus murmured,

"It *is* midday, Quintus," Lucretia pointed out.

"True," he agreed. There was a flurry of movement from within the antechamber. "On which note," Batiatus added, "more refreshment arrives."

A trio of slaves appeared bearing trays heaped with food. Batiatus was surprised to see they were immediately followed by new arrivals. Gaius Verres himself, all smiles and patted backs, leading a balding, serious-looking young man in a hastily chosen toga.

"Well met!" Batiatus cried. "We feared arrival in the wrong arena."

"Quintus Lentulus Batiatus," Verres said smiling, "and his wife Lucretia, and Ilithyia, wife of Gaius Claudius Glaber, may I present Marcus Tullius Cicero, newly arrived on business of the Republic."

"Welcome! Welcome!" Batiatus said hastily. "Your arrival is well timed for the main attractions!"

Cicero managed a pained smile, nodding respectfully toward the ladies.

"You are the editor of these games?" he said politely to Batiatus.

"Not I," Batiatus said. "I am but lifelong friend of the lamented Pelorus, in whose honor these games are held. But if I were editor…" He stopped, realizing that Verres was standing right beside them.

"Speak, Batiatus," Verres laughed. "My programme does not please you, I am sure."

"I would not dream of disputing with one as respected as Gaius Verres," Batiatus said quickly.

"I never claimed expertise in such matters!" Verres said. "I merely muddle through. Now, where is the *wine*?" He left them together, in search of better flagons in the shade at the back of the balcony.

"I sense your disapproval," Cicero whispered confidentially. "And I share it!"

Batiatus grinned at the apparent arrival of a kindred spirit.

"The gods be blessed, this has been a day of utter trivialities," he replied. "You must thank them that you escaped the rabbit hunt."

Cicero shook his head in disbelief.

"Had I the position of editor," Batiatus confided, "by which I mean *truly* the editor of the games and not a mere supplier of gladiators, there would certainly be some more impressive fights to warm the blood!"

Cicero's friendly smile froze in place.

"I… see…" he said. "You are a lanista? I was mistaken."

"I… er…" Batiatus said, unsure of what had just happened.

"Do excuse me a moment," Cicero said, never letting the smile falter, although his eyes had changed their aspect. "I heard whisper of wine and my journey has been long."

"There is wine, wine enough for all!" Batiatus said enthusiastically. He turned to gesture to a slave and the tray of refreshments. "Moreover, there are fine sweetmeats from—"

But Cicero's back was turned, a goblet in his hand as a slave poured wine. He smiled politely as Ilithyia introduced herself in her habitual, flirtatious manner. Batiatus watched as Ilithyia twirled a lock of her blonde hair in one finger, inquiring excitably as to news from Sicilia.

"What strange encounter was that?" he muttered to Lucretia. "You and I are alone on the balcony once more, even amongst a crowd."

"I fear, Quintus, that you were mistaken for a person of position," she said with a sigh. "And then revealed yourself as a trader in human flesh."

"And yet he said Verres's programme was shit. He is connoisseur of quality games!"

"I believe he disapproves of the games themselves."

Batiatus turned to gaze upon the arena, at a dozen smouldering skeletons, charred flesh hanging from their bones. As he watched, one collapsed, its shoulder bones giving way and leaving one arm still clasped within its dangling manacle.

"So," Cicero said to Verres with a smile, "you are to be the new governor of Sicilia."

"Such is my honor and my burden," Verres responded. "You know the island well?"

"Not long ago I was a solid year working in west Sicilia," Cicero said. "But memories were overshadowed by my return."

"How so?" Verres inquired. Behind him, on the sands, a burning body flinched inadvertently, the soul long since departed, its flanks now a firebrand of burning fats and crisped skin.

"The last occasion I returned to Italia, I put ashore not far from here, just around the bay at Puteoli," Cicero said. "Do you know it?"

"By reputation only. Putrid Puteoli?"

"Spiteful rumour spread by rival spa towns!" Ilithyia protested. "It does not smell. The spring waters run rich with minerals and cleansing warmth. The baths are marvelous. It *is* gentrifying."

"I believe your words!" Verres laughed, his eyes unwavering on hers, willing her to leave the men to their talk. Ilithyia backed away with a smile, uncharacteristically tactful, and went to consort with the Batiati.

"I know it to be so," Cicero continued, "from many visits. And I thought I would put ashore near my home, to greet hospes and dignitaries, drop in on old acquaintances and dispatch letters for the east, rather than take them to Rome, only to send them back again."

"Very wise, I am sure."

"And so I stepped ashore, much as you see me now. Sure that the people of Italia would flock to hear my tales of foreign postings and administrative adventure."

"And did they?"

"Flock they did, demanding to know what news I brought *from Rome*."

"But you had not been to Rome!"

"Quite so! All roads lead to Rome, it seems, and all news must similarly issue from there. I protested I had been away in foreign climes, attending to the demanding affairs of the Republic, and some… *fool* chimes in with: 'Oh yes, you have been in Africa, have you not?'"

"Africa!"

"Africa! So I reply that I have been in Sicilia, and some other slow-witted fool interrupts and says: 'Of course, how is Syracuse?'"

"You were not in Syracuse?"

"Sicilia is more than just Syracuse! So I renounced effort. I nodded and declared my time in parts beyond Italia both useful and productive, and feigned thereafter that I was merely another of the Roman herd, taking myself to Puteoli for the baths and relaxation. A valuable lesson learned."

"Puteoli is full of fools?"

"Romans are deaf to facts and correction. My origin mattered not, concern was only for my arrival. And so I made sure I was *seen*. Seen in the right circles, seen at the baths, seen to be at home to callers, whensoever they called."

"To what do we owe gratitude for the honor of your presence here?" Batiatus said, barging into the conversation, fortified with wine.

The assembled Romans visibly winced as the lanista tactlessly broached the subject that propriety dare not raise.

"A… matter religious," Cicero said, carefully.

"Your meaning, exactly?" Batiatus persisted. He was unaware that Verres was backing away from them, carefully separating himself from the conversation lest he be tainted by its collapse. Even so, he lurked, close at hand, pretending to watch the arena even as he listened on the balcony.

"You are refreshingly direct, Batiatus," Cicero laughed.

"I am sent from Rome for the investigation of a possible prophecy."

"A foretelling of a foretelling?" Batiatus said frowning.

"Indeed!"

Ilithyia and Verres stood next to each other both tense, their eyes staring, unblinking, at the burned flesh and writhing flames of the executions, their lips parted in unified anticipation.

"Does not Rome already have prophecy enough, with the Sibylline Books?" Batiatus asked bluntly.

"The Sibylline Books are in a state of… renewal." Cicero said, sucking in air through his teeth. "The priests of the Capitoline ready to consider any additions."

"Add more to them, as water to jug or wine to cup!" Batiatus chuckled at his conversational gambit, and took the opportunity to refill both their goblets.

"It is not so tawdry," Cicero observed. "Rather it is the serious business of the Republic, an effort to shore up our access to numinous portent. The collection of prophecies from all over the known world."

"So it is like a visit to the fortune teller?" Batiatus laughed.

"It is most certainly not!"

Verres and Ilithyia exchanged a nervous glance as Batiatus dug himself deeper. Verres suppressed a smile, as did the Roman lady. Ilithyia stroked her neck with a finger, giving the universal gesture of a slit throat. Verres nodded with a grin, and clinked his goblet against hers as they both stifled their laughter.

"You resemble a giddy maiden," Batiatus went on, "who wants hands held and stories of future husband told. There is an Egyptian down at the docks who will read the lines in the palm of your hand, relating how many children you will have, and how many lovers—"

"The Sibylline Books are not the work of Egyptian fortune tellers!" Cicero said, his voice raised in protest.

"Are you so sure? You said yourself these oracles find source all over the world. Must these soothsayers pass examination before their work is handed over? Or can anyone take part?"

"Clues of particular note mark out the true soothsayers from mere conjurors and charlatans."

"Of what clues do you speak?"

"I believe that the main clues are linguistic. Oracles jabber away in all sorts of nonsense languages. But if a dizzy, drunken priestess in, say, Bithynia, stumbling and coughing under the influence of some Asian incense, should suddenly spout prophecy in the ancient language of Italia, then one can assume with good reason that a message from the Sibyl is being received."

"And that is the business bringing you to Neapolis?"

"Something of that nature. Say that... say that a Syrian girl, blind since birth and permanently addled on the strange, dream-inducing spices of the orient, began to speak in Greek verse about matters particular to southern Italia. A place which she had never been, or even heard tell of. Would that be strange enough for you?"

"You would find me not surprised?" Batiatus laughed loudly at his own joke, smiling at his fellow dignitaries, not noticing their frozen expressions.

"The order of the prophecies is unclear," Cicero explained patiently, as if talking to a child. "Their relevance is not immediately apparent. Where we use everyday names, they supply poetic allusion. Reference to forgotten gods or strange phenomena. There was, assuredly, material in the Sibylline Books that told us how to fight off Hannibal and his elephants, but, tell me, what is the likelihood that your forefathers would have believed a direct reference to African monsters walking over the mountains to the north?"

"Do you seek to tell me that the Sibylline prophecies tell of futures, but can only be understood *after* events have occurred?"

"The books do not fail, only our ability to interpret them."

"So of what use are they?"

"They offer guidance. When an event unfolds as described in the books, it gives us a brief purchase on the text around it. It allows us, for a moment, to see what is happening in the line after that, and *then* we can see what is to come."

"But if everything is pre-ordained, what matters it if we can see the future or not? The future will come to us anyway."

"Imagine Rome as a ship. A vessel with a divinely mandated destination, sailing through unfamiliar seas."

Batiatus thought for a moment.

"And the Sibylline Books as chart? A map through time?" he said.

"If it aids understanding to look upon things in that way, yes."

Gaius Verres shook his head in disbelief and winked at Ilithyia. She smiled in return and they sipped from their goblets. Watching them, Lucretia realized that they were savoring not the wine but the idiocy of her own husband.

"And you are here with promise of chart?" Batiatus continued.

"Not chart, but seer," Cicero said. "I had word from

the late Marcus Pelorus that within his walls there was an oracle of the distant Getae."

Nearby, Gaius Verres suddenly went into a coughing fit, spluttering red wine all over Ilithyia, who scolded him for damage to her silks, and patted his back in accentuated sympathy.

"A slave of Pelorus?" Batiatus asked with a glance at the choking Verres.

"A recent acquisition from Syrian slavers. A savage, untamed priestess who could be persuaded to speak telling portents with the right inducement."

Timarchides frowned and looked from his wax tablet to the holding pen, and back again. He peered into the gloom at the two gladiators.

"Spartacus and Varro?" he asked.

"I am Spartacus," Spartacus confirmed. Varro's face was expressionless, as if he were struggling to keep all reaction, all emotion from view. The two men climbed to their feet, ready for instruction, but Timarchides simply scowled at his tablet, tapping it frettingly with his stylus.

"Do others share your names?" he asked.

Spartacus and Varro looked at each other in confusion.

"*In the House of Batiatus*," Timarchides spat, vexed.

"Only us," Varro said.

"This is most irregular," Timarchides muttered. "You are listed here on two occasions, as catervarii *and* in the primus."

"We could not speak to our master's intention," Varro said.

"But I have fought more than once on occasion," Spartacus added.

"Does Capua lack sufficient numbers of gladiators?" Timarchides asked with a sneer.

"I have killed the rest," Spartacus replied quietly, and Varro laughed.

Timarchides sighed.

"That events have come to this," he said.

"Your meaning, dominus?" Spartacus asked.

Timarchides sniffed, unbolting their cell portal, beckoning them out.

"Years of toil by Pelorus saw his ludus prosper," Timarchides said, turning his back and walking down the corridor toward the waiting area, assuming with the air of a dominus that they would follow him. He continued to speak as he walked.

"He turned men such as I from feeble youths into gods of the arena. He paid his taxes. His slaves received good care. He built up a fine ludus, the envy of all Neapolis. And then…"

Timarchides banged three times on the grating, paused a moment, and then banged again, causing the slaves on the other side to haul the next doors open.

"…and then one slave brings sentence of death upon them all. All! My brother gladiators I have known for half my life. The serving girls. Even the old medicus!"

Daylight streamed through the open door, bringing with it the smell of manure. Varro's eyes widened at the sight of two massive horses, their eyes shielded by blinkers to keep out the worst sights of the arena, their bridles held by grooms. The horses shifted nervously at every shout from the crowd. Varro looked in panic at Spartacus, but the Thracian was listening to Timarchides.

"Fortuna smiled upon you, dominus," Spartacus said. "That you were freed before tragedy struck."

"Quite so," Timarchides said.

"And even more so," Spartacus said, "that Verres seems to favor you with inheritance."

Timarchides said nothing, already preoccupied with his tablet again.

"Now," he said, scratching behind his ear with his stylus, "your names are upon the list as the catervarii. I doubt not that you can ride?"

"Since boyhood," Spartacus said.

"Horses?" Varro asked.

Spartacus and Timarchides turned to look at him quizzically.

"Of course," Varro said, chuckling nervously. "Of course."

X

AD BESTIAS

"YOU HAVE NOT ATTENDED MANY SUCH GAMES?" BATIATUS said, going to refill Cicero's cup, but finding the wine in it still untouched.

"I favor them not," Cicero said.

"Ah," Batiatus said with a wink. "If you had, Cicero, you would know that the world of literature is *alive* in the arena."

"How so?"

"The sight of two men hacking at each other with swords grows dull over time. The most ill-educated of bumpkins will tire of that diversion soon enough."

"It is surely the reason different kinds of armor are employed?"

"Different weapons, different styles. Costumes from bygone ages. Carthaginian shields, Greek helmets."

"The man with the net?"

"Indeed, the retiarius with his net. All serve certain purpose."

"I am sure they do," Cicero said. "But you spoke of *literature*."

"I did indeed. Apologies. For even such variations in weapons and armor are sure to weary the crowd. Perhaps when gladiatorial combat was a rare thing, seen only in funeral celebrations and the most highly appointed of civic games, such things might have been enough."

"But gladiatorial games are commonplace now," Cicero pointed out.

"Indeed! To the benefit of the lanista! There is always a new politician on the rise. Always a priest with a penance to pay. Always a young patrician boy about to wear the toga of manhood. Birthdays, funerals, weddings, even. Many require celebrations, and celebrations in this great Republic require the shedding of blood and the sight of human suffering. And *that* requires a little originality of thought. Masks to disguise repeat performances, and ways to disguise the use of masks."

"Such as?"

"Such as great moments from legend. Re-enactments of famous stories."

"Really?"

"Oh, Cicero, you have not laid eyes on the greatest of games. A good lanista can fulfill requests both strange and wonderful. A good editor will ensure that even the executions are original. Throwing a bunch of slaves to the lions is child's play. Instead they should be attired in the costumes of our rich history, re-enacting wondrous scenes from the past."

"And the coming tableau is…?"

Batiatus squinted at the painted programme boards near the steps.

"Some… people… eaten by lions."

Cicero sighed.

✦

"And what is our purpose in this?" Spartacus asked.

"You arrive late," Timarchides replied, "and kill the lions once they have met their last victims."

The two gladiators looked at each other.

"Like the Thespian cavalry at Thermopylae," Timarchides explained, "arriving too late. A little joke. Nothing can save the victims."

"Are we to be attired as the Thespian cavalry?" Varro asked, but Timarchides ignored him.

"We shall have to watch and wait," the freedman continued. "Executions *ad bestias* are events that cannot be predicted. It is impossible to know the minds of the condemned. The lions are both hungry and angry, giving hope that events will proceed as planned."

"This sounds as if it is being set up for *comedia*," Varro observed, with a grimace.

"You will play the clown if required," Timarchides warned.

"And I surely can," Varro said.

"My friend's meaning," Spartacus interjected, "is that we are attired as heroes: our armor gleams; our lances decorated with bright pennants. If we are seen to *fail*, attired in this manner, they will find it unsatisfactory."

"If we are to fail, arrive late, and not quite save the imperiled..." Varro agreed.

"Then you need to be attired as fools." Timarchides nodded. He bit his lip and glanced fretfully up at the balcony, where the dignitaries could be seen in animated conversation.

"These games have been thrown together with haste," he lamented. "I have been too busy on matters funereal to adequately arrange such spectacles."

"What would you have us do?"

"Perhaps..." Timarchides mused. "I can lay hands upon some comical masks."

"It might make it clearer that we are the comic relief," Varro agreed.

"Hasten! See what you can uncover!" Spartacus said.

Timarchides scurried back into the shadows, while Varro smirked after his retreating back.

"Did you just issue order to free man?" he asked.

Spartacus shrugged.

"Fate itself decreed he go and look. I merely acted as voice of fate."

"Let us hope so, my friend," Varro said. "For a freedman uncharitable might not smile upon such a Saturnalian reversal."

"I am not desired audience," Cicero explained.

"You are Roman. It is tradition," Batiatus protested.

"So I am told. But I fail to see how any—forgive me."

"Please continue, good Cicero. You are among friends, here."

"Very well. I fail to see how any civilized man can derive pleasure from the sight of a defenceless human being torn to pieces by a wild animal. I see little 'magnificence' in a beast under display, if I am also expected to watch it die for my entertainment."

"Aha! You are one of *those* Romans," Batiatus cried.

"One of what Romans?"

"One who denies the blood and pain upon which our Republic has been built. You talk of 'civilized' Romans. Do you mean people who dwell in *cities*? If so, look around at the very rabble you despise. See how they exult at the bloodshed before them. See how they take simple pleasure from the sight of nature in all its raw intensity."

"It is not *natural* to set fire to a man who is tied to a post," Cicero argued.

"Even a man who was complicit in the murder of his master?" Batiastus countered.

"One crime does not excuse another."

"But you are a man of justice. You actively seek to impose penalty upon wrong doers."

"I exact punishments, that is true," Cicero allowed, "but not for the entertainment of braying animals."

"They favor it."

"They know no better."

"Ha! What book would give them *this*?"

The trumpeters gave the fanfare of the March of Beasts, as half a dozen manacled slaves were ushered into the arena, pushed and prodded by armored guards with long spears and full mail on their arms. These were the tamers who would ensure that both men and beasts would perform correctly, and their armor was designed for all eventualities.

The huddle of slaves was herded into the center of the arena. Clothed in rags, each was chained in individual manacles. They were free to move, but unarmed. There were whispers and giggles among the crowd as they realized that one of the wretches was a woman.

"Before you stand the ringleaders," Verres explained. "Denied the right to die as gladiators, instead, they shall be eaten alive like common murderers."

"Ringleaders? Of what do you speak?" Cicero asked, not following.

"And so it begins," Verres said, eagerly.

"And so it *ends*," Batiatus said. "With justice for Pelorus."

"How so?" Cicero asked.

Batiatus looked at Cicero in bafflement. Over the quaestor's shoulder, he saw Verres signaling frantically for him to be silent, although Batiatus could not understand why he should be silent regarding a matter so vital.

"Have you not been informed of circumstances that brought the death of Pelorus?" Batiatus asked the new arrival.

"Of course," Cicero replied. "Gaius Verres showed kindness enough to meet me at the docks and inform me of the circumstances of my meeting's unfortunate cancelation."

"Of the *murder* of Pelorus," Batiatus clarified.

"He was murdered? How unfortunate," Cicero said without much interest.

"By a slave!" Batiatus continued dramatically. But Cicero seem to remain unmoved.

"Tragic," he said flatly.

"By a slave within his own house!" Batiatus declared, with a triumphant look at Verres.

"Poor Pel— Wait. In his *house*?"

Cicero rose to his feet, his dish of sweetmeats clattering to the flagstones. He stared accusingly at Verres, his arms outstretched in entreaty.

"And Verres, you held tongue this whole day! Speaking of no such thing while we dawdled through the streets, and walked in upon the sight of the burning... Oh sweet Jupiter! You burned the household slaves! Have we been seated here, conversing idly, while the woman I seek roasts alive before us?"

Verres scratched his head.

"I know not, Cicero," he said, not meeting the other

man's eyes. "The freedman Timarchides acts as editor. This day before us bears witness to the execution of all slaves of House Pelorus. Only his gladiators yet remain to be thrown to the beasts, and to each other."

"The servants and house slaves?" Cicero demanded.

"Already dead, before your eyes!" Verres confirmed.

Cicero slumped back down in his seat, suddenly heavy with the weight of unseen years.

"I *despise* Neapolis," he breathed. "My presence here is futile."

Batiatus and Verres exchanged a glance.

"I am rarely at the arena early enough for the deaths *ad bestias*," Verres said. "Will it take long?"

Batiatus responded with exaggerated excitement to lift the mood. "We are dependent upon the whim of the animals. In the wild, tigers and lions are simple creatures, but in the arena they swiftly learn to please crowd. Why, in Capua on one occasion of note, I witnessed a Mesopotamian tiger of great majesty ignore with disdain the criminals placed before him for consumption. Instead, he paced up and down before the balcony, as a gladiator himself, head held high, strutting to and fro in long, calculated ellipses. He paused at each end and raised proud head as if in salute."

"I will wager the crowd loved it," Verres said.

"Oh, they lapped it up!" Batiatus said. "He was not wild and hungry like these poor creatures." He gestured at the animals beneath them. "He knew the crowd. He raised his paw, flexed his claws, in what one could call a feline salute. Awaiting acknowledgment and cheering before turning to the business at hand. It was almost touching."

"Except for the 'business at hand,'" Cicero sulked.

"A murderer, or a rapist, or something. I do not recall. But his death was surely justified."

"And its manner, too?" Cicero seemed unable to resist an argument.

"Assuredly! What better way of discouraging crime than by offering such brutal deterrents."

"As you say," Cicero said. "Perhaps I dream, and such displays were sufficient to prevent the murder of your friend Pelorus."

All three men turned to watch the arena, in silence.

Within the entrance enclosure, behind the gate that permitted entry to the arena, Spartacus lifted himself onto his horse, settling in the saddle.

"Lions only know two numbers," he said to Varro. "One and many. Where they see lone victim, they pounce. Where they see a herd, they wait."

"And how is this fact known?" Varro asked, struggling to clamber into his own saddle. He strained to lift himself across the horse's flank.

"Hunting lions is a rite of passage in Thrace."

"It sounds idyllic. A veritable Elysium."

"You envy me?"

"A little," Varro admitted. "For the hunting and the riding."

"Varro," Spartacus said, realizing, "how much have you ridden?"

"Enough!" Varro scowled, shifting awkwardly in his seat.

"Enough to sit on horseback to travel to the next village?" Spartacus asked. "Or enough to control it in an amphitheater full of hungry lions?"

"We shall see."

"Not encouraging," Spartacus said.

"If I had coin enough to own a horse," Varro protested, "I would not be poor enough to have to become a gladiator!"

Medea knelt down and scooped up a handful of the dark Neapolitan sand.

"We are doomed," one of her companions said.

"Doomed to what?" she demanded. "Doomed to die? *All* are doomed to die. But will I bend my neck to my killer like tired deer? I will not."

The others looked at her and at each other. Across the arena, the inner gate rose up to admit the lions. The men gasped as they caught their first glimpse of the tawny flanks and bony shoulders, a prowling, teeming mass of animal hunger. Some of the lions bounded eagerly onto the sands, others paced warily. All marched ever onward, away from the sharp sticks of the guards, ever closer to the huddle of undefended humans.

The lead creature, a lioness, paused and sniffed the air. One of her mates lapped experimentally, almost tenderly, at a patch of blood, but was prodded onward by the tamers. The lions began to fan out as if they sensed the circular nature of the arena, and that some great prize awaited them in its center.

"They are starved," one of the slaves hissed, fear and panic raw in his voice. "Starved and hungry."

"They are," Medea said. "And untrained. Lions to be sacrificed to catervarii the moment we are dead. They may have never before hunted human prey."

"There is no point," another one of the slaves said, sinking heavily onto the sand. "Perhaps we should kill each other? To lessen the pain."

"No!" Medea declared angrily. "We are already dead. What life yet remains to us should be devoted to spiting the Romans that oppress us!"

"We barely dented their armor in our attempted escape," the slave protested.

"And yet for those moments we were free. And we may yet be free again," she urged.

Another companion unfastened his loincloth, to howls of delight from the crowd. The other slaves stared at him in confusion.

"The Thracian in the cells spoke true," he said. "Anything can be a weapon."

He scooped handfuls of sand into the loincloth, fashioning it into a crude cosh.

"*That* against lions?" lamented the man sitting in the dust.

"*Us* against lions!" Medea shouted, her voice full of defiance.

The men needed no further urging. They, too, stripped off, filling their loincloths with sand from the arena floor. The crowd began to crow in appreciation.

"Hopeless," Verres laughed from the balcony.

"Do you think so?" Cicero asked .

"I would sooner wager coin on the white rabbits," Ilithyia said.

"Not so, my friends, not so," Batiatus said, smiling.

"They will die!" Verres cried.

"They will die like *gladiators*!" Batiatus said. "Counting for all in the arena. Their sentence, punitively, denies them opportunity to die with swords in hand. But even so, they prepare to make stand in the arena. That will earn respect of the crowd."

Cicero watched as the victims in the arena tore off their clothes to fashion makeshift coshes and slings. There were cries of appreciation from the crowd at the sight of their naked forms, particularly the woman. As she tore off her tunic to fashion crude bracers on her arms, she revealed in the process intricate tattoos and scarring that crept across half her body. Cicero leaned in closer, squinting at the distant figures, unsure of what he saw.

"Verres, Batiatus," he murmured, his eyes locked on the arena, "I thought you said that all the household slaves were dead."

"Indeed," Batiatus said. "They are."

"Then who is the painted woman who stands now upon the sands?"

"The ringleader," Verres said carefully. "The very instigator of the uprising."

"That little thing?" Cicero was surprised. "A gladiator?"

"A vicious, conspiring, murderous bitch," Verres said. "I fought her myself during the struggle."

"That is her!" Cicero declared suddenly. "The Getae witch yet lives! Stop the games! I want her spared."

Batiatus and Verres looked at each other and laughed louder than they had all day.

"I order you, with the authority of the Senate and People of Rome, to halt these games!" Cicero insisted angrily.

"You cannot stop the games!" Batiatus said. "Justice will be done, in the name of the gods themselves. Would you defy them…?" He pointed at the sky. And then he pointed all around at the yelling crowd. "Or them?"

Cicero's fists clenched in rage, and he leaned forward in his seat, willing the painted woman to fight.

The doomed men huddled around Medea in the arena. About them, in a ragged circle, patrolled the group of lions, their heads held high, their eyes watching for any break in the human herd they stalked.

"Make a weapon!" Medea urged one man who stared fixedly at the hunters. "As we do."

But he seemed not to hear her. Instead, without warning, he bolted from the group.

"Do not!" Medea shouted. "It is what they want!"

But he was already running, straight for the exit gate.

The bulk of the lions maintained their pacing near the huddle of fighters. Two of the animals, however, peeled off from the main pride, and bounded quickly toward the lone figure.

"A denarius on the male!" Verres shouted.

"On the female!" Ilithyia cried, clutching his hand in excitement. It was all they had time to say before the two lions were neck and neck at the fugitive's heels.

As one they sprang, their competition forcing neither into a strong position. Instead, both snatched at the runner's shoulders, each sinking its fangs deep into an arm. The man remained upright for an instant, before tumbling to the sand at the foot of the balcony, wordless, noiseless, his body was hidden beneath two powerful, tawny beasts.

"Was that a draw?" Batiatus asked innocently.

"The lioness was first!" Ilithyia protested.

"Neither yet claims victim for itself," Verres pointed out. As one, the dignitaries peered over the balcony at the prey's last, desperate struggle.

The fallen man had had time to draw breath, and he let it out in a prolonged, tortured scream, as the pair of lions tugged on his arms. The male snatched for purchase with its claws, raking deep ribbons of red through flesh and down to bone. The female matched him, somehow finding better purchase with her fangs in the shoulder, the teeth disappearing from view, buried in soft human tissue.

"Still nothing in it," Batiatus commented.

"They will rip him apart," Ilithyia said hopefully.

"Then perhaps we shall declare the victor to be the one with the *lion's share*!" Verres said with a grin.

Ilithyia and Lucretia tittered obligingly.

"A literary reference," Cicero said. "Unlikely in such a venue."

"It is?" Batiatus said.

"*Aesop's Fables*," Cicero explained. "Surely, as a child, you must have—?"

"Long, long ago," Batiatus laughed with a wave of his hand. "See how I am re-educated, even amid the rabble!"

"Come on, vicious one!" Ilithyia yelled, still fixated on her lion. "Attack!"

"Ten denarii says she cannot," Verres said.

"Only ten?" Ilithyia taunted him.

The subject of their betting screamed anew, his voice reaching high-pitched animalistic shrieks of pain. His legs flailed impotently, trying, and failing to kick at the lions. The noise of their struggle attracted the interest of the rest of the pride—with lions drifting away in ones and twos to investigate the tussle over still-living meat.

"Follow them," Medea said.

"Surely you jest?" one of the gladiators said.

"Let them be distracted in the fight over him," she said. "Let *us* become the hunters." She started forward, beckoning the rest to follow her lead.

Carefully, with unhurried steps, the slaves began to creep toward the balcony end, keeping together, their gaze not leaving the cluster of animals as they fought over their prey.

A dark-maned male lion lurched closer to the fighting pair, snatching one of the still-thrashing human legs, and attempting to drag the feebly protesting prey in a third direction.

"The nature of such wild beasts makes their actions in the arena unpredictable," Verres sighed, watching from above.

"I think not," Batiatus said. "Rather, I think this behavior entirely predictable."

"Only a moment ago you spoke of grandstanding, and beasts playing to the crowd!"

"Trained beasts. Experienced beasts. These are simply hungry. Starvation enough will turn even lions into jackals."

"I see," Verres said. "I was mistaken, it is clear."

"Your suppliers should have raised awareness of the issue," Batiatus said. "A good editor seeks to avoid such uncertainties."

"I *understand*, Batiatus," Verres bellowed in sudden anger. "Apologies if these games do not reach your high Capuan standards!"

"My husband blames you not, good Verres," Lucretia said, giving Batiatus a look of rebuke as she stepped in to smooth things over. "We all know these games were commissioned in haste, amid tragic circumstances."

"And besides," Cicero said, "the crowd appear to be finding enjoyment, regardless."

The yells from the audience threatened to drown out the dying screams of the lions' victim. The three lions each dragged at the human limbs they gripped firmly in their jaws, vigorously shaking their heads. Then there was a sudden flurry of movement as two of the lions leapt free from the fray. The explosive fountains of blood and the state of the body left behind revealed what had happened.

"They have ripped his arms off!" Verres declared with delight.

"A draw for definite, I am afraid," Batiatus said to Ilithyia.

The pride descended upon the armless body en masse, crowding out the original two pursuers, obscuring the dead slave completely beneath a writhing mass of animal bodies. The original lion pair picked at their measly prizes of the ripped arms, and then discarded them, charging back into the brawl.

Medea stared, eyes narrowed, at the heavy iron manacles that now lay discarded on the sands, wet with blood.

Making a sudden decision, she broke from the group, sprinting for the fallen chains.

A lion saw her break from the pack, and bounded toward her, a streak of yellow-brown fur, blurring against the sand.

Medea reached her target scant seconds ahead of her leonine competitor. She snatched up the fallen manacles, whirling one end as a shepherd whirls a sling. Taken by surprise, the lion was not ready for it, and charged headlong into the speeding metal.

The creature reeled from the blow, shocked to meet invisible resistance, shocked even more as Medea pounded the stunned beast a second and third time with her impromptu mace.

Unbalanced by the blows, the lion's back legs gave way, and it tumbled to the ground. Medea took her opportunity and whipped the tough chain up and around repeatedly, smashing the lion's head into an unrecognizable pulp.

The crowd went wild.

Medea paused, panting, and stood over her victim, her arms and chest spattered with animal blood.

Trembling with exhaustion and adrenalin, she kept her eyes trained on the remaining lions.

Her focus on the animal attackers, one of her fellow slaves seized his chance, coming from behind and punching her hard on the side of the head. As the crowd booed in anger, he snatched the chains from her hands. With Medea reeling on the ground, the man now faced the lions himself, whirling the bloody manacles experimentally.

"Interesting," Verres said idly from his exalted view. "The prey turns upon itself."

"The girl was sharp to improvise such a weapon," Batiatus observed. "But too trusting of her fellow slaves."

"If the slaves do not band together, they will present easier targets," Lucretia noted, peering with renewed interest over the balcony. "This cannot end well."

"I think it is coming to an end in a fashion most splendid to watch!" Ilithyia said. She laughed in Verres's direction and he smiled in return.

But the man with the manacles was not quite as alert as the woman. The next lion leapt at him, somehow getting close enough so that the chains slapped harmlessly against its flank. The animal's paws grasped the man's head, in a parody of a lover's kiss, as its fangs closed on his screaming face.

As he fell, another of the slaves saw his chance, leaping onto the back of the lion, heaving with all his might with his arms locked around the creature's neck.

The observers on the balcony leapt to their feet for a better view — all around the arena there was a flurry of activity as the crowd jostled one another for a better view.

"My eyes yet deceive me!" Batiatus yelled. "Lion wrestling!"

"Never was it imagined that these slaves would bring such valued spectacle," Verres said, thrilled. "We could never have advertised such wonders."

"You cannot pay for spectacles such as this!" Batiatus agreed. "The gods smile upon you, Verres!"

"Although…" Cicero said hesitantly.

"What is it?" Batiatus asked impatiently.

"Well, it may simply be my inexperience at such matters? Or does the crowd now rather favor the hunted over the hunters?"

Batiatus glanced from the balcony at row after row of screaming Neapolitans, all yelling encouragement in Latin, Oscan, and Greek, a rolling cacophony of repeated phrases, one merging into the other, creating a strange, oceanic music of screams. It was almost impossible to pick out single words. One had to listen, to sieve through the contending chants. To…

"'*Kill the lions*,'" Lucretia cried, exasperated. "They call for the slaves to kill the lions!"

"My purse rests on the beasts," Batiatus laughed, clinking his goblet enthusiastically with Verres's.

"Not that one, though," Ilithyia said, pointing at the hapless lion with the slave on its back. His arms were locked around the lion's neck, choking it toward its last breath.

The lion's neck snapped, and its body went suddenly limp in the arms of its killer, who swiftly dropped his victim and scrabbled in the dirt to grab up the fallen manacles. Even as he did so, another lion bit firmly into his leg, its claws raking up his thighs.

Screaming in pain, the slave thrashed down with the manacles, the hard metal clanging on the lion as it refused to let go.

"I am starting to wish I had made water before I climbed up here," Varro mused. His horse shifted uneasily beneath him. Instinctively, Spartacus leaned down to steady it by its bridle.

"It comes to a close," Spartacus said. "I see nobody left standing."

But even as he spoke, a bruised, blood-stained figure staggered to its feet.

"Medea!" Spartacus cried in surprise.

"The ringleader is yet alive?" Varro asked.

"The lions never touched her... Stay down!" he yelled. "Stay down and they will leave you be!" But his voice was drowned beneath the screams of the crowd.

"Are they really seeing justice done?" Cicero mused. "Or do they simply relish the fight?"

"Can they not do both?" Verres asked.

"This hunger for spectacle carries strong risk," Cicero said.

"Strong risk of what?"

"Of becoming trial by combat."

"It is *execution* by combat," Verres stated.

"If the executed play their parts," Batiatus noted. "I fear your criminals believe theirs is to entice sympathy from the crowd, leaving the lions woefully unrepresented."

"Then they will be disappointed, but not the lions."

"Never disappoint the crowd, Verres." Batiatus said, leaning forward in his seat. "Where would your Roman virtue be then?"

"They support a murderess!" Verres protested.

"By acknowledging a warrior's prowess."

"Who is in charge here?"

"They are, good Verres. They are."

Timarchides returned to the horse enclosure, flustered, his arms empty of masks, bladders on sticks, or any other symbols of comedy.

"There is nothing, save disaster," Timarchides said. He wrung his hands.

"We save it by saving her!" Spartacus said, pointing at the beleaguered Medea.

"But she is a murderess!" Timarchides objected.

"And she can die for her offence tomorrow," Spartacus said. "Today the crowd is on her side."

"Verification from the editor is needed before any action is taken," Timarchides said. "Your suggestion amounts to stay of execution."

"Then hasten!" Spartacus shouted. "Before her resolve fades!"

Timarchides sped away, up the dozens of steps toward the band and balcony.

Spartacus immediately began pulling on his gauntlets.

"Dress yourself for the fray," he said to Varro.

"I will wait until commanded so," Varro sighed, leaning on his saddle. His horse sniffed experimentally in the dust, searching in vain for grass. "The slaves yet draw breath. We wait until the last of the criminals has been killed."

"Follow me," Spartacus said, "or do not. Let the crowd decide where the true entertainment lies. Open this gate!" Spartacus addressed the unseen slaves on the other side with authority.

Nothing happened.

Varro leaned on his saddle, smirking.

"They only open to a code," he said.

Spartacus looked at Varro for a moment, and then smiled in realization.

He reached out with his lance and smacked it against the gate three times, paused for a breath, and then struck one more time.

Immediately, the gate began to creak open.

Spartacus dug his heels into his horse, and lurched out into the arena before the door was truly wide. His armor flashing in the sun, he held his lance up high to a roar of approval from the crowd.

Varro stared after the Thracian in disbelief, listening to the unmistakable cheers of the crowd.

Timarchides had nearly reached the balcony, and was standing by the band, when Spartacus entered the arena.

"Fanfare!" he hissed hastily at the trumpeters. "Entrance of Pyramus!"

The first trumpeter leapt to his feet and began a simple salute.

The door opened wider, and Varro rode through at a more measured pace than his predecessor.

The first trumpeter repeated his signal, joined now by a second and a third, as if they had been waiting for Varro all along. The crowd cheered once more and Varro accepted their approval with open arms, wielding his lance, and riding carefully forward into the arena.

"Ah, my interest is awoken," Cicero said, sounding almost entertained.

"Batiatus, what is the meaning of this?" Verres demanded. "The execution is yet unfinished!"

"Is this not part of your plan?" Batiatus asked.

Then Timarchides finally reached the pulvinus, wheezing, and clasping at the hand rail for support.

"I... I..." he began, his finger pointing wildly back at the arena. "There has been a change to the plan!"

"Authorization was not given!" Verres protested.

Below in the arena, Spartacus dug his heels into the flanks of his horse, leaping forward, and charging directly at the beleaguered Medea.

She swung her grisly chains about her in a circle, her strength was clearly fading, her chest heaving with the effort. The lions paced just beyond arm's length. Then one lunged forward, connecting by chance with Medea's flailing chains.

The manacles smacked into its eye with an audible crack, causing it to swerve and snarl at her. Medea moved to face it, unaware that its mate was slinking ever closer behind her. The second lion crouched ever lower toward the ground, its paws extending ahead of it in delicious slowness, its haunches bunching and coiling, making ready to strike.

Had Medea not been preoccupied, she might have noticed that the once-braying crowd had fallen ominously silent. There was only the noise of her exertions and the rattle of the chain as she swung at her tormentors, the scuff and skid of the lions on the sand, and cracks and pops of teeth tearing into bodies.

And the hooves. The steady, ever-closer thunder of the horse Spartacus rode, pelting at full speed straight toward her. Medea did not acknowledge his approach, her mind only on her most immediate assailant. But she heard the horse's feet pounding on the ground.

With the last of her strength, she swung the chains again, pushing the first lion back. She looked up to see Spartacus drawing close, his arm raised up to throw the lance.

Medea's shoulders slumped in anguish. She looked, pleading, into the eyes of the horseman, and sank to her knees.

Spartacus hurled his spear at something behind her.

She stared at him in surprise, only half-hearing the anguished yowl of animal pain. A shadow fell across her as the second lion, pierced by the lance mid-spring, tumbled to the ground transfixed.

Spartacus was practically on top of the lions, close enough for his horse to see over its blinkers the deadly creatures nearby. It panicked, rearing up even as the dark-maned lion leapt for its throat. Lion, horse, and rider fell to the ground, just as the crowd regained its breath and began to yell once more.

Spartacus was pinned beneath his horse, the animal screaming as the dark-maned lion bit deep into its neck.

Spartacus strained to reach his sword, his path to it hampered by the thrashing of his dying mount. The horse's screams were deafening, ringing in his ears, drowning out the noise of the crowd as Spartacus wriggled free from the horse, snatching his sword, and plunging it into the skull of the preoccupied lion.

Medea regained her composure, flinging the manacles at the lioness and turning instead to the lance. She tore it from the creature it had speared, and now faced her tormentors with a real weapon.

The crowd continued their chant of "Kill the lions!"

On horseback, Varro ambled through the pride, less attacking the lions than herding them, the point of his lance prodding them toward the other two human fighters.

One of the lions turned to paw at his horse, and the frightened mount reared up on its hind legs. Varro clung on in a panic, unable to see his horse's front hooves mill into the lion's head, the horseshoes smashing lethal curves into its skull, and bringing it down.

Varro slipped from the saddle, landing on his feet as the panicking beast galloped away. The lions ignored the horse to circle the gladiator, even as Spartacus and Medea closed in behind them.

The number of lions dwindled as the butchery went on. The remainder of the pride wheeled and turned, always finding itself facing a spear-point or a sword, as the humans drew closer together and became more efficient. Their bodies were soaked in animal blood, their hands slippery on their weapons as they hewed into the raging clawed beasts that had formerly ruled the arena.

The crowd leapt in ecstacy, hurling fruits in excitement. Strangers grabbed at each other in delight. In the stands, Successa felt the hard bulge of an erection pressing at her behind. She saw a man pawing at her haunches as the lions had all too recently pawed at their prey, and she let her skirt ride up so that he might find moist sanctuary.

She felt his cock sliding inside her with delicious energy as they watched the lions die, felt him pumping into her as the swords and spears penetrated animal flesh in the arena. Successa felt herself one among many, a watching, screaming, fucking audience that lived for such violent delights. She laughed as she was mounted, thinking of the whores by the steps when there were ones such as she giving such favors away freely.

The orgiastic joy of the crowd was not matched elsewhere.

"This was not the intention," Verres fumed. "The bitch must die."

"She can die another day!" Timarchides responded. "This is a difficult situation eased."

"We are wise to trust the will of the crowd," Batiatus said expansively.

"A savage and unpleasant beast," Cicero said, apparently enjoying himself now. "How does one placate such a monster, I wonder?"

Even as they watched, the fighters in the arena faced a single, lone lion. The animal twisted in uncertainty, unsure of how it had suddenly become the hunted. Sensing victory, Medea hurled her spear, but the weapon

flew wide, eliciting a howl of despair from the crowd.
Varro advanced closer, with greater care, still herding
with his lance, as the creature jerked away from him. It
saw Spartacus dead ahead and launched into a desperate
charge, heading straight for the slight, vulnerable human
target on the sands, its jaws extending for the kill, its
haunches tensing to spring.

It never saw the sword: The blade that had been in the
hand of Spartacus was suddenly, unexpectedly, hurled
through the air as a missile, and its point plunged deep
into the chest of the beast even as it sprang. Its heart
pierced midair, the lion fell, limp, the arc of its leap
matched now only by the screams of the crowd, as the
last of the beasts thudded to the ground.

Suddenly, all was silent, as Varro, Spartacus, and
Medea staggered toward each other, seeking support.
They crouched, leaning on their own thighs, catching
breath well deserved, as the shouts of the crowd erupted
all around them, transforming the audience into one
massive, unending howl of praise.

"The lions are dead, the heroine yet stands," Batiatus
yelled above the noise.

"Heroine she is not, rather fucking murderer!" Verres
shouted.

"Everyone in the arena is a *fucking murderer*!"
Cicero said archly. "I am surprised that you are making
such a discovery only at this moment."

"This is not justice!" Verres railed.

"Such reversals should be expected when you leave
justice to wild animals," Cicero commented.

"Roman justice is for tomorrow," Batiatus urged.
"Today finds the justice of the mob."

"They will do as told."

"Would you command the tides, Verres?" Batiatus laughed.

He leaned in close, grabbing Verres's arm forcefully.

"Only moments remain before crowd is lost," Batiatus hissed. "Trust me, and be remembered as hero. Ignore me, and be forgotten absent virtue."

"Something occurs," Spartacus said, "on the balcony."

"They speak of my fate," Medea said. "Verres wants my death at your hand."

"We serve and obey," Varro said coldly, reaching for his sword.

"You will die—!" she spat, crouching ready to spring.

"It will not come to that," Spartacus said. "It appears Batiatus will have his way."

Verres pulled his hand away from Batiatus.

"Do what you will," he spat. "I tire of this appeasement."

Batiatus leapt up onto the band's podium, his hands raised for silence.

"People of Neapolis," he bellowed to the crowd, "you have seen a great warrior fight today!"

The audience roared in response.

"With hands alone, she began this day sentenced to death by beasts. But the gods, and two brave horsemen have intervened. In recognition of her prowess in the arena, and in a further test of her fighting spirit, noble Gaius Verres, editor of these games, decrees that her sentence should be commuted, *ad gladium*!"

He waved at the cheering crowd, grinning broadly, and

gestured with careful deference to Verres, inviting further applause for the governor's apparent wisdom. Verres rose and acknowledged the cheers with a half-hearted wave of his arm, sneaking a gulp of wine from the goblet in his other hand. He shook his head in resignation and sat heavily back in his chair.

"*Ad gladium*? Put 'to the sword'?" Verres hissed. "We are going to have her killed anyway?"

"After a fashion," Lucretia said, "her *fate* is put to the sword. She will fight and die another day."

XI

PRIMUS

THE FIRST OF THEM WAS CLAD IN THE LONG DARK ROBE OF Charon, the skeletal boatman of the dead on the River Styx. He clutched a long pole, as if for punting his legendary vessel, and wore a bright white mask that showed nothing but the bare features of a human skull. The crowd acknowledged his arrival with a series of old gags—mutterings about friends and relatives due to meet him on the river, or pleas to be left alone until the end of the games. Charon played along, venturing close to the stands to point and leer at the front row, inviting their derision and their fear.

He found an old man in the eastern corner, and prodded at him experimentally with his stick.

"Not yet!" his victim laughed, batting away the punting pole. "You will see me soon enough."

Charon held out a hand painted black with dots of white to signify human bones. He rubbed his fingers together as if demanding payment for the ferryman.

The crowd laughed and jeered, and someone threw an apple core at him. The missile bounced comically off his head, and the ferryman looked left and right, then behind him in a pantomime of irritation.

Charon did no lifting, his presence merely signified the arrival of his minions, the harenarii—cleaners and sandmen, who marched briskly into the amphitheater to drag away the dead and the dying. Even as the boatman of the Styx taunted the crowd, and clowned beneath their debris, the cleaners dragged a cart into the center of the arena, hurling the bodies of man and beast alike onto it. Several lions, a smattering of rabbits, and the visceral remains of several human beings. Too big to lift, the corpse of the fallen horse was swiftly wrapped in chains and towed behind the cart as the cleaners dragged it from the arena.

A second cart of harenarii, pulled by two burly slaves yoked to the front, began a fast trot from the center of the arena, spiraling outward in ever widening circles, toward the arena's edge. Piled high with fresh sand, the cart spread a new layer on top of the sticky wet residue of the morning's combat. Their efforts seemed artificially effective—the sand was of bright, sun-bleached yellow, not the drab gray local ash it covered. The cart finally reached the outer edge, scooping up Charon as it went past.

The ferryman climbed aboard, brandishing his staff at the crowd in mock anger, pointing at various hapless individuals among them, as if to say that they were next for a journey aboard his boat. The cart made its final exit, leaving the arena decorated with a wide swirl of new sand, the underlay now forming a dark spiral within the lighter one.

"A pleasing effect," Cicero said, looking over at the freshly sanded arena, "Resembling pattern of snail's shell in sand."

"It will not long be so arranged," Batiatus said with a frown. "Effect ruined by gladiator's first kick. "

"By then, all eyes will be on fighting once more," Verres said dismissively. "With only the primus of the day remaining."

"Perhaps your skills as editor are more advanced than claimed," Batiatus said generously.

He clinked his goblet apologetically against that of Verres.

"The credit is not ours," Timarchides said. "A development pioneered by Pelorus himself when deal was struck with lanistae in Carthage's new colony."

"A deal? For what?" Batiatus asked.

"Sand," Timarchides replied.

There were chuckles all around the balcony as the assembled dignitaries took this in.

"Truly?" Cicero asked. "This Pelorus sold sand to Africans?"

"In truth," Timarchides explained, "Pelorus sent cartfuls of Neapolitan ash across with the grain ships as ballast. When they returned, he asked for a similar measure of local sand."

There was a communal sigh of understanding.

"Making such effect possible in both arenas. Carthage gets a new color, and Neapolis also," Cicero said, approvingly.

"Good Cicero," Batiatus laughed, "your care seems greater for the aesthetics of grounds-keeping than for sport itself."

Cicero shrugged.

"Are you surprised?" he said with a smile.

"All part of the great drama," Batiatus replied.

"If you want drama, attend the theater!" Verres declared.

"A theater is mere semi-circle," Batiatus scoffed, "the crowd seated around the stage, witnessing story unfold. But the *amphitheater* enfolds drama at its center. It offers no respite, no chance of hidden surprise. Its audience bears witness to the most real and most visceral of dramas—the struggle for life itself."

"You have clearly given thought," Cicero said.

"The lanista is witness to the age, an architect of combat affirming and echoing concerns of the crowd itself," Batiatus stated. "When Rome struggled to contend with Hannibal and his elephants, the arena played out our victory before it even happened, as crowds bore witness to the defeat of men attired as Carthaginians. And when, indeed, Rome proved victorious, so they did in the arena. Just as it revealed the might of the elephants, only to see them set upon and butchered by men of Rome!"

"Batiatus, I proclaim there is nothing proper about what you do, but you do it properly!" Cicero said.

"Both of us merely faithful servants to our profession, Cicero," Batiatus said.

Cicero patted Batiatus's arm in approval.

"The arena as instrument for drama and justice. An idea that intrigues me."

"I am but humble servant," Batiatus said.

Lucretia looked on as the two men bowed their heads in excited talk.

"Your husband has made a friend," Ilithyia said.

Lucretia shrugged.

"With a minor quaestor," she muttered.

"For what reason would Cicero take such sudden interest in games?" Ilithyia wondered.

"I care not if it comes with coin," Lucretia observed.

"I enquire," Cicero was saying, "as to the condition of the painted woman."

"The murderess?"

"The witch of the Getae. A sentence *ad gladium*, for me, would be as fatal as a sentence of death. But for her, it sustains life."

"The Getae woman will yet die, assuredly, she will yet die," Batiatus said. "Only the day is postponed. She will fight in the arena as often as her owner decrees, against any odds her owner desires."

"And if she survives such odds?"

"Impossible."

"Impossible? Who is her owner? Legally, who is her master?"

"You have better legal mind than I. Absent those killed in games, property of Pelorus will be inherited by his heir."

"And which man holds that honor?"

"Pelorus died intestate, but good Verres holds his testament."

"He is the familiae emptor?"

"And his intention is to pass all to Timarchides. Apparently the man was on *intimate* terms with Pelorus."

"Perhaps I might make purchase of the woman from them," Cicero said thoughtfully.

"A price unknown if not put to test," Batiatus pointed out. "The banquet would provide audience for such offer to be made."

"What banquet?"

"With Pelorus laid to rest, his death purged from our

fortunes with bloodshed in his honor, we will replace joy with grief within the walls of his house. A celebration of day renewed and final peace."

"She will meet death soon enough," Cicero mused.

"Though she still stands Fortuna blessed," Batiatus countered.

"It is surely not natural for women to fight."

"In Africa, in nature—"

"We are not animals, Batiatus," Cicero said, with a frown.

"No, we are Romans. Even our women fall superior."

"And what if woman gladiator defeats Roman man?" Cicero said, with a quaestor's logic.

"Ah…" Batiatus stopped, realizing that there was more to an argument that simply speaking his thoughts aloud.

"Would it not send opposite message, if foreign woman succeeds where Roman men fail? I would see her fail soon. And permanently."

"But, good Cicero, think only of *spectacle* were she to be pitted against the most expendable gladiators until novelty was spent. What spectacle could rival that of woman gladiator fighting to the death in the arena?"

"I am yet wary."

"Because it offends tender sensibilities?" Batiatus laughed.

"Because…" Cicero glanced behind him to make sure that the ladies were out of earshot. "Fighting is men's work. If women become combative, if they are encouraged by the sight of their sex holding its ground against men, there is no telling what follies they will be led to."

"Your concern is that gentle Roman women will be turned belligerent by the sight of *gladiatrices* in the arena?"

"That is my concern."

"There is danger in teaching *any* slave to fight. Who knows what else they may learn?"

Batiatus laughed long and loud, but Cicero barely smiled in response.

✦

Spartacus upended a pail of water over his head, washing the grime and sweat of the arena from his body as best he could. He grabbed up a strigil and scraped the dirty water from his body in swift, careful strokes, before grabbing a towel to mop up the rest. It was, habitually, the ritual at the end of a day in the arena. But today, there was still the primus to come.

"The sun is hot today," Varro said. "Do not forget the oil."

"And you," Spartacus said, "wash it from you, lest your sword slip in your hand."

Barca poked around the weapons in the corner of the changing room, picking out a large double-handed axe.

"Do we fight with theme?" he asked. "Does some literary conceit constrain us?"

"We are free," Varro replied. "Free to choose whatever weapons we desire."

Spartacus half-smiled.

"Free," he said. "As free as ever, within chains!"

"You know my meaning," Varro said.

"Whom do we fight?" Barca asked.

"Timarchides did not name them," Spartacus said. "But we fight ten men."

"Impressive odds," Barca mused.

"I shall dress as a Greek hoplite," Varro said. "With spear and sword. Enough to take out foe from a distance."

"And us only three," Barca said, scowling.

"Four," a voice said. They turned to see white teeth and eyes shining from a dark shadow at the gate. The guards opened it and pushed a new figure into their holding cell.

"Bebryx!" Varro said. "You cannot fight—your wounds hinder you!"

"I am a gladiator," Bebryx said, determination in his voice. "While I live, I fight."

The African stood proudly, but with his left arm all but dangling at his side.

"We fight ten men," Spartacus said thoughtfully. "Your presence will be useful, even as distraction."

"Distraction?" Bebryx spat. "My presence will be useful as *killer*!"

Barca laughed appreciatively.

"Attire yourself as murmillo," Spartacus said. "The heavy armor affords better protection with shield to cover wound."

"A shield tied with extra bindings would restrict movement—" Varro suggested.

"But at least protection will be assured," Spartacus agreed.

"I need no crutches as though fucking invalid," Bebryx snarled.

"I seek to prolong your life, in this fight, and the next," Spartacus said mildly. "Do as I say and survive."

"And what will you fight with, Champion of Capua?" Barca asked, voice tinged with sarcasm.

Spartacus thought for a moment.

"The twin swords of the dimacherius," he said. "As with the Shadow of Death."

As he spoke, Timarchides passed by, a doleful look upon his face. The freedman nodded curtly at Spartacus, and Spartacus leaned as far forward against the bars as he could to watch where he went.

The freedman lurked nervously before the bars of a nearby cell. Shadows from within played on his face, as he addressed the occupants.

"I come to say farewell," Timarchides said.

There was no response from inside the cell.

"My brothers," the freedman continued, "let it not end this way."

Someone threw a helmet at the bars.

"Is there choice?" an angry voice spat. "Perhaps you would like to join us, Timarchides?"

"I do not share your sentence."

"You shared our fates. You shared our bread. You shared our victories and our defeats."

"I did, and proudly."

"And now, we die, while you watch from the pulvinus."

"Apologies."

"You apologize for nothing! Where are the rest of our number?"

"Already dead."

"And you place us here, in the far cells, denied consideration of watching them fall."

Timarchides looked away awkwardly.

"My hands are tied," he said.

"They are *not*!" the man snarled. "You are master now, and we yet slaves."

"Indeed!" Timarchides said, his eyes narrowing. "I am no longer slave. I bought my freedom. Paid for with hard-won coin, and such is the receipt upon my wooden sword. I *labored* to avoid a slave's fate, and purchased that right with Fortuna's blessing."

"Fuck you. And fuck Fortuna."

"Perhaps, Scaeva, you should have spent less coin on wine and whores, and more on saving for your manumission."

"Mark that well, Varro," Spartacus murmured quietly to his friend.

Varro frowned at him in confusion.

"There is no talk among them of the love of men," Spartacus hissed. "Only of freedom freely purchased."

Down the corridor, the insults still flew.

"I will show you how a *gladiator* fights."

Timarchides turned away and strode purposefully back toward the arena steps, with the gladiators' jeers pursuing him through the corridor.

"You were no fighter!"

"You were no gladiator!"

"Hoarder!"

"Thief!"

"Coward!"

As he passed Spartacus's cell, Timarchides tried to turn away, his hand rising to his eyes in an attempt to brush away his tears.

The gladiators of the House of Batiatus walked out to the fanfare of a primus, a mismatched platoon of four, marching beneath the roars of the crowd. Spartacus bore two blades, each with a cruel curve near its point. Barca stood, half naked, swinging the great axe. Varro advanced with the almighty oval shield and crested helmet of a Greek warrior. Bebryx wore the heavy armor of a murmillo, his shield held a little too stiffly, clutched a little too close to his chest.

Their opponents were all attired exactly alike. Ten

warriors clutched round shields painted with the two-horned symbol of House Pelorus. Ten hands clutched leaf-shaped swords, dirty and pitiless, each, too, bearing the twin-horned mark on its blade. Ten pairs of greaves, battered and worn, protected shins from low blows.

"So this is the last stand of the House of Pelorus," Cicero mused.

"Their fate is sealed," Verres said with a nod. "Though they were gladiators locked in their cells, they were slaves within the house of a master cruelly murdered. They will all die."

"I confess myself surprised that they play along," Cicero said.

"Your meaning?"

"Were I a slave, told I would die whatever my actions, I doubt that I would care to put effort into honoring my master."

"What would you do?"

"Take my own life! Deprive them of opportunity to gain coin from my suffering!"

The other dignitaries chuckled at the thought.

"Spoken like a true Roman," Verres said with a smile. "That, Cicero, is what separates us from the barbarians."

"You dismiss matters intricate with too much ease," Batiatus said. Lucretia shot him a warning look, but he ignored it.

"I would understand your meaning," Cicero said.

"Gladiators suspected to harbor such self-murdering desires are watched with vigilance," Batiatus explained. "Prevented from pissing without guard to hand, and absent items by which to harm themselves. A gladiator is stock of great value, and as slave, he has not right to damage what belongs to another. Including himself."

"I am a free man, now," Timarchides said with a wry smile. "But if Fortuna had been late with favor, I might find myself on sand."

"Do not let us keep you!" Batiatus laughed. "I am sure a sword and shield can be procured!"

His joke, however, fell flat on an expressionless crowd.

"Quintus!" Lucretia said. "My husband merely jests."

"I am quite used to it, my lady," Timarchides said with a weak smile. "It takes true virtue to acknowledge it in another. Often it is the newest of men who have trouble accepting others to their ranks."

"What is your implication—?" a red-faced Batiatus began, but Lucretia carefully blocked him with her back, pouring more wine for Timarchides as if her husband had ceased to exist. Batiatus stomped back to the dwindling supply of grapes and olives, cramming both into his mouth indiscriminately.

Cicero edged over to Batiatus.

"What is his meaning?" he whispered. Moving away from the refreshments, the two men leaned on the balcony, staring idly at the swirling pattern in the sands below.

"He imagines I despise him because he is newly freed." Batiatus spat an olive pit down onto the pristine sand. "I despise him for being an oily little cunt. A true gladiator knows his place. A slave is already dead in the eyes of the law, a gladiator doubly so. There is nothing left but to fight well."

"In hope of freedom?"

"A gladiator that wins his freedom is rare indeed. Fight well, and die well."

"I struggle to conceive of that."

"You do not live with death day by day, witnessing gladiators fight poorly in the arena, only to find redemption by manner of defeat, baring neck to slayer. If the gods are kind, we shall see such nobility today."

———+———

Spartacus led the way, his swords at the ready, Barca and Varro looming at his flanks, Bebryx bringing up the rear, to best hide his wounds from their opponents. The doomed gladiators from the House of Pelorus stood, their shields up, their swords ready, standing in a wide "V," its mouth facing their oncoming nemeses.

"They draw us in," Varro said. "Their hope to surround us."

"We are not fools," Spartacus muttered, halting.

The two groups of men faced each other across the sands, while the crowd grew restless.

"Split up," Barca said. "Two to each end of the 'V.'"

"No," Spartacus said. "That is what they want."

"We charge," Bebryx said. "Straight into the middle, and fuck them all if they think they can win by surrounding us."

"No," Spartacus said again. "That is also what they want."

"I want to fight," Varro said.

"I want to *live*," Barca said.

His fellow gladiators turned to stare at him in surprise.

"I shall fight," Barca said, scowling. "But let us not be fools. I wish to return to Capua absent injury, that I may buy my freedom."

"Begin!" a familiar voice shouted from the balcony.

"Dominus instructs us," Varro noted.

"I do not accept their will," Spartacus said, nodding at

the enemy gladiators. "Let us ruin their patterns."

"How?" Varro and Barca chorused.

"We attack as one, on one point of the 'V' alone." He gestured with one of his swords at the man closest to the balcony. "Let them break rank to come to his aid. Or stand still and see their advantage worn away."

His fellow gladiators nodded gruffly, and without a further word, Spartacus turned and ran toward the man who stood furthest from the base of the 'V,' far out at the tip of its limb.

Spartacus leapt into the air as he approached, scything down with both his blades, barrelling into the man, the full force of his bodyweight crashing into the shield and pitching them both to the ground.

The man swiftly stood up, but made no attempt to riposte. He was still standing, unmoving, when Barca's great axe hewed into the side of his helmet, hurling him through the air and toward the sands, still. Dead.

Varro and Spartacus exchanged startled glances, seeing the rest of the men remain still. Initial cheers from the crowd soon subsided into a quiet unease. Death alone was not enough.

"This is not right," Verres muttered. "Where is the resistance? Where is the fight? Where is the blood!"

"I fear," Batiatus said, "that the men of the House of Pelorus seek to deny us entertainment." He leaned over the balcony and yelled at the men whose shields bore the twin-horned mark of Pelorus. "Fight, you miserable bastards!" he shouted, a sentiment that met with cheers and jeers from the nearby crowd.

"They raised not a finger to save their master," Ilithyia

noted. "Absent such loyalty it does not surprise that their skills are limited, too"

"They were locked in cells below ground, while their master lost his life," Cicero pointed out.

"Such behaviour has no excuse. They line up like lambs to the slaughter," Verres said.

"I cannot help but feel," Cicero mused, "that they stand bravest of all."

"Then thank the gods that you were not in charge of defending us from Hannibal!" Batiatus said good-naturedly, and all on the balcony laughed.

Spartacus stood before the next man in the line.

"Fight me," he said.

The man simply stared at him.

"Fight me!" Spartacus shouted.

"Why?" the man said, quietly.

Angrily, Spartacus raised his twin swords, but faltered. He realized he could not do it.

Bebryx had no such qualms, and darted ahead of Spartacus before the Thracian's hesitation could be seen. Laughing wildly, Bebryx hacked at the still gladiator with the sharp sword of a murmillo, slashing a wide red gash in his neck. The man collapsed to his knees, pitching over, his blood pumping into the sand, his arms twitching in spastic jerks, and then still.

"Who is next?" Bebryx roared at the crowd, brandishing his sword high to ragged cheers. He advanced to the next man in line, who stood, as his fellow had done, motionless. His mouth was pinched in a snarl but he did not move. As Bebryx loomed closer, he closed his eyes and opened his arms, as if to embrace his slayer.

"This is an *honor*, you ungrateful swine!" the voice of Verres shouted from the balcony. "This is an honor!"

Bebryx hesitated for but a moment, and then thrust his blade firmly into the man's neck, with enough force to smash between the gladiator's vertebrae and out the other side. Bebryx's victim crumpled before him, sliding off the blade, the head all but severed.

In the crowd, someone booed. Soon, the noise was joined by others, low at first and then with growing volume, like a conference of owls.

"I have never found easy victory so hard-won!" Varro muttered.

"Nor I," Spartacus replied.

"It matters not," Barca said. "Let blame fall at editor's feet." He marched toward the opposite line of men, intent on matching Bebryx's slaughter on the other arm of the "V."

Bebryx approached the next man in line. As he drew near, Varro hefted his Greek spear and hurled it at the still warrior. It whooshed through the air in a lazy arc, and clanged harmlessly off a suddenly raised shield.

Realizing that instinct had intervened where will had not, the gladiator sheepishly returned to his stand-to-attention. Bebryx eyed him suspiciously, and then swung his sword at his neck.

The gladiator's sword sprang up, blocking the path of Bebryx's.

"At last!" Batiatus shouted. "Fight!"

Bebryx chuckled in surprise, delighting in the scattered applause that now began to spread around the arena.

"That is better—" he began to say, before the edge of the man's shield smashed into his face.

Spartacus and Varro heard the crowd before they saw

the strike. Bebryx stumbled backward in surprise, his mouth a mess of jagged teeth and seeping blood. Dazed, he raised his sword to strike, only for his opponent to hack down at his right arm, severing it at the elbow.

Bebryx screamed, his stump spurting blood. He twisted to the side, dropping to one knee as his opponent came up behind him, taking careful, deliberate aim at the junction of his neck and shoulder. The doomed gladiator drove his sword straight down into Bebryx's heart from above. Bebryx fell, a lump of twitching meat, as his killer bellowed an angry yell of imprisoned rage.

The killer's face contorted in a sneer, he turned to face the surviving three gladiators of House Batiatus. He banged his sword upon his shield, flicking trails of viscous blood across the sands in elongated strings. Then he pointed the dripping blade at the three men and waited, his feet firm on the earth, his shield raised and ready.

"What true gladiator can resist final fight?" Batiatus exulted.

"And not before time," Lucretia breathed, "it was to become the worst primus in memory."

"It may yet be," Ilithyia observed, "if this warrior's fellows cling to their deluded protest."

"Not so," Batiatus crowed. "Not so! This sudden change in fortune will soon be mirrored. Mark my words."

"Why so elated, Batiatus?" Cicero asked. "You have surely just lost another slave!"

"Bah, one who already proved himself useless at the graveside," Batiatus spat. "Bebryx has died in the best way he could, by bringing this primus *to life*!"

"How so?"

"The death of Bebryx has delivered a dose of the drug that no gladiator can resist."

"Blood?" Cicero asked.

"Applause!" Batiatus cried, gesturing about him at the bellowing hordes of the audience as they roared their support.

"See!" Batiatus cried. "Their feet shift and paw at the sand like unruly horses in their traces! See them turn to face Spartacus and my men. The death of one enemy awakens them. They are sentenced to die this day. They sulk and spit and complain that there is no justice, but now they remember. There *is* justice here, amid the blood and sand, for the man who will *take* it! And if they fall, they die as gladiators!"

The line of the "V" broke in sudden animation, as six men ran to join their fellow warrior. The sands erupted in clashes of steel and wood, as the seven men of House Pelorus joined battle with the three of House Batiatus. Some in the crowd cheered for a gladiator called "Pelorus," unaware that he was not present on the sands. Others yelled for Varro, the Roman Conqueror, clad today in the armor of a Greek warrior. Some, still, cheered for the Beast of Carthage, once a symbol of Rome's greatest enemy, now tamed upon the sands, fighting at the Romans' will, hewing into his enemies with a double-headed axe.

One name rang out above the others, taken up by the crowd, propagating through the stalls and along the steps with each slice toward victory. They cried it out as his twin swords cut into shields and helmets, flesh and bone, he was the "Slayer of the Shadow of Death."

He was the "Bringer of Rain."
"The Champion of Capua."
Spartacus.

XII

SPOLIARIUM

FEW SAW THE SPOLIARIUM. OR RATHER, FEW SAW IT AND LIVED to tell the tale, and no Neapolitan ever asked to venture within. Why would they? It was a place of death and messy endings, of pleadings and suffering. It was no place for a good Roman, only for slaves and beasts who did not know how best to die. It reeked of death, of exotic, unnameable meats left to rot in corners, of scraps of flesh best not identified, putrified on spikes and caught in gratings. The stench could choke a man unready for it; it sent newcomers retching and heaving for the outside world, as if the human body itself recognized, at some atavistic, animal level, that this was a place cursed.

The slave boy shut the door behind him. A hatch opened in the roof above his head, illuminating the chamber for a moment with bright light from above, rays falling on walls stained with black, ancient blood.

Almost as soon as it had arrived, the light was dimmed again by a hail of falling bodies. Lions, men, rabbits and a single horse, dropped through the hatch from the back of the charnel cart, thumping onto the grated floor like sacks of grain. A shield from the House of Pelorus, battered and bent, clattered incongruously with the flesh. A gladiator's body thudded against the wall and crumpled to the ground. Red blood vibrant against black African skin, the knotted hair matted with blood, one arm missing at the elbow. The absent forearm was thrown in as an afterthought, bearing a raised branding scar, a simple letter "B."

The light returned as the last of the bodies hit the floor, then gradually dimmed as the hatch was drawn shut, until only pinpricks shone through once more.

The slave boy listened to the continual trickle of a dozen streams of blood dripping through the grate and into the sewer directly below. He wearily lifted a pair of outsized tongs, and grabbed at the first lion, still bearing the mark of the Thracian's spear. He dragged it in a dozen heaves over to a free space, and then went to grab a meat cleaver from the wall.

"Wait!" a voice said from the doorway. Charon, boatman of the River Styx, stood in the half-light, his hands lifting to his face to remove the skull mask, revealing the wizened head of an old man beneath it.

The slave waited, the meat cleaver poised to fall.

"The lion skins are worth good coin, boy," the man said. "Do not cut them up. Skin them later."

Wordlessly, the boy nodded and picked up the tongs once more. The man who had been Charon hung his long dark robes on a peg, next to the mask. He surveyed the chamber with his hands on his hips, observing the long task ahead.

"I want this room clear by tomorrow," he said. "Lions skinned and separated—teeth, too, if you can. Best cuts from the horse. We feed the dogs tonight."

There was a low groan from the floor. The boy peered at the battered, savaged form that had once been a man.

"This one lives," he said, his voice still in the process of breaking, his accent redolent of the coasts of Sardinia.

"Always the way," Charon sighed, snatching up a long knife from the wall.

"Please…" whispered a voice from the floor. "Help me."

"What do we do?" the Sardinian boy asked.

Charon peered down at a ruin of a man, his features ravened by lion's teeth, one eye seemingly gone, his arm dangling limp and bloody, his chest rent by long, deep claw marks to the bone. Even as he breathed, blood seeped from his wounds and dripped through the grate in viscous, dwindling cascades.

Charon handed the slave the knife.

"Do you yet nurse dreams of fighting in the primus?" he asked.

The boy nodded, hopefully.

"Then here marks the commencement of your training," Charon said. "Kill your first man."

"Wait," pleaded the weak voice from the floor. "Show mercy… mercy…"

"Mercy this is," Charon said flatly. "Well, boy, hurry up."

The boy moved forward and leaned over the wounded man. He then drew his knife across the man's throat, spraying them both with a jet of further blood, filling the chamber with an agonised choking noise that went on and on.

"You must press deeper," Charon said calmly. "That is not a killing wound. Here. Give me the knife."

Charon took the wet blade from his apprentice, and grabbing the curly hair of his victim firmly in his left fist, he drew the knife hard across the wounded throat in a vigorous sawing motion. A trembling, bloody hand clutched momentarily at the apprentice, but sank to the floor, limp and unmoving.

Charon dropped the head to the floor.

The Sardinian boy made as if to say something, but Charon silenced him with an upraised hand. He listened, intently, in the dripping darkness.

"Do you hear it?" he asked.

Through the drips, through the trickles, there was another noise: a labored, shivering breath.

"Another is alive," the boy said.

"For but a few moments longer," Charon said. "Bring the knife. I will show you how to hit the heart."

The boy clambered over the dead horse to reach Charon, who had found his prey among the lions.

"This one might survive, doctore," the boy suggested.

Charon looked at him glumly in the half-light.

"I cannot be medicus. With luck and prayer and the greatest of herbs. With careful cosmetics to hide the worst of the wounds. With help to walk on those broken limbs. He might survive. Will you pay for him?"

The boy stammered, unsure.

"I am but a slave, I merely meant— "

"He is already dead," Charon said. "We are here to remind him of it."

He held out the blade once more, and gestured at a space on the chest as it rose and fell.

"Here," he said. "And slowly. I want you to see the moment that your blade makes a difference."

The boy carefully placed his blade at the allotted spot

and began to push. The flesh puckered beneath the knife's slow advance, then suddenly gave way with a loud pop. The injured man snarled in anguish, began to scream, until Charon silenced him with a hand on his mouth. The noise continued, muffled, while Charon carried on with his lesson.

"Now," he said, "see how his chest still moves. You have barely pierced the flesh. There would be more blood, but he is near bled out. Push on... push on, and see now how he flinches. And here... there!"

There was a sudden upwelling of blood, and the struggling ceased.

"You have pierced the heart," Charon explained. "Measure well the depth required with such a blade."

Some were already leaving as the acclamation of the primus died down. Cicero had seen retreating backs ambling down the steps, even as Verres and Batiatus made their closing announcements. The rabble had already forgotten Marcus Pelorus, if they had ever remembered him. They had forgotten many of the gladiators, too, and the reason that ten fought against four. But there was talk of the remarkable turnabout in fortunes during the fight with the lions, and much gossip of the painted woman who had lived to see her sentence postponed. It was, he heard patrons saying to each other, a fine day of games put on by Gaius Verres, in memory of Someone-or-Other. Pilorux or Plorus or something like that, may he rest in peace.

As Cicero stumbled down the steps after Timarchides, he heard some children giggling about some business with rabbits, which Cicero was grateful to have missed.

"A woman without worth," Timarchides said to him.

"A judgment made by me alone," Cicero said.

"As you seem judge of all things," Timarchides muttered.

"Your meaning?" Cicero said sharply.

"Coming to Neapolis in search of a... what was it? A foretelling of a foretelling? Picking over the spoils of plundered cultures."

"It is necessary, for the continued well-being of Rome."

"Is the past, present and future of Rome not already inscribed in Sibylline Book?"

"A matter of some sensitivity," Cicero sighed.

"Why is that?"

"For the reason that we no longer have them in our possession."

Timarchides turned to look quizzically at the quaestor.

"But they reside in the Temple of Jupiter, on the Capitoline Hill!" he said.

"Burned ten years hence, the books destroyed with it."

Timarchides stood, speechless for a moment. Then he looked about him at the firm, unyielding stone of the arena.

"So Rome is ended? Your history is over?"

"Fortunately, it appears that there is a window in the wall of Fate."

"I would hope so," Timarchides laughed humorlessly.

"The books may be restored."

"You jest!"

"The priests maintain a prophecy is neither created by words inscribed upon a scroll, nor destroyed by burning."

"Really? That is not what I have been told."

"Regardless of what you have been told, no doubt by uneducated Libyan nurses and ill-informed Bithynian house-slaves, the future of Rome may be preserved through solicitation of replacement oracles from around the world."

"If only the late King Tarquin the Proud had been told such a thing, he might have saved himself much grief."

"Do you mock me?" Cicero bristled.

"Of course not," Timarchides smirked. "I mock the priesthood," Timarchides declared, "conniving swindlers with interest only in lining their own coffers."

"Enough! The Sibylline Books can be replaced. Prophecies have been sought from all edges of the known world. They are to be collated in Rome and examined by the assigned priests. History will go on."

"Thank the gods for that."

"And gratitude to you for preserving one."

"Of what do you speak?"

"The woman Medea."

"She is not preserved."

"I would buy her from you."

"She will die for her crime, and soon."

"Then may I at least examine her tonight?"

"Unfamiliar words for familiar request."

Batiatus found himself descending the steps at the same pace as Verres, with little hope of speeding or slowing his progress.

"I envy you your governorship," he said, after a pregnant pause. "Such opportunities await."

"Perhaps," Verres said. "Opportunitiy to be the object of hatred. The Sicilians are as yet unprepared for Roman government. They still yearn for the rule of the whip."

"Why so?"

"Sicilia was that part of the Greek world where the old ways endured the longest. Their cities once ruled by tyrants—the strongest of men, the worst of men. Perhaps, in rare moments of fortune, also the best men suited to the task."

"And how does one achieve status of tyrant?" Batiatus asked.

They paused to let a veiled woman pass before them. Her head turned to stare at Verres, her hand raised as if to say something, but then she hurried ahead of them, weaving through the dawdlers on the steps so that she was soon receding from sight far below.

"Application is simple," Verres was saying. "Requiring only that you kill the previous incumbent. But it is not a responsibility that most mortal men would relish. The constant threat of similar attacks upon oneself? The constant need to make the toughest of decisions about one's people and one's supplies. A tyrant's life is not easy, and a successful tyrant might come from the lowest of the ranks. Might alone endures the worst that fate has to offer, refining him through such hardship, honing him as a whetstone does a blade, until he is the fittest for the job."

"I see no problem."

"And when the tyrant dies. Who succeeds?"

"His son?"

"But the tyrant has fought his way up from nothing. He has learned the justice of the battlefield and the honesty of misfortune. He has clawed his way to the pre-eminent position in his domain, and that is what has made him what he is. But what is his son?"

"The son of a tyrant?"

"The *son* of a tyrant, exactly! Raised in a palace, perhaps? Cossetted and fussed over by a coterie of adoring women and hopeful slave girls. Given the best mentors that money can buy, and opportunities denied his father for poetry, song and epic. He will know his *Iliad*. He will know his Socrates and Anaximander. He will read Greek…"

"The tyrant should anticipate such obstacles. He should ensure his offspring suffers the correct hardships."

"You are serious? You think it possible to create some form of ideal hardship?"

"Gladiators train body through exercise. Why not train mind through rigour? Banish him, perhaps? Force him to be raised by shepherds, unaware of true heritage? It might work…"

"And if it does not?"

"Then seek a new tyrant. The son will lose his place in the hierarchy."

Verres laughed.

"Congratulations, Batiatus," he said. "You have just invented the Republic!"

"We had our kings and found them wanting," Batiatus agreed. "Following the bad days of Tarquin the Proud, we replaced them with our Republic. With men such as yourself made to run the course of honors as their training for rulership. With men such as Cicero to learn the best course of political action."

Verres seemed to suppress a flinch, as if he had stubbed his toe, although Batiatus did not see him stumble on the steps.

"Rome has no tyrant," Batiatus continued. "That is what makes us great—great enough to overcome the backward Sicilians."

"Perhaps," Verres said. "Yet we do have tyrants. Several occasions have seen the Republic falter and the appointment of new dictators to cut through the knots that senatorial government could not. Why, within living memory, Sulla was made our dictator in order to restore order to Rome."

"And resigned office, once job was completed."

"Fortuna smiles upon us. But what befalls the Republic should a dictator not resign?"

They reached the base of the steps.

"Then a king would rule once more."

Each turned to head in a different direction.

"You depart?" Verres asked. "My litter awaits."

"First I must attend to the gladiators, and sign off on the departed Bebryx. The show is not over for the lanista!"

"Of course. Forgive me. Till tonight, then."

Lucretia stared listlessly at the colors and muted sights of Neapolis as her litter swayed past them. But no distraction could put the prattling of Ilithyia from her ears.

"I practically *envy* your husband!" Ilithyia said. "To see all those victorious gladiators."

"You will lay eyes again soon enough, Ilithyia," Lucretia replied. "Tonight is the silicernium banquet, when all grief for Pelorus is put from mind."

"Another gathering!" Ilithyia sighed dramatically. "For a man of no consequence to me."

"He was nothing but a name, to me," Lucretia admitted. "A stranger unmet. A fragment of my husband's history that has brought us little fortune. Would that my father-in-law had never freed him!"

"He need not have."

"Pelorus saved his life in some forgotten act of kindness. He felt an obligation."

"A master has no obligation to his slaves," Ilithyia said. "Nor does a mistress. Slaves are the spoils of our superiority. They are the prize for our labors. We can do as we please with them!" She raised her eyebrows conspiratorially. "Anything!"

"Not anything," Lucretia said. "Slaves do not spring into the world fully formed. They must be found or bred, raised or trained. They must be clothed and fed. Their illnesses attended to. With such an investment in a human possession, it would be foolish to abuse it."

"I can no more abuse a slave than I can abuse a table. I have even heard it said that a slave with no tongue is not diminished in value."

"It is true slaves are not expected to speak," Lucretia agreed. "In most cases, the tongue is an unnecessary organ. Unless to command other slaves, or serve as nomenclator to remind you of appointments and distant acquaintances. A food taster checking for poison would be of no worth without tongue. As would a pleasure slave!"

They giggled together at the thought.

"Not all men share the entitlements and honors of a Roman citizen," Ilithyia said. "If a foreigner wishes to be Roman, it is the work of generations to learn the etiquettes and culture required. Why, one such as myself is the very pinnacle of such development, representing generations of breeding."

"How could we forget?" Lucretia noted, flopping her head back onto her pillow.

"But I fear I am not the type to ever give consideration to freeing a slave. Not unless he is of no possible use to me, and impossible to sell on."

"You mean if blind, infirm, or senile?"

"Certainly. Why waste coin upon him? Would you have me purchase *another* slave to care for the one that already drains my resources?"

"Would he not be burden on our city, when found wandering the streets?" Lucretia asked.

"I would see him taken him up into the hills. Left beneath the heavens for the gods to decide his fate."

"Is that not a little cruel?"

"Such a method gave us Romulus and Remus, suckled by the she-wolf. Rome itself came into being by such means."

"Does that not seem like a strange comparison?"

"How so?"

"Between the legend of the foundation of Rome, and the abandonment of old slaves in the wilderness!"

"You should have a scribe set this down. A treatise on the management of a state, resembling Plato's *Republic*, but absent the *good* ideas."

"You think I am a lady of bad ideas?" Lucretia asked.

"In such a state, no work is done, but coin mysteriously appears to clothe the idle and feed the indolent. Your world is the most terrible of Saturnalias, where slaves sit in luxury while their masters scurry like mad to make sums enough to keep everybody happy."

"You misunderstand meaning, I suggest not an end to slavery," Lucretia scoffed. "but small kindness, when merit allows."

"I keep them fed," Ilithyia said, a small frown crinkling her delicate brow. "I give them a roof beneath which to sleep. I call the medicus if they injure themselves. Already I am the very model of charity."

Bebryx's body was already gone, hauled away by the harenarii to an unknown fate. Batiatus applied his seal to the proffered document of recognition, and prepared to leave the unpleasantly warm, blood-soaked inner hall.

His three surviving gladiators were led past him in manacles, ready for transport.

"A word, dominus?" Spartacus hissed.

The guards tensed, but Batiatus waved them on, leaving the Thracian by his side.

"What is it, Spartacus?" he demanded impatiently. "Today has been very trying."

"Apologies, dominus," Spartacus said. "I meant only to impart news."

"News!" Batiatus laughed. "Neapolis has news in abundance! A day at the arena that saw a whole ludus despoiled! An entire school of gladiators massacred in the name of justice! And a painted woman fighting a pride of lions practically bare-handed, before the Champion of Capua rides to her aid! Already the tongues wag. Already words cast at country cousins enumerating the sights they have missed."

"Even so, dominus—"

"And you! You are fortunate, Spartacus, that you only fought in the arena! My fellow citizens near blows. A quaestor seeks to debate politics with a governor and a freed slave. And I suddenly found to be warden of wise words on matters gladiatorial! You fought well today. Thank the gods for you, able to conceal the shame of Bebryx's defeat."

"Bebryx fought as best he could, dominus. Tired and unprepared, absent the care of a medicus—"

"Gratitude, Spartacus! When I need a new doctore to chastise me, I shall give your application due consideration. You may go."

"But dominus…"

"What?"

"I wished to have word with you."

"Your wife again? I pursue her to the ends of the earth and beyond. I had the departed Pelorus scouting every Syrian slaver listing a dark-haired oriental priestess. Others besides. She will turn up, in due time."

"I have concern for Medea, and the discharge of the will of Pelorus."

"What concern is it of yours?"

"Its entirety has been awarded to Timarchides."

"An annoyance, it is true. Would it have killed Pelorus to offer some small scrap to the House that gave him his freedom?"

"And this was the wish of Pelorus?"

"With dying breath. With dying breath he fucks us over by leaving estate in unworthy hands!"

"Medea spoke to me of her actions in her escape."

"Her futile rebellion?"

"Her brief bid for freedom, a single blow to the throat of Pelorus."

"Dramatic!" Batiatus said. "Such a slice in the arena is always beloved of the crowd." He grew wistful, staring out of the portal at an unseen amphitheater of dreams. "Aim correctly and moments pass before the victim knows his fate. He might even keep fighting, unaware his last breath has already been drawn."

"I have used that cut many times in the arena," Spartacus agreed. "But—"

"Suffocation commences but the victim fights on," Batiatus continued. "The crowd knows before he does that he is already dead. His sword is dropped, he clutches hands to throat. And then, only then, do knees buckle and body drops to sands." Batiatus's eyes glistened with the memory of many battles witnessed from the balcony. "The doctore favors a neck wound for bringing down a prominent opponent in single combat," he added. "The audience given opportunity to savor the moment of death. Recommended also for dispatching less experienced gladiators who perhaps cannot be trusted to die well. Wait. Is your meaning that Medea is yet professional? Already trained?"

"No, dominus. I believe that she had the advantage of surprise, the distraction of her nude form."

"And the expedience of a sharp blade close to hand."

"But, dominus…"

"What is it, Spartacus?"

"I speak of this because of the nature of the wound."

"What of it?"

"A man with a cut throat cannot speak."

"Well, his mind is surely elsewhere!"

"He *cannot speak*. He is not able."

The lanista's eyes widened in shock.

"Pelorus *did not have* any last words!" Batiatus breathed with sudden comprehension. "Verres is lying."

"That is my meaning, dominus."

"The strange binding of the body of Pelorus at the funeral procession did catch the eye. I thought it merely some Egyptian fancy, swathing a body in tight bandages, but… Now it seems that they were making attempt to keep his head in place? Spartacus… Spartacus… I *saw* the wound. Gaping like a second mouth. I assumed it one of many, but now you say it was the sole cut?"

Spartacus shrugged.

Batiatus chuckled with excitement, patting his own chest in satisfaction.

"The whole testament is a sham. Timarchides merely a figure convenient and believable to take on the estate. And Verres gets to play the magnanimous Roman all along, shielding himself from accusation of wrongdoing."

Spartacus bowed.

"It would seem so, dominus."

Batiatus smacked the Thracian upon the shoulder in elation.

"Spartacus! Such spoils of battle you have brought your master. You have won great favor for the House of Batiatus! You have just conquered an entire estate!"

XIII

ARGUMENTA

They were armed to the teeth with swords and axes, lances and tridents, but nobody feared them. Their armor was the bulkiest ever seen, and yet the lightest, for it was made of stiffened cloth. When they entered the atrium of the House of Pelorus, they did so en masse, without any of the shoving and pushing that might have accompanied other gladiators. But none of the play-gladiators ran to their habitual position in the center, instead they brandished their arms to make way for new celebrities.

Ahead of them, waving his arms in mock fear, ran a male figure attired with false breasts and a long, dark wig, his hands "chained" in manacles made of rope. Behind him, in chaotic, bounding pursuit, ran a handful of other men attired in bright yellow skins. The "lions" bumped and tripped over one another in a parade of pratfalls, eager to chase their prey, until a fateful moment, carefully timed to reach the middle of the chamber, when they realized that their prey had turned on them, and was whipping them with the chains.

While the false Medea and the false lions clowned in the middle of the chamber, two new arrivals pranced in. Each wore a carefully fashioned skirt in the image of a horse's torso, leading a fake horse's head by a bridle. Their masks were outlandishly large, amounting to false heads. One bore a stubbly beard and piercing eyes picked out in blue. The other had a shock of garish blond hair and an exaggerated expression of horror.

The first raised his arms up, exorting the crowd to acknowledge him, which they did, with cries of *SPAR-TA-CUS, SPAR-TA-CUS*! The other feigned an inability to control his mount, teetering from side to side, lurching back and forth, and bumping on occasion into his fellow rider.

"Is that supposed to be us?" Varro fumed.

Spartacus smirked.

"I believe it is."

"They mock us," Varro said.

"Is that not their job?" Spartacus asked.

"Until I find the man and put an end to it," Varro said. "We stand here, originals forgotten!"

The clown riders rode to the rescue of the clown Medea, bumping and jostling with the clown lions. The crowd laughed, as the "lions" retreated, their arms held up in a mock echo of Medea's entrance. But as the clown riders took their bow, the clown Medea began to kick and berate them, chasing them off. They exited fast behind the lions, but for an interlude in which the clown Varro missed the portal, smacking into the wall instead, to milk one last laugh from the crowd.

The clown Medea stopped suddenly, alone in the arena, as if hearing the crowd for the first time. "She" looked about her and began to point threateningly at the crowd, in a way that had been seen before.

"Charon," Varro said. "It is the same old bastard who plays Charon in the arena."

"You are famous," Spartacus said.

"I am *infamous*. And your clown was more handsome than mine."

Spartacus laughed.

"Gladiators, already your legend supersedes your fleshy reality," Batiatus said, appearing behind them. He gestured toward the stairs downward. "Perhaps it is time that you returned to the cells, and leave the guests to their phantoms and delights."

At the far end of the courtyard, Verres and Timarchides were locked in a futile argument. They bellowed and pointed at one another, such that men who did not know them well assumed that they were about to come to blows.

"Do you suggest the love of women is natural?" Timarchides said, already somewhat the worst for wear.

"Do you suggest that it is not?" Verres sputtered.

"Women serve to bear and rear children. But when it comes to *fucking*, there is no comparision to the real thing."

Some of the assembled guests laughed nervously. Cicero stood among them, had a pained look on his face as the contest continued.

"Spoken like a Greek!" Verres scoffed.

"Spoken like the greatest warriors the world has ever known!"

"Are we really going to have discussion of this now?"

"The Sacred Band of my native Thebes! A phalanx of fearsome warriors that drove all Greece before them. The most beautiful youths on the front line. Their older lovers bearing spears behind them, encouraged to fight all the more in order to protect the ones they loved so dearly."

"Were not the Sacred Band annihilated at the battle of Chaeronea? Killed to a man? Not a single one left alive."

"Killed by Alexander the Great!" Timarchides cried, slurring victoriously. "Whose love of his male companion Hephaestion surpassed that of man for any woman. Whose 'Persian boy,' Bagoas—"

"Enough! My ears grow weary of this," Verres said. "You are drunk beyond coherent speech."

"Quite so," Cicero said. "Citing occasional exceptions to a general rule is no argument worth using, except to fool the gullible and easily persuaded. Not an exercise in rhetoric, rather two drunks shout at one other. If you seek to duel with words, then do so with some panache! As the gladiators of good Batiatus, here, duel with their blades!"

Batiatus, ascending the stairs from the now almost-deserted ludus, brightened at the sound of his name spoken with approval.

"I have gladiators under my command," Batiatus said, "who subscribe to the same obscenities as Timarchides describes. Their performance in the arena uneffected."

"My concern rests with the claim that these *foreign* lovers of men are 'the greatest warriors in the world,'" Cicero said. He appealed to the crowd. "Will nobody answer this? At a dinner in the heart of Italia, will nobody stand up to defend the honor of the Republic?"

"The Republic needs no defence," Verres said. "History is its shield. Free Greece is no more. Conquered by *Romans*. And Timarchides knows this, for it was a Roman that set him free."

The house shook with laughter, and the chastened Timarchides staggered away, laughing himself, as Cicero and Verres clasped arms in friendship and approval.

"Let us argue on another topic!" Verres proclaimed, to extended cheers. "I would see how quaestors approach true debates!"

"Apollo's shit pipe," Batiatus muttered to himself. "Not *more* talk!" He crept from the gathering as carefully as he could, feigning an interest in a retreating platter of fruits and the slave that bore it.

"Name your *argumenta*," Cicero declared, "and I shall speak upon them."

"Concerning slavery!" a red-faced Timarchides shouted, leaning on a statue of Pelorus, barely able to stand himself. "Let Cicero argue that all should be as liberated as I!"

There was a hushed murmur of approval among the other guests, and scattered outbreaks of applause. Cicero mimed shock, and then deep thought, and then turned to address the crowd with a smile.

"In nature, we are all born as squalling infants, unable to fend for ourselves," he began. "We are all born in need of succour and sustenance. This is natural. But we are not born *equal*, and it is a fallacy to suggest otherwise. Why? I shall tell you why…"

"I cannot stay!" Ilithyia proclaimed. She collapsed onto the couch and grabbed an entire bunch of grapes to pick at. "I leave tonight in hope my bearers may convey me to Atella while I sleep. So this is farewell, till reunion in Capua."

"What can possibly have tired you?" Lucretia said.

"You have done nothing all day but watch other people exert themselves for your entertainment."

"Good Verres spat wine all over me at the arena. My dress destroyed, I was forced to search for another for hours in Neapolis. Weary hours passed waiting for the slaves to model it. Dickering with the merchants. Such efforts!"

"I see you found suitable replacement, eventually," Lucretia noted.

"It will do, though it is not of the latest fashion," she said. "I chose blues and greens, to resemble the seas of the bay of Neapolis."

"Were they without grays and browns, decorated with fish-heads and floating shit?" Batiatus asked.

"The waters as I imagine them to be," Ilithyia continued, undaunted. "In summer before such autumnal upheavals.

"And you chose wisely," Lucretia said. "You look most becoming."

"I do," Ilithyia agreed. "But that is not what has taxed me most! Have you heard?"

She pointed over at the menfolk in the middle of the room, where Verres and Cicero were engaged in heated debate. Other guests lurked around them in rapt attention, piled onto couches and chairs, leaning on arm-rests, seated on tables in row after serried row.

"They look like they are reconvening the senate in the atrium," Lucretia observed.

"Indeed they are!" Ilithyia giggled.

"They drone of politics and faraway lands," Batiatus said, "of men and legends I never heard. Bringing reminder of two senile old men striving to remember the past. And they will brook no interruption."

"I think they find you rude," Lucretia said.

"I am the very model of fucking politesse."

"You interrupt."

"I await suitable opening for discourse," Batiatus protested.

"You do not! One can barely get a sentence out before—"

"Cicero can wag tongue all day. He is a fucking lawyer. Every time he opens his mouth his tongue speaks another argument for the defence."

"It is a considered example of superb rhetoric from a master of the form," Ilithyia said.

Batiatus's eyes bulged.

"It is a—? It is a *what*?"

"Can you not hear it when he speaks?" Ilithyia said. "Everybody hangs upon his every word. His speeches provoke new thoughts, and report ideas from educated men all over the world. It is a performance rarely seen outside the Senate itself!"

"Hold tongue and let him speak!" Lucretia agreed. "Look at them. Hearing of distant countries and mad ideas. The guests entertain themselves, and still proclaim they have had the best of times."

"Timarchides has engaged the dancing girls already at great cost," Batiatus protested. "Unless Cicero is going to strip off…"

"All will go home speaking of the wonders of this night."

Batiatus shook his head in amazement.

"Lucretia, your words turn insufferable bore into unexpected blessing."

"Now speak with the kitchen," Lucretia said. "Timarchides is not in sight, and refreshments wanting."

But Batiatus was drifting back toward the two

Romans in the center of the room, listening with newly found interest to the way they spoke. He saw the excited gleam in the observers' eyes, their respectful silence as they watched. And he realized where he had seen it before.

He turned back to his wife.

"My ears are awakened," he whispered to Lucretia. "They duel like gladiators. But they duel with words and ideas."

"Indeed they do," Lucretia sighed. "*I* will deal with the refreshments then, shall I?"

"Fuck the refreshments. I wish to dine on *ideas*, Lucretia. Ideas!"

Ilithyia laughed and raised her hand in farewell, while Lucretia shook her head in exasperation.

"Sicilia is a special case," Verres was saying.

"Every province can claim its own particulars and peculiarities," Cicero said. "I speak to the wider issue, of slavery itself, and its future."

"Slavery is a fact of life."

"A fact that has gouged holes in our memory of our history. No monuments stand in Rome to the Sicilian slave revolt. No great plays or poetry that commemorate either it or the proscriptions that ended it. We prefer not to dwell on the massacre of innocents, the rape and murder of good Roman citizens, not only by slaves, but by low-ranking peasants who chose to join the slaves rather than die alongside the wealthier freeborn."

"Hardly a subject suitable for drama," Verres laughed, to supportive cries from some of the crowd.

"Why not? It is the most perfect and terrible of tragedies."

"We *learn* from tragedies," Verres said. "We must purge the revolt from living memory, not for matters of aesthetics, but simply to ensure that it does not spread such ideas."

"Do you think the slaves who rose up in Silicia needed drama to inform their anger? Do you think they read books about the precedents? Of course not! They rose up because they had nothing left to lose."

"And that, good Cicero, is why I say that as governor of Sicilia I must be ever vigilant, and to stamp out with firm hand indication of further revolt."

"And that, good Verres, is why I say that Sicilia is not a special case at all. The uprising in Sicilia could have come to pass anywhere in the Republic. At any time! And might still again."

"Where is your evidence?"

"By the time I had *evidence*, it would be too late! Rome is not founded on bricks and cement. Whisper it, that only your inner circle may hear. Rome is founded on the blood and sweat of slaves. Our borders must expand ever outward to bring in new slaves to till fields, rear children, wash clothes... And we sit at our tables and cheer each other with tales of nobility and virtue. But cast eyes around you. One in every three people in this house, in this town, in this land, *is a slave*!"

"And kept in their place."

"For now. What if they found opportunity to rise against us?"

"You see, *now* I am concerned!" Verres said. "But consider, slaves are in a state of perpetual revolt."

Cicero looked around him in mock concern.

"I see no burning buildings. No fleeing citizens," he said archly, to titters from the crowd.

"Of course not. But there are ways far subtler of fighting back. And you would know it, too, if you spent more time managing your household."

"How, then, do slaves revolt?"

"Stupidity feigned to manage their master's expectations. Pilfering from the house or on return from market. Selling their master's things. And worst and most prevalent of all, by not working hard enough!" This last was greeted with grumbles of approval from the menfolk present, and hearty outbreaks of applause.

"How is that revolt?" Cicero asked, frowning at the audience as if they had insulted him.

"If I buy a slave," Verres said, "I buy everything that he is. I buy his every waking moment, and his dreams if I wish them. I buy every day of labor while he is under my authority, and if that day ends too quickly, or is not busy to my satisfaction, if that day is truncated by illness feigned or otherwise, then my slave is *stealing from me*."

It was dark. The openings to the outer world were small, and little light shone through from the cloudy night beyond the walls. The gloom was such that Medea could not even see the bars on the far side of her cell. She held up her arms, able to pick out only the most striking of her painted symbols. She prodded unhappily at the bowl of gruel left for her in her solitary cell.

In the next cell, she saw something watching her.

"What is this offal?" she said to the darkness.

"There is offal? We are fortunate tonight," the voice of Spartacus replied.

"Almost. It is a foul paste of pulses and leftovers."

"It is your miscellany."

"My what?"

"Your miscellany. The food of the gladiators."

"It is no better than pig food."

"There is all you can eat."

"But I can eat none of it!"

"Then truly, there is all you can eat."

She smiled. They looked at each other through the bars.

"Does my body excite you?" she asked, suddenly.

"It does not," Spartacus said.

"You lie to me. Come close to the bars, Thracian. I shall relieve your animal hungers."

"My appetite is not for you."

"I suppose I owe you my life," she said, in Thracian.

"Think not of it," he replied, in the same language.

"I repay my debts," she said.

"Live," he replied. "Live to spite them. That is repayment enough."

"Now I see it. You love men, like the Carthaginian."

"I do not."

"You love animals? Like the Cretan queen!"

They laughed together at the suggestion.

"I do not," Spartacus chuckled.

"Then what is it, Thracian?"

"I love a woman," Spartacus said.

"All men love women," Medea said.

"I mean," Spartacus said, "I love one woman, and one woman alone."

Medea was silenced.

"You have a wife?"

"I do."

"Then where is she?"

"She was sold into slavery, as was I. I fight here for

the House of Batiatus, that she will be returned to me."

Medea leaned her head against the wall, staring up at the moon.

"Now I see it, Thracian. Now I see why you prize the life of Batiatus above your own. But what will happen when your wife is returned to you?"

"We shall live together at the House of Batiatus, until I win my freedom."

"And if she is not returned to you?"

"She will be."

"And if she is not?"

"She will be. There can be no alternative."

"You are a trusting man. Too trusting."

"I have nothing else."

"They call you Spartacus," she said. "After the Thracian king of old?"

"The only Thracian they have ever heard of." He shrugged.

"You are fortunate that they have heard of even one."

"But what matter?"

"Indeed. What do we care now? We are all barbarians to the Romans. One great seething mass of savages. We all look alike. We all think alike."

"We do not."

"Perhaps we should. The woman you see before you is already dead. It is merely a matter of how many Romans I can take with me."

"If you fight as a gladiatrix, most of your opponents will be fellow 'barbarians' and criminals the Romans are happily rid of."

"I think not of myself, but of thousands like me. Thousands of barbarians, rising up as one."

"It is not possible."

"You only say that because nobody has yet succeeded. Look at us. Look at this happy pair. So much more unites us than divides us, even if we once fought in rival clans."

"We are both caged by Rome."

"It is a matter of perspective, Thracian. Why are the Getae your enemies?"

"You plundered our villages. You stole from us."

"Did I steal more from you than the Romans you now so loyally serve…?"

"Batiatus has given me his word. My wife shall be returned to me."

"And then? How many times must you risk death to buy back your freedom? How many to buy back hers?"

"Winning in the arena is a simpler matter."

"The cost of your board, the cost of your training. The cost of the acquisition of your wife. How many years do you think you will fight for the House of Batiatus before you gain your freedom?"

"Nevertheless, I shall gain it. Batiatus has—"

"Given his word, so I hear. Have you had much luck with the word of Romans in the past?"

Spartacus brooded silently. Medea laughed to herself.

"I thought not. The Syrian merchants are sure to delight when the Thracians come to town. You fall prey to thieves and then labor willingly to buy back what should already be yours. The Getae are not your enemy, Thracian. The Getae could never hope to hurt you as much as you seem to have hurt yourself."

"I can buy my freedom."

"You can. Although your master can also choose to withhold it."

"He would not."

"He already does! Your freedom may be granted by a

mere wave of the hand. A whim. Why not you? Batiatus could free you this very moment if he truly desired it."

——✦——

"You speak, Cicero," Verres was saying, "of a world absent slaves! As ludicrous an idea as a world absent trees. Where would they all go?"

"Why would they have to *go* anywhere?" Cicero asked, his palms upraised in an appeal to the crowd. "Why not let them live on?"

"*For the reason that a great number should already be dead!*" Verres shouted, as if volume alone made his case for him. "On the battlefields of Numidia and Hispania! In Carthage! As the result of countless crimes thwarted! Thieves arrested! Murderers apprehended!" There were cheers from their audience with the name of each Roman victory, cheers with each success of justice itself in the name of the Republic.

"Slavery is the lowest state to which a man can fall and yet live," Verres continued. "It is the moment before death itself, prolonged perhaps for an entire lifetime. But it is better than death itself. Ask the slaves of this house their preference. Death on the battlefields of Thrace and Africa, or food, shelter and purpose here in the bosom of the Republic?"

"Ah, but it is not *their* Republic. Their presence here not of their own volition."

"Their minds should have dwelt upon that before mounting attack, stealing, or—"

"Or having the misfortune to dwell on our borders?"

"You would set them all free?"

"Not every man is fit to be a Roman. But mere cursory observation within these walls reveals the faces of men

238

and women who have yet *become* Romans within living memory. But a handful of years have passed since the rest of Italia was allowed into the warmth of Roman arms. Many generations hence we may admit the people of Hispania or Greece."

"But you think there is such a possibility?"

"Of course! And if we may, in time, raise Italians up to glorious rank of Roman, surely slaves can become freemen. Take Tiro, my manservant."

"What of him?"

"He is a slave, lifelong loyal servant of the Cicero family, practically a member."

"Would you permit him to marry your daughter?"

Cicero ignored the ludicrous suggestion.

"He did not merely hand me clothing in the morning, or hold basin for my ablutions. He carried my books to school and sat alongside me. In his station as a slave, he witnessed the best education that money can buy. He learned to read Latin and Greek, not merely in the classroom but as my living textbook for revisions. The Cicero family has invested thousands of denarii in Tiro. Think of the working hours lost to us while his mother carried him and nursed him. Think of the food and clothing bestowed upon him while he grew to manhood. The Cicero family has invested far more coin in the rearing of its slave than a Capuan merchant might spend on his own children, and Tiro is the better for it."

"But is he free?"

"No, he is not free, although he can claim more freedom than a fisherman hauling nets at dawn, or a litter-bearer straining to carry heavy load that final mile at the day's end. And at some future time, it may be that the Cicero family will release Tiro from bondage, altogether.

But with responsibility."

"How can one free a slave *with responsibility*?" Verres scoffed.

"By committing such an act when the slave is fit to offer contribution to Roman society, of course. What purpose is there in discarding a slave's collar if he will become nothing but a beggar? I have no desire to create one more mouth clamoring for the grain dole; one more scream added to the hordes in the arena. Such behaviour is irresponsible. Should Tiro ever be freed, I would desire him to become valued citizen. But we shall see. We are in this position through application of untold generations of our forebears. The day a forgotten great-great-grandfather toiled with extra rigor upon his farm, and had grain surplus for the purchase of more land. No matter what the priesthood may dictate, we are not here solely through the whims of the gods. Venture into the very center of your household, look into that little shrine, and what do you see? A mirror to tell you that you are the axis of your world? No, you see your household gods. You see the symbolic statues and *imagines* of the uncountable ancestors, your family stretching back into time immemorial."

"Such is the protestation of a New Man, not a patrician family," Verres said, waving his hand dismissively.

"We were all New Men once. Maybe not in this generation, but some time in the past. We were not sprung, fully formed, from the brow of Jupiter. Only a fool does not honor his father and mother, and theirs before them, and theirs before them."

"Where will it end? Do you expect legions led by German generals? Rome ruled by an African?"

At this, there were some titters from the crowd.

"Why not?"

"Ludicrous! Preposterous!"

"And yet but a generation ago it was thought 'preposterous' that men from Capua might be regarded as citizens of Rome itself. If Rome extends its reach to include men of worth in Neapolis—men of Greek descent, incidentally—then why not men of other provinces?"

"Why not women, too?" a voice shouted.

"Why not dogs?" a man blurted from the crowd.

"Why not woodlice?" Verres added, to hearty guffaws.

"My horse could be consul!" another man shouted from the sidelines, leading to more laughter.

"What sophistry is this?" Cicero said. "I make a serious, intelligent point, and you seize upon it like Oscan buffoons."

"A gladiator may win the rudis," Batiatus interjected.

"Quite so!" Cicero said. "As my good friend Batiatus has taught me! A gladiator fights *for his life*. He may fight with such bravery, and win such victories, that he might be presented with true freedom and permitted to leave the ludus. Why, what is there to stop such a gladiator, or perhaps his freeborn son, enlisting in the Roman army, and rising to rank of centurion or tribune? What is there to stop such a man becoming a farmer with a life of honest toil? And from there, perhaps, the same course of honors that awaits men of patrician families."

"Or," Verres interrupted, "his brutish ways might lead him to fail at farming. His unbridled nature might lead him to desert the army. He, or his hypothetical freeborn son, might turn to criminal acts, becoming robber and brigand. Within a generation your freeborn man might be dead in the street, or choking up our prisons, or reduced once more to slavery."

"Of course!" Cicero cried in elation. "You are so right, my friend. We are entirely in agreement."

"We are?" Verres asked.

"We are!" Cicero smiled. "Any New Man stands at a portal of opportunity. Before him lies the uncertain life and prospects of any free individual. Above all there is the opportunity to become a man of virtue. Blessed or despised by the gods, women and wine, prosperity and decline, the chance to reach for greatness."

"And behind him?"

"Behind him lies the mire from which he came. Temptation toward crime and corruption. Perhaps, indeed, he or his descendants will soon fall back once more into the bestial, ignorant world of slaves. But can we not agree that there is at least the *chance* of rescue? You say that slaves are slaves because they are irredeemable, but not all slaves are so. What of the African king fallen on hard times? What of the noble Roman soldier captured by Pontian pirates?"

"Death before dishonor!"

"Thus speaks a man who has never held a sword in battle!"

"Nor have you!"

"Roman law recognizes that good Roman citizens may fall upon hard times. Slavery is a state of suspended death, but providence may bring the fortunate soul back from its brink."

"That cannot be true!"

"Ask your scribes, ask your magistrate. Ask them of the status 'postliminium.' It exists for those Romans who lose their freedom as prisoners of war, but have it restored to them by the inevitable military victory that is sure to follow wherever an insult is raised against the Republic!"

Cicero glanced around him at the expectant faces in the lamplight, and saw that all were waiting for him to explain. Verres quaffed at a flagon of wine, unused to the prolonged exercise of his voice. His opponent was occupied, and that meant that Cicero could strike. He took a deep breath, and gazed around his audience with wide eyes, inviting attendance, and imagination.

"My friends! My friends!" Cicero called. "I would ask you to paint a picture in your minds… that even as we duel with words here tonight, Lydian pirates, hundreds of miles from their Asian haunts, steal ashore and raid the house! Oh, how the Romans fight. The women scream and flee, and we menfolk make brave stand with table knives and candlesticks.

"Brave Verres cries: *'You shall never take me alive!'* but he is struck from behind and falls into the arms of Morpheus. Asleep. When he awakes, he is bound in chains! He is tied to a bench as a galley slave! What should he do? Should he sit, arms folded, as though half-witted, unable to fight back as the slave masters whip him for his lack of labors? Or should he grit his teeth and pull on his oar in virtuous confidence, secure in the knowledge that every sweep of the oars surely drives his galley closer to a moment of retribution and revenge?"

The echoes of Cicero's voice died away in silence, as he surveyed a hushed, thoughtful crowd. He paused just long enough for his words to sink in.

"Sure enough," he continued, "be it days, weeks or even months later, the Lydian pirates' run of good luck comes to an end. Fortuna smiles upon our Roman hero as marines storm the ship! In the chaos, seizing opportunity, Brave Verres grasps the harsh slavemaster and, with his own chains, strangles him! He takes possession of the keys from the cruel pirate's belt and unlocks his manacles. Then he turns to the expectant mob of his fellow rowers, and casts the ring of keys into their grateful midst!

"Brave Verres tells them: *'Free yourselves!'* And he takes up a sword and runs swiftly onto the deck to give aid to the Roman soldiers as they extract vengeance upon the pirates!"

The chamber erupted in cheers at Cicero's story, crushing Verres beneath a flurry of pats on the back in appreciation of his imaginary heroism.

"WAIT!" Cicero shouted, arms raised, calling the merriment to a sudden quiet. "I ask you now: Is Brave Verres a *slave*? He has toiled under the lash for many days. In appearance he is indistinguishable from the slaves on either side of him, who pulled on the same oar. And yet we know him to be a virtuous Roman, this man we see before us today. The Roman law of postliminium says that his slavery was but a temporary condition—a misfortune visited upon him, but soon evaded. He can return to Roman life as if he has returned from death itself. But what of the man next to him? What of thousands like him? What of those who toil in the silver mines or scratch letters as scribes or haul rocks as builders? We are all born free! Should *all of us* not aspire to remain so?"

There was applause, wild applause.

"Good Cicero," Verres laughed. "I still feel you have proved nothing, and spoken of wild ideas, but you can boast of having laid claim to the hearts of the crowd." He held up two fingers in a parody of gladiatorial submission. "The day is yours!"

There was enthusiastic and admiring applause, while Cicero bowed graciously.

"A prize!" Batiatus called. "Give him a prize!"

"Whatsoever you desire," Timarchides laughed, slumped half-awake at the base of a statue. "From what little remains in this house."

"An audience," Cicero said immediately.

"With whom?"

XIV

FENESTRAE

"WHAT, THEN, MEDEA?" SPARTACUS GROWLED THROUGH THE metal grate that separated their cells. "What would you have me do? My wife is sold into slavery. My labor is beholden to the one man who can bring her back to me. My body fights in the arena for the glory of the Republic I despise. What would you have me do?"

"Despair," Medea replied. "Lose hold on those last of your hopes."

"If I give up hope, I will have nothing."

"Nothing but vengeance. Nothing to lose but your chains."

"And my life."

"What does your life matter if you have no hope?"

"I hope for Sura. While she yet lives."

"And if she does not?"

"Do not speak such words."

"The gladiator is hurt by words? The gladiator is injured by mere prospects? *What if your wife is dead?*"

Spartacus rattled the bars between them, but Medea stood

unflinching before him, her nostrils flared with passion.

"Then I will kill them all," he said.

"And for that you will need help."

"No help but my arm. No help but my fists."

"Thracian, you have more friends that you can imagine. You have seen the Romans and their customs of hospes and hospitality. 'The friend of my friend is my friend,' they say."

"What of it?"

"If you seek to destroy Rome, then forget your past antipathies and seek future alliances. Rome's enemies should be your allies. Look to the pirates of the east. Look to the rebels in Hispania and the allies of Mithridates. Consider the disaffected peoples within Rome's festering, king-slaying Republic."

"I do not seek to destroy Rome."

"Oh, but you will. You will."

Footsteps approached, accompanied by the sputtering illumination of a torch. Its firelight glimmered upon scraps of the scene—a body in a distant cell, a pair of eyes glowering between the bars. It picked out Spartacus, briefly, in profile, and then he too was back in darkness.

The light, however, was strongest now upon the front of Medea's cell. She shielded her eyes as they adjusted to the glare.

"Open the door," Cicero commanded.

"That I cannot do," Timarchides said.

"I am a quaestor," Cicero said. "I speak with voice of the Senate. If I demand that you unlock this portal, you will obey me."

"And I am a freedman," Timarchides responded, hotly. "I am a man whose wrists yet bear the marks of chains he no longer wears, in the house of a murdered master."

"That makes no difference."

"It does to me, Cicero. She overpowered Verres himself, a Roman gentleman. She fought her way into the main house. She led a revolt that claimed the lives of free citizens."

"I do not fear a naked woman."

"Then you are a fool, quaestor. Where are your powers of investigation and intellect? You yourself watched her fight lions, naked in the arena. And you would have me let you inside her cage?"

"What harm does it do you?"

"Every harm, if I am implicated in your foolish death."

"I say to you, Timarchides. I command you."

"And I say to you, Cicero, go fuck yourself."

His lips pressed together in grim resolve, Timarchides shoved the torch into its wall bracket.

"Parley with the bitch if you must. But do it through the bars."

The two men stared at each other in the flickering torchlight.

"Very well," Cicero said eventually. "I shall not fight you."

"A wise choice," Timarchides said. "I have torn out the hearts of greater men."

"Leave us, then," Cicero said. "This is for the ears of no other."

Medea glanced at the shadows to the place where Spartacus had been, but he had crept away from the bars so that he was not visible from her cage. She smiled to herself at the petty rebellion. Spartacus listened. Spartacus listened, because a Roman did not want him to.

"As you wish," Timarchides said. "Watch your footing

on your return. It would *sorely* grieve me if you tripped and broke your neck."

His footsteps receded down the corridor, shuffling drunkenly.

Cicero peered through the bars at the painted woman of the Getae, unaware that Spartacus watched in secret.

"I have come for you," Cicero addressed her.

"Come and get me, then," she said, flatly.

"Pelorus told me of you."

"He sent message from the afterlife?"

"While he yet lived. He wrote to me of a sorceress of the Getae, who had the power of prophecy."

"I said I would kill him. That came true."

"You have wit," Cicero observed. "Quick-witted and wise."

"And look where it led me," Medea said. "See my palace and my servants, my bath and my banquets."

In the dark, she glimpsed the white of Spartacus's teeth as he smiled in silence. She willed herself not to look in that direction, lest Cicero realize that they had an audience.

"I am a quaestor," Cicero said.

"I am a condemned woman."

"It is my purpose to investigate."

"I was apprehended with Roman blood on my hands. I do not think my case is in doubt."

"Matters legal and spiritual. I am collecting prophecies."

"Here is one for you. *You will die with a Roman sword in your neck*."

"I mean real prophecies. Oracular utterances."

"Is that not real enough for you? It will be real enough when the iron bites your flesh."

———+———

Her hair was brown, tied up in careful whorls, and set with pins of Greek bronze. Her legs were long, her rump pleasingly rounded. Her name was unknown. Verres saw no more, nor desired any greater view. Instead, he reached out and grabbed a handful. Verres snatched the girl by her hair, twisting her head back to stare into her face.

"You will do," he said.

"Dominus!" she breathed in terror. "I have committed no wrong."

"None indeed," he said, dragging her toward the darkened room. "There is nothing wrong with your beauty. Nothing wrong with your firm body. Tell me there is nothing wrong with your cunt."

"Dominus?"

"No matter," he said, as they neared the bed. "I shall discover for myself presently, and hear you call me dominus with quickened breath—" He threw her onto the bed, which unexpectedly shrieked with surprise.

Lucretia threw off the covers, awoken but disoriented by the sudden intrusion.

"Domina!" the girl breathed apologetically.

"What is the meaning of this?" Lucretia shouted. "Get out! Get out!"

The girl scurried away without another word.

"Gaius Verres?" Lucretia spat.

"Apologies, lady Lucretia," Verres said, not sounding at all apologetic. "I did not know you were here."

"I must have dozed off as the silicernium fluttered into embers. I was not expecting to be awoken by your... nocturnal predations."

"I am no predator. I cannot steal something that does not even possess itself. Slaves are there for the taking."

"For their master, not for any passing citizen."

"I am a hospes here."

"Obligations extend both ways."

Verres shrugged.

"Timarchides cares not."

"He will if you cost him extra coin. The servants here are on loan. Damages have to be paid for."

"Your directness is most becoming. I spoke of the joy a man feels in reminding a slave of who is dominus."

"Find a resting place for your cock somewhere in town. Neapolis has plenty of brothels. The House of the Winged Cock is but a few steps from our gate."

"Brothels are for slaves and laborers. Uglies and beggars. I would not eat at the same table as a street sweeper. And I would not fuck the same hole as him either."

"But, where…?"

"If not in the bedchambers of a gracious host, then there is no lack of serving wenches and weaver girls who will take a day's pay for an hour's work. Every woman has her price, Lucretia."

"*Every* woman?"

"Well, not *every* woman, of course."

"I should think not!"

"After all, there are many ladies who would not dream of accepting any payment for something in which they take such pleasure."

"You are speaking to a Roman lady."

"And we all know the proclivities of the Roman ladies, do we not?"

"I am sure I do not know what you mean."

"Do not be so coy with me, Lucretia. You are a beautiful woman. I am sure you have desires."

"For the attentions of my husband and the *respect* of his friends."

"Is that all, Lucretia. Is that really all…?"

"It certainly is."

"Your blushes tell me otherwise. Who is he, I wonder? A childhood sweetheart, sweet memories never forgotten? A true love abandoned when you agreed to a proposal of marriage from the lofty House of Batiatus? No… nothing like that, I am sure."

"Nothing like that."

"But perhaps it is something *wilder* you seek? I wonder what it must be like for the lanista's wife living each day with a balcony view of the strongest, the most dangerous men in the Republic. Are your eyes drawn to them, Lucretia? Do you look down on your husband's warriors and imagine what it would be like to take one inside you?"

"The very thought of it," Lucretia sputtered.

"Of imagining? Yes, for you have done more than imagine, have you not? What female would not sample the delights she owned? I am sure there is not a woman in Rome who hasn't wondered what it would be like to summon her kitchen slave or gardener to her on a warm summer's night. To order him to stand, unmoving before her. To whisper in his ear that subsequent events should be a secret shared only between the two of them, on pain of torture.

"I only tease. I am a rude old man and your blushes are so beautiful I cannot help but encourage them. Forgive me, I beg you! Forgive Gaius Verres and his drunken talk of such indiscretions. I am certain you are as pure as your namesake."

✦

"Cicero! My congratulations for the entertainments," Batiatus said, breezily. "I have never seen orators in full flow before! Most illuminating."

Cicero stared half-heartedly back at the lanista, and shrugged.

"I claim victory in the battle of words with Verres when it concerns matters theoretical and hypothetical," he sighed. "In my daily labors, I am thwarted at every turn."

Batiatus patted his arm in an attempt at reassurance.

"Let me ask you about a gladiatorial matter," Cicero said, "If I may?"

Batiatus grinned expansively.

"I surely lack your rhetorical tongue. But when it comes to the arena, I may speak of what I know."

"The woman of the Getae."

"Ah yes, a natural," Batiatus said. "Her frame is small, but she has a truly murderous intent. Her pleasure in killing warms the soul."

"She will not be the last, I am sure."

"She lives for it. But her survival thus far seems but an accident. She cares not for her own life."

"I spoke with her in her cell. She is a spitting cat. Full of fire and vigour, but not prophecy. And while she has had better fortune than a cat, even cats meet their end in time."

"Are you surprised? These prophecies are doggerel. The priests are artful swindlers. Who cares what nursery rhymes are in the Sibylline Books if they are only found to be true after the event? The Getae woman's rantings are of no importance to you, to me, to any noble citizen."

"She has no 'ranting,' as you put it. She is lucid. Angry, but not… prophetic. But Pelorus would not have lied to me. There must be some way to unlock her sight of futures and posterities."

"The oracles of the east surely do not spring from their beds spouting prophecies. They are induced, their site aided by elixers and opiates."

Cicero patted Batiatus on the arm.

"You are too kind, Batiatus. But I fear that my time is limited."

"Perhaps not, good Cicero. There a matter I wish to discuss with you."

"What possible help can you offer in this situation, good Batiatus?"

"I can claim ownership of the Getae witch."

"She is not for sale."

"That is of no import, if I proved her rightful owner. I wish to engage your services."

Batiatus beckoned Cicero toward the inner rooms of the house. Cicero followed, indulgently, a cup of wine forgotten in his hand as they strolled toward the shrine of the household gods.

"Verres's case seems solid," Cicero said. "It seems but a formality for him to present Timarchides to the magistrate tomorrow and sign over what remains of the estate of Pelorus."

"But what if I have examined Verres's armor and found gap?"

"A *fenestra*."

"Indeed, I have a window. A window for us both!"

"My policy is always to be available to petitions," Cicero said. "But I cannot promise anything unless the facts of the case warrant my involvement."

"In truth," Batiatus said, "it is a relatively simple matter. Pelorus has died absent a will. He has no heirs, no family."

They reached the shrine of the Pelorus household gods. The lamps sputtered in the near darkness over a sparse tableau. A figurine of Nemesis spread threatening wings across the table. Mercury, too, frozen in time as if in mid-run; Diana, the huntress, her statuette's bow bent as if ready to release an arrow, although it lacked any string.

"You are sure of this?" Cicero asked.

"I am certain."

Batiatus gestured at the altar, where the figurines of violent gods stood. There were no ancestral tablets among them; no representations of parents or cousins, children or friends. The altar in the house of Pelorus had only representations of the gods themselves, and no place for man.

"I see," Cicero said. "He was alone."

"Pelorus and I have been associates since childhood."

"How so?"

"Ever since my father bought him—"

"Wait. Pelorus was a slave?"

"For some time, yes. He was freed by my father. He saved him from roadside brigands, and in a moment of uncharacteristic charity my father promised him whatever he desired. Naturally, he asked for his freedom, and it was granted with deep reluctance. And thenceforth, my father refused to have slaves as his bodyguards, lest similar happenstance place the same burden upon his goodwill and purse."

Batiatus pointed at the only other object in the shrine—the wooden sword that hung on the wall.

"The proof yet lies there," he said.

Cicero plucked the sword from its hooks and squinted in the dark at the crude words etched in its side. The abbreviations were drastic, largely hacked down to clusters of two and three letters, but the meaning was clear. *Pelorus, a gladiator of Capua, freed for valor, with the blessings of his master Titus Lentulus Batiatus, and in thanks to the gods.*

"From where did he come?" Cicero asked.

"The slave market. Purchased as a boy to be my companion, and sometime guardian. His family were Cimbri from the far north, captured in the campaigns of Gaius Marius."

"Well, Batiatus, I fear that you will be disappointed. None but a Roman citizen can write a will."

"That is surely not the case," Batiatus said, seating himself with a smug sigh upon the altar itself. "What about that king of Asia who left his entire kingdom to the Republic?"

"The state can make exceptions where it suits it. But for private individuals, the matter still stands."

"But we are all Roman citizens now. The franchise has been extended over all the Latins. You may have been *born* a Roman citizen, Cicero, but even humble Capuans such as myself are now admitted to the ranks. Pelorus, too."

Cicero leaned his haunches on the altar next to Batiatus. He smiled to himself in appreciation of a new and dangerous loophole.

"Batiatus, my friend," he breathed, "you are entirely correct. Yet another problem to occupy the lawyers of the Republic for decades to come."

"So if Pelorus can claim to be a citizen of Rome, what consequence to his estate, if he is left without heir?"

"His citizenship is less of an issue than his status as a freedman."

"And as freedman who departs this life absent a will, his estate becomes property of his former owner?"

"Indeed. His owner being your late father, who himself leaves his estate to you, Batiatus. I can see why this interests you so. You have identified a window of immense size."

"You will take my case?"

"There is a case?"

Batiatus leaned in as close as seemed proper.

"Verres is self-appointed," he said. "He makes claim to be familiae emptor."

"The 'buyer of the family,' meaning he has charge of disbursing the estate as Pelorus would have wished it?"

"Well, what the *fuck* would Verres know of Pelorus's wishes? What gives him the right to make decision, absent guidance?"

"Your points have validation, good Batiatus," Cicero said. "What is Verres's claim?"

"That as he died Pelorus willed him to dispense his fortune, largely to the freedman Timarchides."

"So?"

"The evidence of such an intent is strangely absent."

"Pelorus intended differently?"

"I do not imagine Pelorus had any intentions at all, one way or another."

"Why?"

"I was well acquainted with the man. Such a man as he lived for the moment. Pelorus lived a life both safe and secure—or so he thought. He had no enemies. He had wealthy friends. He did not expect to depart life at such early age!"

Something clattered in the corridor outside. The men looked up but saw nothing in the moonlight.

"I sense a Thracian's disapproval," Medea said, scratching her head. Her chains rattled in the dark.

"It is your life," Spartacus said from the neighboring cell.

"It is not my life," Medea replied. "It ceased to be my life when Roman legionaries fell upon the Getae and captured me."

"The story is familiar," Spartacus said.

"With variants, I am sure," she said. "I never yet saw Asia, but from the road as I was marched to Bithynian slave markets. Sold to the Syrians. Acquired by agents of Pelorus, with his strange predilection for sorcerous women. And thence to Italia."

"Where you will die in the arena."

"So be it."

"Unless you cooperate with Cicero."

"Fuck him."

"Give him what he wants," Spartacus said. "Give him what he wants, and you shall be taken from this place in his custody, taken to Rome as a seer and prophetess."

"As a slave."

"For now. But your life will be longer and more luxurious if you foretell portents of Rome's future than if you sit in such a cell as this, and wait for the trumpets to call you to the sands."

Outside, the moon peeked from behind rainclouds, allowing gentle, gray light to glow through the small window near the ceiling.

"See," he said. "Luna agrees with me."

"I am worth more to the Romans as their seer, than as

their animal of the arena?" she mused.

"Truly," Spartacus said, "you are worth more to the Romans alive than dead."

"In which case," she said, "I shall make sure that I die."

Lucretia awoke, again. This time, there was a scratching at the window, a pawing at the shutters. Her eyes narrowed in annoyance as she snatched up a statuette as an impromptu weapon.

"Governor or not," she breathed, "I will mark you for such insolence."

"Governor…?" slurred the voice of Batiatus. "I am but the governor of your heart."

Lucretia flung open the shutter, to find her husband attempting to climb through the window—a maneuvre that seemed to tax him more than it should.

"In Luna's name," Lucretia cried, "what are you doing?"

"I am coming to bed," Batiatus mumbled.

"Through the window?"

"It was the swiftest means to reach you. As windows are, I have discovered, in matters legal or marital."

"What are you talking about?"

"Tonight I am going to fuck you. And tomorrow, we are going to fuck Verres!" He finally found purchase with his other leg, swinging himself over the ledge and into the bedroom, where he tumbled on the floor at Lucretia's feet. She made no attempt to help him up.

"It delights me to see you so animated," she said dryly, returning to the bed and climbing back beneath the coverlet.

"Indeed I am, Lucretia. Your husband has found a new course through the obstacles set up by Verres and

Timarchides. A new chance, even, that you and I shall become the owners of the House of Pelorus. And Cicero himself engaged as my advocate!"

"I hope his success is greater with your case than his success in collecting prophecies," Lucretia said. She turned over fitfully, only to discover the hand of Batiatus grabbing at her shoulder and traveling swiftly toward her breast.

"My cock rises!" Batiatus whispered in her ear, pressing the evidence into her back.

"Quintus," she said smiling into the dark, "you find me not yet unlocked."

Batiatus harrumphed with the apparent effort required.

"Well," he said, realizing, "it is strange that you and I are in our bedchamber unaccompanied."

"Absent our usual servants of the cubiculum," Lucretia said, "we lose many modern utilities."

"Here in Neapolis," Batiatus said, rolling onto his back. "I shit and do not know the name of the man who hands me the sponge."

"And can you fuck, Quintus?" Lucretia shifted to look at him. "Without some tight-mouthed Illyrian to tease your cock into readiness?"

"I am ready for anything!" Batiatus declared, his tunic tented with the evidence.

"As a Roman lady," Lucretia said delicately, "I am not so swift to desire."

"Well," Batiatus said, looking about him in confusion. "I can… help…"

Lucretia smiled and draped her arms around him, pressing herself against him.

"Can you… help…?" she breathed in his ear.

His hand found the place where her legs met, sliding in between them, rubbing mechnically, joylessly for the merest moment. He then grabbed her hair and pulled her head back, pushing her roughly onto the bed.

"Quintus!" she protested. "Such things take preparation."

"And there is nobody here to prepare you."

"Remember when we were young, and we would prepare each other?" She smiled at him teasingly.

"I do," he sighed. "But that is what slaves are for."

"Then begin," Lucretia said, her face turned away from him. "Or occupy yourself elsewhere until we are returned to our Capuan comforts."

Verres dozed alone. He dreamed of quivering slave girls and fountains of wine. He dreamed of Sicilian riches and the plunder due a governor. The shutters to his room hung partly open to let in the night breeze, which blew unheeded through his hair.

"Verres!" came a stage whisper from the window.

Verres sat up, confused, and banished thoughts from his mind of the warm, wet and willing.

"Who is there?"

"Timarchides. I desire only to talk."

"Can this not wait until the morning? It is but a time for wolves and whores, and guards with poor luck."

"This cannot wait."

"We have the magistrate tomorrow morning. You will be a man of means. Wait until then."

"It concerns the magistrate," Timarchides said. "We are undone."

Rubbing his eyes, Verres climbed unsteadily to his feet, willing them to manoeuvre him to the window. He allowed his gaze to settle, with errant unsteadiness, on the face of Timarchides.

"What is it, then? Timarchides, you bring all the fretting of a wife, absent her amatory benefits."

"The quaestor moves against us."

"Whatever for?"

"In the name of Batiatus. He suspects us."

"I care not if he *suspects*. What is in his arsenal?"

"Testimonies of slaves. The ingenuities of Cicero as lawyer. Those windows in our scheme that are as yet unshuttered."

"Then it is time to shutter them."

"And risk further investigation?"

"We sail shortly, and I am untouchable in Sicilia. Remove obstacles and see targets hit. Batiatus, Successa, and the Getae witch. It will ease our arguments tomorrow."

"And Cicero?"

Verres thought long and hard.

"As an inquisitor, he seems like an unruly dog that will not give up a bone once proffered."

"Then him, too?"

"Not in this house. Outside. Make him *disappear*."

XV

SICARII NOCTE

HE BANGED ON THE DOOR, NOT CEASING LONG ENOUGH FOR A reasonable reply before banging on it again.

"Open your doors!" he bellowed. "And then open your legs!"

Welcome silence briefly reigned, before he reached to hammer his fist on the door again, only to find it opening before him.

A woman's bright eyes peered at him over the top of her veil.

He stood, a wiry Roman in his toga, a hulking Carthaginian by his side.

"The hour is late," the veiled woman said.

"It is! What kind of brothel is this place?"

"One whose staff sometimes needs sleep," she said firmly.

"My cock knows not night or day," he boasted, snickering alone at his own wit.

"Do you have coin?" she asked, businesslike and brisk.

"Of course." He seemed insulted at the implication that he did not.

"Then I am sure we can accommodate you... Batiatus?"

"Apologies, lady, you have me at a disadvantage. It is the veil."

"As well it should. I am Successa and the veil does me no credit by its removal."

"Of course, the funeral! My mind recalls."

She beckoned him into a courtyard illuminated only by the barest, dying flickers of red lanterns. He raised his hand behind him, signaling to Barca the bodyguard to wait outside.

Barca looked about him on the veranda, found a bench on which to recline, and wrapped himself in a discarded blanket, expecting no trouble till dawn. He shifted a couple of times for comfort, and then began to snore.

Within, a lone figure, stout and heavy-set, mopped the floor without looking up. Batiatus wondered if the janitrix was on the menu, and hoped the establishment had better merchandise. He stared instead at the rear of Successa as she led the way.

"What brings you here tonight?" Successa asked.

"Cunt," Batiatus grunted.

"I see I need not offer you any more wine. Any particular kind?"

"A willing one, requiring no maintenance. There was a dancing girl, at the cena libera yesterday's eve."

"We sent several dancing girls. All from Pompeii, all equipped with the organ you so delicately describe."

"Golden hair. White skin. Lips like she could suck the face off a denarius."

"That would be Valeria. So different in appearance from your good wife."

"Let me have her, and taste youth once more."

"I shall have her brought to you, as the villa of Pelorus is so close at hand."

"No, here, here."

"That is no cheaper."

"I shall have the coin. I shall have the coin soon enough, once the magistrate has had his say."

"How so?"

"The House of Pelorus shall be mine."

"The House of Pelorus is cursed."

"We have expelled those demons."

"Not I. They haunt me in every mirror."

Lacking windows except at the topmost edges of the cells, the corridor of the ludus sleeping quarters was black with the night. Occasional moonbeams shone through the dust, between the bars, stretching their dim light into the corridor. But the torches were dead and the lanterns dismounted.

Most of the cells were deserted, emptied by the catastrophe of the Neapolis games. A blond Roman snored in one, lost in dreams of freedom, not hearing the light footfalls that approached.

A figure peered into Varro's cell, and then moved on, its steps creeping with careful deliberation, barely rustling the rushes, barely scuffing the sand.

Somewhere, a female moaned in her sleep. The figure sped up its movements, darting toward the far end of the corridor, where the woman Medea lay chained on the floor of her cell.

The key did not jangle, as it had no fellows. It was a single large slab of iron, designed to open the simple locks of any of the cells. He fumbled at the lock, seemingly no longer caring about the noise.

Medea opened her eyes.

"Who is there?" she asked.

"Nemesis," he whispered.

"Nemesis is a woman," she yawned.

"Not for you. Not tonight."

He drew his knife with an audible scrape.

"A sicarius?" she observed, without emotion. "A nocturnal knife-man, sent to end me?"

"Be quiet, and I shall be quick," he whispered, advancing into the cell.

She climbed to her feet, her chains scraping on the stones.

"I will not make your task easy," she said.

"You should welcome death," he said.

"I will," she said. "But you are a Roman, so I will take you first."

Her chains rattled again, spooking him. She saw only the nervous jerk of his arms in the moonlight, as he sought to ward off a blow that never came. It was the reflex of a man accustomed to fighting.

"You are a large man," she said. "And I am chained."

"Fairness concerns me not," he said, hesitating, peering in the half-light, circling her, unsure of the length of the chains.

"But you still fret that I have the advantage," she said.

"I do not."

"Then make your play." She snapped her chains as if they were a whip, startling the sicarius in the dark. He lunged and she grabbed at him, propelling him back toward the bars of the cage. He kicked her away, and she came at him again, her chains snapping taut a safe distance from him.

He leaned against the bars and chuckled.

"You cannot reach me," he smirked.

Medea stopped struggling against her chains, and stood in the dark, her hands on her hips.

"I do not need to," she said.

He frowned at the odd reply, and drew himself up, ready to strike again, but something enfolded him. He stared down in surprise to see a strong, tanned arm, reaching through the bars behind him, enveloping his chest, grabbing fast onto his neck. He made as if to protest, but the air was choked out of him, his throat held tight, the arm pressing down on his windpipe, dragging him against the bars.

Unseen in the dark, the face of the sicarius turned red, his eyes bulging as the grip grew ever tighter, his head was forced against the sharp-edged, rusty cell bars, drawing blood. His legs thrashed impotently as something gave way in his neck with a distant pop, and then he went limp.

True to his training, Spartacus drew several breaths, waiting for any telltale signs of fakery. Only when he sensed the body was truly dead did he let it drop to the floor.

"It seems I owe you my life again, Thracian," Medea said softly. "But as a slave I have nothing to give, except that which you do not desire to take."

"You have the key," Spartacus pointed out. "Throw me the key."

Medea scrambled across the floor, dragging her chains to their maximum extent, her arm straining to reach the fallen key. Her fingers nudged against it, found purchase and drew it into her grip. She hurled it over, through the bars and into Spartacus's cell.

He wasted no time, shoving his arms through the bars at

the front, twisting in order to get the key in the lock.

"That was the only key," Medea said. "And it is clearly too large for my manacles."

"I do not seek to escape," Spartacus said, not meeting her gaze. His eyes concentrated on the task at hand as the key slid ponderously into the lock.

"Do not lie to me, Thracian," Medea said. "Give me that, at least. Run. Run while you can, and I shall not hold it against you."

"I am not escaping," Spartacus repeated, turning the key inch by inch, a process made tortuously slow by the need to bend his hand back on itself.

"Then find the key to my manacles," Medea said. "And I will 'not escape' with you."

"There is no time," Spartacus responded as the lock clunked out of place. He kicked the cell door open and sprinted into the darkened corridor.

Medea said something incredibly obscene in the language of the Getae. But there was nobody there to hear it. She peered expectantly down the hall, but heard nothing save for the Thracian's receding footsteps.

Eventually, she returned to her pallet and curled up to sleep, her back turned to the dead body slumped against the far wall of her cell.

Batiatus lay back, breathing heavily on the pallet, spent.

"You were right," he panted through laughter.

"Concerning my accomplishments?" Successa smiled.

"Indeed," he said, barely able to gulp air. "You are the Champion of… the Champion of… Fucking."

He heard her reply tugged by a smile, even though he could not see her.

"All cats are gray in the dark. My career yet has a course to run."

"Undoubtedly," he agreed, draping his arm around her, feeling her draw closer to him. "You are a mistress of mistresses. You did well to dissuade me out of that stupid little girl."

"Valeria is a fine young woman," Successa said in polite disagreement. "But age brings sophistication."

"Something to which I aspire in all things. In bed. In business. In the course of honors."

"Really?" Successa propped herself up on one arm, intrigued. "You seek political office?"

"In Rome any man may become anything, given enough time, and luck, and virtue."

"Any man?"

"Well, no, not any man," he conceded. "There are those who are subject to *infamia*."

"What brings a bad reputation?" Successa asked. "In a world where men murder each other for the entertainment of the crowd?"

"A public official who accepts bribes; a soldier who flees the battlefield. Those who sell their flesh for the entertainment of others."

"So I shall never be a Vestal virgin," she sighed in mock disappointment.

"You are eminently disqualified," he agreed.

"And what of the lanista?"

"What of me? My reputation is unsullied!"

Successa laughed. "You trade in men like a madame pimps her whores. Unlikely to be the sort of man to be welcomed into virtuous circles."

"You make comparison to prostitutes and panderers, but surely this is merely a matter of perspective,"

Batiatus declaimed, as if addressing an imaginary crowd. "Regard us instead as generals with *flexible* armies? As warriors who fight to win people's hearts? The lanista performs a noble function. He occupies the rabble, true enough, but he instils in them a deep-seated respect for the martial virtues upon which Rome was founded. In the hands of the lanista, our people are regularly reminded of the power of the sword. In the hands of the lanista, we are taught repeatedly the lesson that death may be tamed for the pleasure of Rome, and that it is our destiny to witness bloodshed and pain, but to walk away from it sated."

"Well, you *could* say that."

"Gratitude!"

"Or you could say the same of the whores. Let me think, now... Why, yes, you could say that whores are good for Rome because they present fine scabbards for Roman swords. That they allow you to remember your position in the hierarchy by presenting themselves for your pleasure."

"Now you speak foolishly."

"Without the noble whore, where would you be? They remind you that whatever the world has to offer, it is there for the taking. The ugliest of Romans, the most pock-marked, disease-ridden citizen, may fuck a Grecian goddess if he has coin to pay for it."

"And possession of a heavy purse is a Roman virtue."

"Roman virtue surely leads to the acquisition of wealth."

"Which allows one to acquire prostitutes."

"Among other things," she said.

✦

A lamp smashed against the wall, its flaming oil licking swiftly against a hempen curtain. Suddenly, the room was illuminated, as yellow flames curled and flickered up the wall.

"Put it out, Tiro," Cicero murmured sleepily, rubbing his eyes. Seeing that the flames were rising faster than expected, he dragged himself to an upright position.

"Tiro!" he said, still not awake.

"Dominus!" his slave answered with a panicked voice. Cicero turned to look, and saw a black-clad figure lurching toward him. He held up his hands to ward off the attack, only for Tiro himself to stand in the way.

Cicero watched, dumbly, as Tiro and the attacker grappled. The boy was no match for the bigger man, and struggled fitfully as he was first pinned, then lifted and flung at the far wall. He slid to the floor and lay there unmoving.

Reluctantly comprehending that this truly was no dream, Cicero drew himself to his feet.

"What is the meaning of this?" he demanded, only then seeing the short, curved knife in the shadow's hand.

"Marcus Tullius Cicero," said the unknown figure. "Come with me."

"Absent cause or reason? I think not."

"Come with me, dead or alive," the man hissed.

"Is that a Gaulish accent?" Cicero mused, trying very hard not to look at the figure of Spartacus, who had appeared at the doorway and was now stealthily advancing on the would-be killer.

"Silence," the man said.

"It is!" Cicero said. "What is a man of Gaul doing so far from home, I wonder...?"

"Dying?" Spartacus suggested, as he locked his arms around the man's neck.

The man's eyes widened, his knife-hand stabbed backward, but the blunt edge of the blade bumped harmlessly against Spartacus's skin. The gladiator tightened his grip. Desperately, the Gaul propelled himself backward against the wall, smashing the Thracian into it, causing the plaster to crack away from him in a spidery star. Before Spartacus had time to yell, he was lifted and smashed again. Chunks of the white walls caved away, revealing terracotta bricks beneath.

But the firm purchase of the wall gave Spartacus extra leverage, allowing him to drive his forearms yet closer together, pushing ever harder against the man's neck, until it suddenly gave way, and the Gaul's head lolled, unseeing, as he slumped to the ground.

"Thracian!" Cicero said happily. "I owe you my life, it seems."

"Where is my dominus?" Spartacus demanded.

"I know not."

Tiro the youthful slave struggled to his feet, pressing tenderly at the bump on his head.

"You!" Spartacus said, throwing him the key. "Unlock Varro. Set him to your protection."

"Varro…?" the youth mumbled.

"The blond gladiator!" Spartacus shouted.

"Do as he says, Tiro," Cicero said.

Spartacus did not wait for any further acknowledgment, running instead for Lucretia's bedchamber, leaving Cicero to pat fussily at the burning curtains.

"What is happening?" Lucretia demanded drowsily as Spartacus burst into her room.

"Where is dominus?"

"For what meaning do you stand before me absent guard?"

Spartacus grabbed her hands, causing her to gasp in surprise.

"Where is he?"

There was a knock at the door.

"I believe it unlikely that I would receive two midnight callers," Successa said.

"Perhaps your fame spreads," Batiatus replied.

The knock came again, louder this time.

"Let your slaves answer it," he mumbled, turning his head back toward the pillow.

"They are largely employed this night at the House of Pelorus," she replied, tugging on her gown. "I, alone, am not permitted to cross its threshold."

"Come back to bed," he wheedled. "I yet have appetite unsatisfied."

Outside, she heard the janitrix setting her mop within its bucket and sauntering toward the door.

"As you command," Successa said, and turned back to her client.

Outside, the slave wearily peeled open the shutter in the main door.

"Who is it?" she said.

"A message for Quintus Lentulus Batiatus," a man's voice said.

"There are no names here," the slave said carefully. "For this is the House of the Winged Cock."

"Then let me deliver papyrus that Batiatus may gaze upon it should he *happen* to be nearby," the voice said with some irritation.

"Very well," the janitrix sighed, not wishing for any further trouble. She slid back the bolt and began to pull on the door, and hence had little time to register the sudden foot that kicked it wide open, or the short sword that plunged into her neck. She struggled, fitfully, against the hand that was clamped on her mouth. Her lungs heaved, but drew in no air as blackness crept at the edge of her vision — then nothing. Her last thought was that her newly cleaned floor was stained with blood.

The new arrival strode inside, his figure hidden beneath a bulky cloak. He pulled back the hood to reveal a shock of red Teutonic hair, and a knotted beard and mustache. The cleaning slave slid off the end of his blade, crumpling on the floor, her blood seeping across the newly scrubbed tiles.

The interior of the House of the Winged Cock was silent and dark, and the Teuton smiled to himself as he walked further inside. He was hence entirely unprepared for the bellowing cry of: "BATIATUS!" and the sudden onslaught of a Carthaginian giant.

Barca leapt out of the shadows, his coverlet still clinging to his chest, his hands grabbing for the sword-arm of the surprised Teuton. The two men pitched over onto a table, rolling across it until it gave way under their weight, dropping them both to the floor.

Successa and Batiatus appeared at the doorway to her chamber, baffled.

"Your bodyguard earns his keep," she mused.

"Against what dangers?" Batiatus said.

Barca and the Teuton seemed equally matched, their fists smacking into each others faces, their hands clawed to grab at clothes and flesh, their muscles straining to heave the other off-balance. They scrabbled across the tiles, smashing into pots and pans and pieces of shattered furniture.

"Such brawls are regular occurrences in a house such as this," Successa noted, unmoved by the drama unfolding in her courtyard.

"Drink and cunt makes many men merry," Batiatus agreed, nibbling at her shoulder.

Then they both caught sight of the dead slave.

"Get dressed," Batiatus said, suddenly deadly serious. "This is no drunken brawl."

Successa ducked back inside the room, only to scream in shock.

A man was climbing through her window, sword in hand.

Batiatus followed her into the room. He swiftly snatched up a blanket, throwing it over the new arrival. He grabbed Successa and guided her quickly to the stone steps that led to the upper floor.

Their pursuer charged after them, throwing off the blanket, and revealing the squat, black, scarred face of a Numidian warrior. Even as Batiatus flinched from him, he leapt through the air, sword outstretched toward Batiatus's neck—

Only to stop suddenly and smack to the ground, hard.

Someone had grabbed his ankles mid-flight. The Numidian kicked savagely with his legs at his new assailant: a Thracian, newly clambered through the same window.

"Spartacus!" Batiatus cried in surprise and relief.

Spartacus did not pause to greet his master, instead he dragged the Numidian down the stone steps and back into the central atrium.

In the distance, Barca and the Teuton punched each other on the floor, still neither had the upper hand.

The Numidian seized the fallen mop, jabbing it up at Spartacus like a spear. The assault threw the Thracian off-balance, affording the Numidian a vital chance to kick himself free and clamber back to his feet, sword in hand.

Spartacus and the Numidian eyed each other warily for a moment, before the laughing Numidian lunged at the gladiator with his sword. Spartacus lunged forward, too, to the side, snatching the Numidian's sword-arm behind the wrist, and tugging him forward.

The Numidian lost his purchase on the wet floor, tumbling a second time. His head cracked with a sickening thud against the stones of the hearth. He lolled, his arms and legs twitching, as blood and gray brain matter seeped out onto the flagstones. Spartacus turned to the other side of the hall, where Barca and the Teuton wrestled.

The Teuton had gained the upper hand, hefting Barca by the waist and throwing him toward the hearth. Spartacus leapt over the fallen Carthaginian, grabbing the Teuton by his long hair, a foot sliding out to trip him up.

The Teuton snarled in anger, whirling to snatch up his own fallen knife, not seeing the great dangling cauldron hook behind him as the Thracian dragged him by the hair, shoving him with irresistible force, inch by inch, toward the piercing, sharp prong.

The room was suddenly silent, but for the creaking of the chains that held the cauldron hook, and the gentle pattering of the Teuton's blood on the floor and table, as the dead body swayed gently, his feet dragging on the flagstones.

Spartacus helped Barca to his feet, and their hands clasped in momentary unspoken brotherhood.

"Gratitude," Batiatus said, stepping forward. "I owe you—" He stopped himself suddenly, remembering his father's folly with enslaved bodyguards. "I owe you gratitude," he finished carefully.

"Two sicarii," Successa said, trembling as the reality only now began to take hold. "Did they come for you, or me…?" She sat down on the floor, shaking in shock.

"Or one each," Spartacus said, "as one was sent to kill Cicero, and another to kill Medea."

"Are they—?"

"Both are safe. I made sure of that."

"This place is not secure," Barca said.

"Gratitude, Barca, for observations unrequired," Batiatus said. "Absent a confession extracted from one of the killers, we must work with what we have."

"Your meaning?" Spartacus asked.

"Someone seeks to kill a select group, or perhaps merely to silence us. All the targets are presences usefully absent from the magistrate tomorrow…" He looked at the rosy light of dawn beyond the balcony. "… or rather, later this morning."

"This is Verres's doing?" Successa said tentatively, willing it not to be so.

"Verres? Timarchides? Perhaps the pair," Batiatus replied.

"Absent proof, you might as well be accusing the winds," Spartacus said. "They have the protection of freedmen against idle accusations."

"I seek not proof, I seek safety," Batiatus said. "Ilithyia is already on her way to Atella. Lucretia should take litter and join her to place herself beyond harm."

"Someone must stand guard over her," Spartacus said.

"Barca. He has ties to the ludus that he would not dare sever with flight," Batiatus said, meeting his bodyguard's eyes.

"Dominus," Barca responded curtly.

"Rouse Lucretia now!" Batiatus instructed. "There must be no delay. Return with her to Capua!"

"You, too, should flee," Spartacus said. "There is nothing left here for the House of Batiatus."

"Cicero and I have business to attend with the magistrate this morning, with Varro as our protector. And you will stand guard over the witch. *My* witch."

XVI

GLADII ET CINERES

VARRO WALKED WITHOUT COMPLAINT BY THE SIDE OF THE litter, along the morning road, unheeding of the birdsong.

Batiatus left the curtain open so that he might speak to his prize as the slavers carried him along the hill road. Cicero sat upright by his side, his brow furrowed in concentration, his lips moving silently as he practiced imaginary rhetorics.

"We pause at the undertakers on the road," Batiatus said to Varro, "seeking testimony as to the manner of Pelorus's death."

"Dominus," Varro said.

"Evidence to further good Cicero's suit today against the boy-loving Timarchides."

"I doubt his predilections," Varro said.

"He never ceases to speak of them," Batiatus said.

"Yes dominus, but it occurs to me that he might overstate his interests?"

"For what reason?" Cicero asked, pausing in his mutterings to join the conversation.

"Timarchides' motivatation seems to be antipathy toward Romans, rather than love of men," Varro said carefully.

"Why tell such falsehoods?" Cicero said.

"For the forging of a chain of deceit," Varro said. "A chain that links him to Pelorus in a more intimate fashion than truly warranted, to smooth the passage of the inheritance."

"I would need proof for that," Cicero said.

"Before the primus, I was witness to Timarchides bidding farewell to his brother gladiators from House Pelorus," Varro said.

"Warm embraces all round no doubt," Batiatus laughed.

"They were less than kind?" Cicero asked.

"I imagine so!" Batiatus said. "To the gods-favored bastard who gained his freedom but hours before all the slaves within the house were condemned to die. And all because he happily sat on the master's cock!"

"Perhaps not," Cicero said.

"Come now, good Cicero. Verres all but proclaimed it at the funeral. Timarchides was beloved to Pelorus more so than any woman."

"Was he, dominus?" Varro put in. "Spartacus and I heard the insults of the gladiators as he departed. They called him many names. They accused him of cowardice and theft. But not once of being the lanista's lover. Surely, if a gladiator wished to cut another with words, such obscenity would be made prominent abuse?"

"The hearsay of dead men," Batiatus said dismissively, "attested by gladiators in my employ. Such testimony is of no use."

"Indeed, dominus. But Timarchides himself refuted it."

"Go… on…"

"He swore to them that he *purchased* his freedom. And that the price of his purchase was recorded upon his wooden sword."

Batiatus looked expectantly at Cicero, who nodded enthusiastically.

"It would be," Cicero said. "And such evidence that Timarchides dare not destroy, lest any citizen in the future question his manumission. This is useful. As is the news that the first victim that Medea's violence claimed that night was Verres himself."

"How do you know that?" Batiatus asked, shutting the curtain on Varro.

"Timarchides admitted as much himself when I went to parley with the witch. He spoke of her overpowering Verres, and thence proceeding to her murders."

"*Verres* unlocked the door to her cell? It was *him*? While tormenting the Getae girl. Successa did not name him, but if that is the case…"

The bearers came to a halt before the lone house of the undertakers, far from any other dwelling, set within wide-set grounds of ponds and orchards.

"Business is good, I see," Cicero commented.

"Death is sure investment, one with guaranteed buyers," Batiatus said with a shrug, swinging his legs out of the litter.

Cicero chuckled.

"Stay in the litter," Batiatus said. "We shall but be a moment."

"Considering last night's events," Cicero said, "I would feel safer accompanying you and your bodyguard."

"Of course. Come, then."

Batiatus advanced through the gateway, seeing no sign of the skulls and bones that would characterize the carvings in a cemetery. Instead, the decoration of the undertakers' residence was all flowers and beasts, gods and piety. And yet, the grounds seemed unkept, the hedges untrimmed. Apples, newly ripe but worm-eaten, were scattered on the flagstones.

"Where are their slaves to tend to such disarray," Batiatus murmured, as the trio reached the house. "They take such pride in disposition of dead, but not their own residence."

A gust of wind tugged at their clothes, causing a shutter to slam in on itself and creak open again. Varro reached out to stay his master, drawing his sword.

"What is it, Varro? Has the Getae witch infected your mind? Now *you* see the future, too?"

"Not the future, dominus. A trouble past."

Varro advanced slowly toward the house.

Batiatus began to register the signs of a dwelling deserted. Torn curtains, damp from earlier storms, flapped in the gusts of the wind. The door stood open. The ponds were not merely untended, but overflowing; their drains clogged with weeds and fallen leaves, their waters forming a new-made stream that trickled between the flower beds, toward the gutter in the road outside.

With the tip of his sword, Varro pushed the door open and peered inside.

The house was arranged around a central atrium, open to the sky, with a colonnade around its edge leading to the various rooms. In its midst was a continuation of the external garden. Or rather, had been.

It was different now. The entire walled garden was now a barren waste of blackened timbers and scorched bones.

"A bonfire has burned here," Batiatus said, following behind Varro.

"Of corpses," Varro said, poking at a skull with his blade.

"What has occurred…?" Batiatus breathed.

Varro squinted thoughtfully at the walls.

"The fire was some days ago. Note the dust carried into doorways and splashed by rain on walls." He stepped down onto the charcoaled timbers, bones snapping beneath his sandals. "I count perhaps a dozen skulls," he said. "Maybe more."

"A funeral pyre?" Batiatus said, surveying the scene in bafflement. "For what reason?"

"It is hidden," Varro said, "within the eaves, and few houses stand near by, who would know?"

He pushed aside a charred timber, to find a nest of edged weapons, bent and blackened by the heat, their hilts burned away. Turned from a soldier's tools into so much scrap metal.

Batiatus peered into the closest room, finding a sleeping pallet spread out upon the bloodstains, and scattered breadcrusts and animal bones.

"Someone has taken up residence here after the bodies were burned," Batiatus said. "But why kill the undertakers?"

"Whoever the killers were," Cicero said, "they dwelt for several days among swords and ashes."

Now, the House of Pelorus had but two occupants. The putative owners and hospes had gone into town. The slaves on loan from the House of the Winged Cock had returned to their home. Cooks and cleaners, serving girls and workmen, all were gone. The manifold guests had long departed, leaving little of the wine cellar but piss in the cisterns. And Spartacus, guardian to a hollow mansion.

Wearily, Spartacus approached the cell of Medea. The barred door still sat ajar. The resident of the cell still sat on the floor wreathed in her chains.

"Alone at last," she said calmly. "And the door to my cell is open."

"I am not here for you," he said.

"From free Thracian to man with a mop? Such a Tarpeian plummet."

"Eat this," he said, throwing her a hunk of bread. "I must remove your cellmate before he starts to smell."

"Gratitude," she said, "for his elimination from this world, and from this place."

Spartacus grabbed at the corpse's arm. The flesh was already strangely yellow, the blood having pooled lower down the sprawled body. On the face bruises and the flower-shapes of popped veins attested to last moments of strangulation. Spartacus dragged the body toward the door, its clothes snagging on the rough stone floor, pulling back its sleeves and half-opening its tunic.

Suddenly, Spartacus stopped.

"What is it, Thracian?" Medea asked.

"He has a mark," Spartacus said, "upon his arm."

"So noted," she said. "What does it mean?"

"Such a mark denotes current or former status."

"As a criminal?"

"As a gladiator who has passed the test of his house."

"Just like yours."

"Not so," he said, brandishing his forearm for her to see. "Mine is B, for Batiatus. His is P."

"But I thought the slaves of Pelorus all dead?"

Spartacus stared down at the arm, thoughtfully. His mind spun with the events of the last few days, with arguments in cells and whispers in corridors; with threats in hot moments and chilly reason. He thought of all the possible reasons why a man with the brand of Pelorus could somehow appear in the dark of night, when the brand of Pelorus was supposedly banished from the world of the living. And then he realized.

Spartacus dropped the body and darted from the cell.

"Where are you going, Thracian?" Medea called after him.

"To retrieve key to your manacles," he replied. "We must leave. Now."

"Gaius Verres, welcome, welcome," the magistrate said. "And congratulations upon your appointment!"

"Gratitude," Verres laughed. "Magistrate Gnaeus Helva, it has been too long since we last met."

"And will be long again, if you soon sail for Sicilia."

"Duty calls."

"It surely does. Be seated, be seated."

Helva beckoned to a slave to bring a small stack of scrolls, and took the topmost one from it. Verres slumped into a chair, his leg hooked over one of the armrests in a languorous pose. Timarchides sat carefully in the next chair, his back straight, and his expression serious.

"This seems a simple matter requiring little more than seal and salutation," Helva said. He glanced down at the papyrus, his eyes running along the neat letters written in a scribal hand, then frowned. "The death of Pelorus was indeed unfortunate," he continued, "but these are straitened times. One murder still moves me, even after the purges of the Social War when such things were commonplace and found in their myriads."

Verres nodded in a conciliatory fashion.

"I loved Pelorus dearly," Timarchides said, his interjection attracting a scowl from Verres. "His sudden death was tragedy."

"Indeed, indeed," Helva said, "and at the hands of a slave. So... the value of the estate is considerably diminished?"

"There is little here but the tying of loose ends and the agreement of settled accounts." Verres said. "As familiae emptor, I carried out the necessary disbursements of Pelorus's funeral. Unfortunately, that also included the necessary execution of the entire household."

"Entire?"

"Of course."

"My meaning," Helva said, "is that the *entirety* of the household has been disposed?"

"All but the Getae witch Medea," Verres said, "who is sentenced *ad gladium* and sure to die."

"Very well," Helva said. "It is your finding, as familiae emptor, that the freedman Timarchides is the man most appropriate to inherit the estate of Pelorus?"

"For certain," Verres confirmed. "Timarchides was as son to Pelorus, and his sole associate of free status."

"You exclude yourself, Verres?"

"As familiae emptor, I desire not to abuse my position."

"Well then," Helva chuckled, "gratitude to you for a sense of duty most pious. With a certain degree of relief, that I call for the sealing tar." He clapped his hands to summon the slave again, and tugged a prominent signet ring from his middle finger.

The door opened, but not upon a loyal servant. Instead, it revealed a commotion outside as servants tried to bar new suppliants from the courtroom.

"By all that is sacred," Helva muttered impatiently. "What now?"

"Magistrate Helva!" a voice shouted. "This case is yet unheard."

"I think," Helva said, "that I shall be judge of that. I speak most literally." He laughed at his little joke, only to stop short when he saw that Timarchides and Verres were not so amused by the intrusion. They stared at one another wordlessly, their eyes and brows animated in a silent discussion, as if each had left the other to perform a task, and now found him wanting.

"Marcus Tullius Cicero, quaestor of the Republic," Cicero declared, announcing himself. At his shoulder stood Batiatus, tugging his tunic back into shape after an unseen tussle, and the gladiator Varro, who stared threateningly at unseen scribes in the next room.

"What is the meaning of this, Cicero?" Helva said. "I heard of your arrival in town, on business Sibylline, if I recall."

"A quaestor questions where he may," Cicero said. "And I seek clarification of some matters regarding this estate."

Helva looked dolefully at his signet ring, already off his finger and ready to apply to the papyrus.

"Very well," he sighed. "What is your contention?"

"A misunderstanding," Cicero said carefully.

"Mis—!" Batiatus began, only to be stayed by his counsel's upraised hand.

"A misunderstanding," Cicero continued, "that would see the estate of Pelorus wrongly assigned, absent diligence."

✦

Butchers worked their carcasses on stone tables in front of their shops. Grocers haggled with household slaves over vegetables. Two painted whores leaned lazily on the staircase to a cheaper, second-floor establishment, and did not even bother to call out to passers-by. The street was damp from earlier rains, but already warm. It was as if the buildings sweated in imitation of their residents.

Spartacus pushed through the crowd, his attention focused on the forum building that loomed above the smaller houses and insulae. He dragged Medea behind him, their wrists chained together.

"Where are we going?" she demanded.

"Batiatus seeks audience with the magistrate," Spartacus said, ducking around an ambling pair of blacksmiths.

"Then let him," Medea said, barely circumventing them herself. "It makes no difference to us."

"It will if he dies," Spartacus said. "Enemies are at large and yet unknown to him."

"Let me go," Medea said thoughtfully. "Unchain me that we can move faster through this crowd."

Spartacus laughed despite his concern.

"I am a slave, Medea. I am not a fool."

Autumn came early to the hills. The air swam with yellow leaves, spiraling and circling in a downward slant, like flocks of birds circling toward one single prey. Always, they swept along with the wind, darting and in occasional eddies, but always downward, down toward the damp, grimy flagstones of the road.

Far below, the forest gave way to hills, the hills to fields, the fields to the sea. A dark, angry mountain marked the general location of Neapolis, now far behind

Lucretia's litter. Her four bearers plodded on without a word, and she left the sidings to flutter in the mounting breeze. It let her see the ceaseless corridors of trees that avenued their path; it let her see glimpses of the featureless road ahead; and it let her see Barca, faithful Barca, marching at her side, his hand ever on the hilt of his sword, his eyes scanning the trees for invisible foes.

There was a flutter of wings ahead. A platoon of surprised crows darted for the sky, like black shadows against the confetti of leaves.

Barca gestured for the bearers to stop.

"Something lies up ahead," the Carthaginian whispered.

"Home!" Lucretia said. "Capua lies but hours before us. That is the sole destination for which I care."

But she was talking to Barca's back as the giant stepped ahead, his sword half-drawn.

Cursing silently, Lucretia dropped from the litter, gathering her silken robes against her to ward off the mountain chill.

"Barca!" she fumed, tottering after him on legs not yet fully awake. "We flee dangers Neapolitan. They will not lie ahead of us. It would please me not to dawdle so long upon this road."

Barca had stopped at the side of the road and knelt beside something.

"Tell me what it is." Lucretia asked, nearing the hunched giant.

Barca's gazed down upon his findings.

"There are no bandits here," Lucretia said. "No dangers for us to—"

She stopped at Barca's side. He was knelt before what had once been a man.

The corpse lay sprawled in the gutter, its back arched by

the tightening tendons of the dead. One arm was stretched out, imploringly, the other clutched at what had once been its side. The eyes were gone, the flesh torn from the face in strips. Chunks had been wrenched from the limbs by animals with larger jaws, leaving gobbets of meat and gristle scattered on the road nearby. One foot was missing entirely, along with the lower portion of the leg.

"What do you see?" Lucretia asked.

"A slave," Barca replied.

"How do you know?" she asked.

"Because I was witness to his abandonment," Barca said. "As we journeyed to Neapolis, our drover left an old man at this place."

"That is no concern of mine," Lucretia said, with a sigh. She began to walk back to the litter.

Barca looked back at his mistress for a moment, and then rose to his feet. He said a short Carthaginian prayer, little more than a cantrip, for the departed slave.

"I vow I will not meet similar end."

Cicero had started softly, but his voice now thundered around the chamber. He left his chair, pacing in front of the magistrate, stopping only occasionally to fix the glowering Verres with a knowing stare.

"The property is not yours to disburse!" he said. "Pelorus died by your negligence, and now you scatter his coin in your own honor!"

"My negligence? My negligence!" Verres sputtered. "Do you accuse a Roman citizen of murder? Witnesses innumerable saw the Getae witch slay Pelorus at his banquet."

"Removed now to their estates in Pompeii and

Herculaneum, Baiae and Capriae in circumstance most convenient, and unable to discuss Pelorus's final moments," Cicero countered.

"Not even I was present at his moment of death."

"Pelorus was killed with a knife. His throat slit with brutal thrust. How might he impart last words of such import when he was incapable of utterance?"

"He whispered."

"To a man who 'was not present'? You expect us to believe such words?"

"I can only speak truth."

"Yet voice seems capable of lying. Perhaps we should call the pollinctores who dressed the body of Pelorus, and demand description exact of his wounds? Let us see what they tell us of the nature of his death."

"Call them! Call them!" Verres bellowed. "Apologies, magistrate Helva. Call adjournment, pending testimony of the undertakers."

"That will not be necessary, magistrate," Cicero said. "Batiatus and I called upon the undertakers today. And Verres surely knows what we found at their residence."

"I do not," Verres said. "I have not had cause to visit undertakers, a task more fitting a slave."

"*Someone* has visited them," Cicero said. "Someone visited upon them a knife in the dark, and burned the dead bodies within their own household. The pollinctores, dead. The fossores, dead. Another household visited by grim Nemesis, absent cause, absent reason, absent honor."

"And you would put blame toward me for that as well?" Verres asked.

Batiatus watched carefully, not the argument between Cicero and Verres, but the reaction on the face of Timarchides.

"See," he whispered to Varro. "The freedman makes clear attempt to conceal his countenance. He knows something. Cicero has found them out!"

"Do you question the words of a Roman citizen?" Verres was saying.

"I do, Gaius Verres. That is my job, after all," Cicero responded.

"If I were going to speak false of Pelorus's wishes, why would I not make claim of his worldly goods for *myself*?"

"Why indeed? Your decision to award Timarchides shows virtue most praiseworthy. I understand that Timarchides has also been offered a position in your own entourage."

"He is a good man."

"Perhaps so. But our purpose here is not to discuss the virtues of the freedman Timarchides. We are here to discover whether you are empowered to sign over the estate of Pelorus into his hands."

"Then hasten decision. I am due in Sicilia shortly, on the business of the Republic."

"My question, Gaius Verres, concerns the unfortunate events that led to the death of Pelorus."

"An answer already given. Pelorus met with unfortunate death at the hands of escaped slave, Medea of the Getae."

"And what was the manner of her escape?"

"I do not know."

"Let us ask someone who does. Call the witness."

Helva smiled in surprise.

"You have a witness at the ready, quaestor? Such dedication!"

Cicero stood still, staring at his fingernails in search of imaginary dirt. He smiled calmly at Batiatus, and then turned to stare at Verres. The governor fumed in his chair, his eyes narrowed in vengeful slits.

In a distant chamber, there was the sound of footsteps and guardians' spears clanking aside. The hurried footfalls of a household slave, mixed with the light rustle of a woman's steps.

She entered the courtroom, her veil hiding her face. She bowed, demurely and without a word, to the magistrate, and then advanced to the podium.

"Gratitude," Cicero said, "to this fine, upstanding lady of Neapolis, who steps forward to offer account of events of fateful night. Your name?"

"Successa," the veiled woman said. Only her eyes, dark and flashing, could be seen over the dark silk that stretched across her face.

"Of what house?"

"Of no house, save that of the Winged Cock," she said, naming the famed symbol that matched her Pompeiian accent.

"Lady Successa, I understand that you were present at the banquet on the night of Pelorus's murder," Cicero said.

"I was."

"In what capacity?"

"So it please the court, I was hired as companion."

"Let us not be coy. You mean in the amatory manner?"

"I do. My favors are highly regarded. *Were* highly regarded."

Batiatus raised his eyebrows in agreement.

"By the people of Neapolis?" Cicero asked.

"By Pelorus himself. He said that I was the best fuck in Campania, and that I was to ensure that his honored guest, Gaius Verres, was to depart Neapolis thinking the same."

"And, if I may ask, lady Successa, how did Pelorus

come to know that you were the 'best fuck in Campania'?"

"He was a regular visitor."

"At the, what was it now, the House of the Winged Cock?"

"Yes."

"He was intimate with you?"

"Upon multiple occasions."

"And with other ladies of that establishment?"

"With all of them."

"And with the men of your house?"

"Never."

"For what reason?"

"Pelorus had no interest in cock."

"I must protest!" Verres exclaimed. "Cicero employs hearsay against hearsay. Taking the word of a whore against that of a Roman citizen!"

"In my defence," Cicero suggested, "the lady Successa is present and able to testify. She is neither conveniently dead, nor miraculously able to convey her wishes with a slit throat."

"She has already *attested* that she sells her cunt for a few denarii!" Verres said. "How much cheaper is her mouth?"

"I cannot claim knowledge of pricing policies of Neapolitan brothels," Cicero said dryly.

"My meaning," Verres said through gritted teeth, "is that this woman's testimony must surely be available for a price. It is not, after all, very likely that she will be amassing much more coin on her back!"

Cicero waited politely while Verres's words resounded around the chamber.

"Really, Verres?" he said after a time. "For what reason is that?"

Verres swallowed nervously and turned to the magistrate with calm composure.

"Time comes that this farce must reach conclusion," he said.

"I have interest in hearing Cicero's closing arguments, nonetheless," the magistrate said.

"As it pleases you," Cicero said. "I would ask the lady Successa to remove her veil."

"I have removed far more than that in the past," Successa said, a smile clearly audible in her voice.

She reached up to withdraw a hook from an eye in her headdress, allowing the veil to fall away with exquisite slowness. It was the practiced tease of a woman who knew how to reveal her body — but now revealed a horror rather than a delight.

"Tell me, lady Successa," Cicero said, "what it is you owe to Gaius Verres."

"He promised me a stipend," she replied. "I do not know how to—"

"Let me try to parse it for you," Cicero suggested. "Gaius Verres, the kind-hearted governor-designate of Sicilia; Gaius Verres, the apparent long-term friend and hospes of the deceased Marcus Pelorus, is well known as an honorable man. And, following events of the night of this last *ides* past, Gaius Verres, that noble Roman, took pity on the lady Successa, so badly wounded in the fray at the House of Pelorus, and made promise to her that he would provide a stipend of five hundred denarii for years remaining. This agreement so notarized in the records of the Neapolis magistracy, and impossible to deny. And what must you do to earn this impressive honorarium, lady Successa?"

"Nothing, Cicero," she replied.

"Nothing!" Cicero laughed. "And so it please the magistrate, 'nothing' is precisely what it says upon their contract. But I am lover of words and puns and poetries, and I must say that the meaning is ambiguous. It might be taken to mean that you need do '*no thing*' in order to receive the charity of the good-natured Verres. Or, it might mean that your silence has been purchased, and that the coin is yours so long as you say and do '*no thing*' regarding the aforesaid Gaius Verres."

"Sophistry!" Verres shouted. "You will be claiming next that black is white."

"Gaius Verres has been most kind to me," Successa protested. "I had no complaint against him."

"I am sure you did not," Cicero said. "Not until this last night past, when sicarii ambushed you in your home and sought to send you to the afterlife."

"And I am responsible for this, too?" Verres cried raising his arms in supplication to the ceiling above and the gods beyond. "Why not lay blame at my door for earthquakes and storms?"

Cicero ignored him, and continued in his questioning.

"Lady Successa, with bonds of silence dissolved, speak of events passed on the *ides* of September. How did you find yourself so injured?"

"Precious time wasted on worthless words," Verres said.

"If it pleases the magistrate," Cicero said. "The slave Medea was wild beast, in locked cell, from which she was somehow set free to bring destruction upon House Pelorus. The slave Medea, as her later actions in the arena have demonstrated with ample clarity to all, is a living weapon, capable of infecting great harm upon her victims. Whoever unleashed her on that night is as culpable in the death of Pelorus as falconer who looses bird, or hunter who frees hounds. Lady Successa, I implore you, who set Medea free that night?"

"It was Gaius Verres," she said.

"Open eyes and see stipend's end," Verres spat.

"A thing never seen recieved," she snarled at him, suddenly roused. "Nor would it buy me much in the afterlife!"

"Enough!" Helva declared, banging his hands on the arms of his chair. "Enough!"

"Magistrate, I implore you—" Verres began.

"Magistrate, I am yet unfinished—" Cicero began.

"Silence, I beg you!" Helva said. "This matter full of thorns, and attended by many deliberations, twists and turns. However, representatives for both sides have identified a means through whispered threats and honeyed promises. In the matter of Batiatus versus Verres, I find reasonable doubt in the assignation of rights familiae emptor to the aforesaid Verres. Perhaps Verres misheard his friend's last words; perhaps he misinterpreted them."

Batiatus made to stand in protest, but Cicero stayed his arm, a finger raised in a weak parody of the gladiator's gesture of surrender. Batiatus saw the signal and read it for what it was—a sign that they would have to concede some ground.

"However, I can have no doubt that the intentions of the pious Verres were wholly honorable," the magistrate continued. "In treatment of the injured lady Successa, he has displayed a noble quality in the dispensation of charity. In his attempt to do right by the freedman Timarchides, he has shown great kindness."

Verres permitted himself a sly half-smile.

Batiatus stared at Cicero, his nostrils flared in anger.

"Do you misremember whose side you represent?" Batiatus hissed to the quaestor. "This fool has ignored every one of your words."

"Patience, Batiatus," Cicero whispered out of the side of his mouth.

"In the matter of the accusations leveled against him," the magistrate stated, "I remind the plaintiff that Verres became the governor of Sicilia at midnight on the night of the event in question, and that henceforth, even if Cicero were to pursue his insinuations of wrongdoing, the person of Gaius Verres is sacrosanct, protected and above reproach."

Verres smiled at Batiatus, the smile widening into a grin fit to contain the world.

"In the matter of the estate of the late Marcus Pelorus, I shall retire to deliberate on its best dispensation. It may take some days, considering the light of these crimes peripheral, now entered into the record."

"If I may speed the process, magistrate?" Verres asked.

The magistrate shrugged and gestured for him to continue.

"Since my duties are not required in the role of familiae emptor, I have no matters to address in it. May I suggest that I withdraw all opposition to the suit of Batiatus, and depart as friend."

Timarchides leapt to his feet in surprise, grabbing at Verres's toga.

"You said that purse was mine!"

Verres held out his arms in conciliation.

"Timarchides, please!" he said. "The magistrate has spoken. We must abide by Roman law or we are no better than barbarians."

"But—"

"What purse?" Helva asked, indicating the pile of scrolls. He held one up for them to see. "You will see from the accounts that the estate of Pelorus is already well discharged, almost into nothingness."

XVII

POSTERITAS

"DO I DREAM," BATIATUS SAID, STANDING ON THE STEPS OF THE forum, "or did we just get bent over and fucked?"

"I have no idea of your dreams, Batiatus," Cicero said, his eyes set ahead. The two men sighed in unison on the steps, and began to dawdle toward the street level. Varro walked behind, ever watchful.

"The magistrate made no note of our evidence," Batiatus protested. "Rather keeping up the nonsense of the 'last words'!"

"The magistrate showed himself to be a masterful diplomat," Cicero replied. "Governors are not truly sacrosanct, but it is beneficial for the smooth running of the state if we assume that they are. Absent a truly monstrous cause, it is better to remove all talk of crime. The magistrate allowed each man to depart unsullied by accusation."

"But I want Verres fucking *sullied*! I want him up to his neck in shit! He walks away with head held high."

"But absent control of the Pelorus estate."

Something was moving to the side of the two men, something oncoming with the speed of a charging gladiator, something in bright white edged with Greek borders. Batiatus turned to see, and found Varro bodily holding back the angry Timarchides.

"You will pay for this, Cicero," the freedman snarled.

"Will I?"

"You steal from me. You rob the grave of a great man."

Timarchides hurled Varro to one side, leaving the blond gladiator reeling in the dirt. But the slave had served his purpose, calming the angry Greek just enough to prevent him coming to blows with a noble Roman. Instead, Cicero faced no more than a pointing finger and a torrent of abuse.

"I merely made investigation into a suspicious abuse of power," Cicero said calmly, when Timarchides eventually paused for breath.

"Listen well, Timarchides," Batiatus crowed, "You and Verres have reached agreement's end, your sullied fingers remain empty as will Pelorus's house when next you seek shelter!"

"I am disinherited!" Timarchides growled. "Left with nothing!"

"From nothing left nothing!" Batiatus replied. "Returned to the heavy work of arm twisting, save now for Verres in Sicilia."

"Pelorus would not have desired this."

"I grow weary of this ludicrous performance," Cicero said, suddenly impatient. "Pelorus did not *want* to die."

Timarchides stood, fists clenched, before them breathing heavily for lack of words and direction. Varro clambered back to his feet, rendering the odds once more against the Greek. Batiatus stared directly into

Timarchides's angry eyes for a moment, before walking away with a dismissive wave of his hand.

"Might I suggest," Cicero said, "that the freedman Timarchides composes a will forthwith. If you were to die intestate, in the fashion of your former master, then your property would revert to Pelorus, who reverts to Batiatus, and you would end up leaving everything to the man you so despise."

"Enough of such legal knots," Timarchides spat. "I depart for Sicilia, and curse you all."

"Knots of your own making. Matters would be eased if you but had a son."

"Then I shall go out and sire one tonight!"

"A difficult task when men lay with men." Cicero called after Timarchides's retreating back. He sighed with the effort of a day's work well done, and sauntered after Batiatus, who slowed his pace now that the danger of physical assault was past.

"Cicero, I stand amazed," the lanista said.

"Do not be," Cicero said, oddly sour. "There is no victory to be celebrated here."

"On the contrary, you have executed every action exact."

"I have done nothing. It is a disaster."

"You make reference to the business of Verres being governor? An inconvenient 'window,' to be sure."

"The means by which he could be held accountable destroyed, and if he is not accountable then he is removed entirely from deliberations. He disappears. As if Verres was never here."

"Which means?"

"Which means that Pelorus died by means unknown in a slave attack. Absent will, which means everything lands upon you."

"My meaning exact! The slaves are dead and purse empty, but the villa is mine!"

Batiatus puffed out his chest and looked around him at the bustle of Neapolis, wondering what to buy first. He hailed a vendor with a pole draped with wineskins.

"Not so, Batiatus," Cicero said glumly, as the lanista handed over coins. "I possess knowledge enough of legal mind to know where thought alights."

Batiatus offered him a swig from his celebratory wineskin, but Cicero pushed it away.

"Tell me," Batiatus said, wiping a red smear of wine across his cheek, "why the result disappoints."

Cicero backed into the shade, narrowly evading a cart drawn by two horses. He stared after the retreating vehicle, watching as its driver skillfully negotiated its passage through the next junction, and on to the road out of town.

"Look upon that horse, Batiatus. If horse breaks free and charges through street, with whom does the responsibility rest?"

"What is your meaning?" Batiatus asked.

"Is fault with horse?"

"Of course not."

"And if horse ends life of passing woman and grieving husband seeks redress. Can he seek it from horse?" Cicero asked.

"You expect apology from a horse?"

"That is not possible, you are right," Cicero said. "So would you stone the horse to death?"

Though tasked with remaining silent, Varro could not resist a chuckle.

"That is ludicrous," Batiatus replied. "You cannot lay blame with dumb animal."

"Then who bears burden of responsibility?"

"The owner of course!"

"And what if criminal is not animal, but slave?"

"He will be killed. In the same manner as the slaves at the House of Pelorus."

"Ah," Cicero said. "That is *their* punishment, but what of damages they did to others?"

Batiatus had been midway through another long gulp of wine. Instead, it somehow caught in his throat, causing him to spit and splutter a pink mist into the street.

"What?" he coughed. "Your meaning is that liability will rest with me for everything?"

"There will be dispensations to Timarchides, to the musicians, to all the guests that claim some blemish or inconvenience, in atonement for the actions of the slaves *you have just inherited.*"

"It cannot be inheritance if subjects are already in Hades!"

"Oh, but it can. Or rather, their debts are your inheritance! It would surprise me not if the beneficiary of Pelorus's estate received strong encouragement to honor 'noble' Verres's obligations and was forced to pay pension rashly promised to Successa. With lesser stipends for other whores. And band. And citizens present. There will also be liability for bills outstanding to caterers and vintners."

"Payment for banquet never attended?"

"Worse than that. Much worse."

"What could be *worse*?"

"I must remind you of the funeral games."

Batiatus clutched at his chest in fright.

"The fucking funeral games! You mean that is mine to pay as well? I owe coin for fucking dead rabbits?"

"The bill was surely charged to the estate of Marcus Pelorus, and as his sole heir…"

"JUPITER'S COCK!"

"Look well at your new villa in Neapolis, Batiatus. Soon obligation will come to dispose of it to honor new-found debts."

"Gentlemen, gentlemen!" Verres called. He stopped in front of them in a litter born by four glowering men in dark robes, two of whom did not seem quite fit to be porters—a boy who seemed too young, and a man who seemed too old. Varro found himself staring at the lead bearer, confused with a sense of familiarity. The old man nodded back, as if in recognition.

"Charon…" Varro breathed.

Timarchides sat by the side of Verres in the litter, staring straight ahead.

"I take my leave of you!" Verres said cheerfully. "I sail for Sicilia. Well played, Cicero. Well played, as in our nocturnal debates. The victory is yours, but the spoils are inconsequential."

"That is your game, is it not, Verres?" Batiatus snarled. "*Everyone* your slave. You rape estates. You plunder provinces. You seek the chase. You burn the bridge you crossed. You kick away ladder by which you ascended."

"You will not be governor of Sicilia forever, Verres," Cicero said. "I will be there to witness you fall."

"And I, you," Verres said, the smile still pasted on. "When time comes Cicero, you will run like frightened deer."

"I hope very much to die of old age in my bed."

"Our lives are lived in troubled times, and enemies flock to you like flies to honey," Verres said, pointedly.

"The price of seeking truth, I fear," Cicero said. "But I

know nothing of the way of the warrior. If chased by man with sword in hand, I shall certainly seek to avoid him. This is not cowardice, but sense."

"But if he catches you, Cicero. What then?"

"Further debate?" Batiatus muttered. "Another argument, even as he sticks his cock in ass. Leave hold, Cicero, absent cause!"

"If your hypothetical pursuer catches me with his notional sword," Cicero was saying, "and I theoretically have nowhere left to run?"

"If then," Verres said, with a nod.

"Then I shall put into practice lessons learned from gladiators. And I shall extend neck to assailant, dying like a Roman, unafraid of the afterlife."

Verres laughed, and motioned for his bearers to continue on their path. His litter wove through the people and soon passed from sight.

"Dominus!" called a voice. "Dominus!" In a market street full of masters, none paid it heed.

Batiatus offered the wineskin to Cicero, but again the quaestor refused, deep in thought.

"BATIATUS!" shouted the voice, finally gaining the correct dominus's attention.

Spartacus arrived, panting, manacled by his left arm to Medea.

"What comedia is this?" Batiatus demanded. "Are ears blocked that I find you not standing guard at the house of Pelorus!"

"Your will, dominus," Spartacus panted. "But doing so uncovered vital news."

Cicero looked up.

"More vital than that of a slave that deserts his post and runs through the street chained to a murderess?" he said. "My ears are pricked and ready to hear such news."

"The sicarii last night," Spartacus said, "were men of the House of Pelorus."

"How do you know?" Batiatus questioned.

"They all bore his mark."

"But they are all dead."

"Not all."

"They were the undertakers," Varro said, suddenly.

"Hold tongue, Varro," Batiatus snapped. "Spartacus, give explanation. How can the men of Pelorus be yet alive? I witnessed their end in the arena."

"Some," Spartacus said. "The cells are vast. Did they only contain a small number of gladiators on that night? For that was all that died in the arena."

"They took upon themselves the garb of the undertakers," Varro insisted. "And the clowns. They were the cleaners of the arena. Before our eyes unseen—"

"Varro, be silent... Oh..." Batiatus said.

"Even at the games, I heard the damnati protest that not all their brother gladiators were present," Spartacus said. "Timarchides laughed off accusation, but what if he tried to save those most beloved?"

"The slave speaks sense," Cicero said. "And it is a scheme worthy of Timarchides, to preserve lives of those fellows of his ludus whom he yet called friends. To kill undertakers, absent witness, and place favored slaves of Pelorus in their stead. They burned evidence and partly melted swords that did the deed, and used undertakers' mansion as refuge."

"They leave no evidence," Spartacus said, "save the bodies of the dead, who cannot testify."

"And swords lying in ashes," Varro added, "with ludus mark melted."

"Yet they marched in procession funereal!" Batiatus sputtered. "With fucking balls forged of iron!"

"Masked and long-sleeved to conceal their brands!" Spartacus agreed. "His favored gladiators mourned him, and some of their number yet work for Timarchides and Verres, as knife-men and bearers. And now the survivors journey to Sicilia, where they will doubtless toil in the entourage of its new governor."

"Spartacus, Varro," Batiatus said, "stop them before they reach harbor."

"We need but one," Cicero insisted. "Apprehend but one living slave that bears mark of Pelorus, and Verres is undone."

"Are you sure it is charge 'monstrous' enough to warrant case against a governor?" Batiatus asked.

"As sure as I can be," Cicero said, equivocating as a quaestor must.

"Halt them!" Batiatus shouted.

"Dominus!" Varro said in assent, immediately taking off at a run through the crowd.

"Dominus!" Spartacus said, moving to follow him, Medea at his side.

"Leave the witch!" Batiatus said in annoyance.

"I cannot, dominus," Spartacus said, raising his chained left hand. Slaved to his actions, Medea was forced to raise her right. "I left key to our chains at the house, that her escape could not be engineered."

"Then take her with you. It is so fated."

Batiatus shook his head as the three figures darted through the crowd after the litter, the towering Varro yet visible, Spartacus and the chained Medea soon hidden.

"A diligent slave, that Spartacus," Cicero commented. "To rush to your side with such immediate purpose."

"Merely being true to his obligations—to see to the best interests of his master!"

"And what price does he exact for such interference?"

"A very simple coin. A woman."

"Any woman?"

"Not any woman. His wife. Sold into slavery. To be returned to him on my word."

"How will you find her?"

"I asked fellow lanistae to bear watch in slave markets for Syrian merchant, selling seer-women from Thrace and its environs."

"Oh, did you…?"

Batiatus bit on his own knuckle in shock.

"Diana's crack! Pelorus bought the Getae witch *because* of me!"

"Because of Spartacus. It all comes back to him."

"Spartacus does not spin the wheels of fate," Batiatus scoffed.

"Oh, but he does. Medea would never have entered the House of Pelorus if she were not caught in net you cast for the Thracian's worthless wife. In your own fashion, you and Spartacus are as much to blame for Pelorus's death as the witch herself."

"Absent any other culprit. Although the gods be thanked there are many."

"Are there? Was it not Spartacus who came to her rescue? And was it not he who revealed to you that Pelorus died with throat slit, and hence precipitated your legal suit?"

"…Spartacus…"

"He controls actions as if you were puppet. Your actions give indication you are master of your destiny, but every element of your mounting misfortune has been at his instigation."

"He is the Champion of Capua, the bringer of rain! We have an understanding. We have a bargain."

"Then you had better keep your side of it. Spartacus is yet loyal servant. I would hate to see how such an iron will would cleave to vengeance."

But Batiatus was lost in thought, listening not to Cicero, but instead gazing at the iron railings that descended from where they were standing, lining a long stone staircase that plummeted for several streets into the distance.

"We may yet meet them at the harbor," Batiatus said suddenly.

"What?"

"The litter must take winding road that slopes toward sea. But we, Cicero, *we* may take the steps that lead direct."

"Lead on, Batiatus. Lead on!"

"I did not know," Timarchides muttered sourly, "that so little of the ludus remained. These four slaves that bear us to the harbor are all that we could salvage."

"Come now, Timarchides," Verres said, toying idly with the curtain of the litter. "You have your freedom. Pelorus had his funeral games. The estate has been run into the ground, but our purposes here in Neapolis are achieved."

"*Your* purposes."

"Yours, too. Sicilia is not prize command. It does not have prospect of triumph presented by military consulship in the east. Nor does it have old-world allure of Greece, or frontier excitements of Gaul or Hispania. But what it possesses in abundance is vast, simmering volcano of slaves, many of whom learned stories of rebellion and atrocity at their mother's knee."

"A dangerous posting."

"For the wrong man, it would be. But you are seated next to the man who is right for such a job, and you shall be my right hand. We shall tolerate no suggestion of revolt. We shall be merciless on slaves, and merciless on masters who do not adequately manage such beasts that reside beneath their roofs."

The litter swung about as the bearers negotiated a hairpin turn, the street turning back on itself as it descended toward the harbor.

"You will force masters to take blame for slaves' rebellions?" Timarchides asked.

"Are not owners responsible for their animals? There shall be fines. Confiscations. Inspections. Under governorship of Gaius Verres, slaves will be kept in their rightful places, or *owners* will suffer consequences."

"I have been slow to realization. A price must be paid."

"Most certainly."

"A price paid, no doubt, into the coffers of Gaius Verres."

"Fines and forfeits, tithes and taxes. To both our fiscal posterities."

"We must reach Sicilia first," Timarchides cautioned, looking behind him. He gestured, causing Verres to twist in his cushions and follow the direction of Timarchides's pointing finger.

"What is it?"

"Varro, blond Roman slave of Batiatus. He follows us. His face set to purpose."

"Deal with him."

"Deal with him yourself."

"Bearers, speed your pace!" Verres called, tapping on the curtain supports for emphasis. The porters increased their march, and the litter began to sway as if on troubled seas.

"I say to you, Timarchides: get out at the next turning," Verres said, "and *deal* with the slave."

"And I say to you: fight your battles with your own hand."

"You are free, Timarchides, but you are not a tyrant of your own dominion. You still have superiors."

"Meaning youself?"

"Of course, *meaning me*! You serve at the pleasure of the Governor of Sicilia. And it pleases me that you will put an end to Varro's pursuit. Now!"

"Wait," Medea said, suddenly ceasing her steps, and dragging Spartacus to a halt.

"Follow me," he said pulling her forward.

"Why?" she asked.

"Because I must catch them."

"Why?"

"Medea, there is not time for this."

"I have time entire to stay here and breathe sea air."

"Medea!"

"You seek to apprehend slaves. Slaves who will die if caught. I will not aid you in that enterprise."

"I seek to apprehend slaves who will bring down Gaius Verres. A Roman governor."

"Now," she said with a delighted smile, "now, you secure my assistance. Run!"

She sprinted on with such speed that Spartacus first had to struggle to keep up, her chain stretching taut behind her, all but dragging his arm.

Suddenly, it was Spartacus who stopped and Medea to

be jerked to a standstill by their mutual manacles.

"Spartacus!" she shouted. "The chance awaits to wound a true Roman. Do you not appreciate the scale of this undertaking?"

"Scaling is my thought," he said briskly, pointing to another of the several stairways that descended toward the harbor. "These run perpendicular to the road that the litter must take. We can dart ahead, as if spurred by Mercury himself."

"Then why do we tarry? Down the steps! Move!"

Varro quickened his pace as he approached the turn in the street, ducking and swerving between merchants and vendors, sliding deftly around chatting ladies in demure veils. And then a man who sidestepped at the same time as he.

Varro darted to the left, but so did the man in front of him.

"Who do you seek?" Timarchides asked, throwing back his hood.

Varro glanced past the Greek's shoulder, seeing the litter receding through the crowd. He made to shove Timarchides aside, but the burly Greek grabbed his hand.

"You miss my touch, Varro? Is that it?"

Varro bellowed with anger, and punched with his free hand, a blow that Timarchides easily dodged. The freedman twisted and turned so that he dragged Varro's right arm with him, throwing the Roman over his shoulder and hard to the ground. But Varro grasped at his tormentor, tugging down on his tunic, and planting his foot in Timarchides's stomach as he fell, propelling the freedman in a somersault over his head and hard into a stack of earthenware jars.

A crowd began to gather, calling and jeering at the fighting men.

Teeth gritted against the pain of a dozen jagged cuts, Timarchides threw himself at Varro. But the gladiator rolled deftly out of the way, and snatched up a meat cleaver from a butcher's table. He advanced toward Timarchides, swishing the iron blade experimentally.

"Think on what you are doing, Varro," Timarchides said, backing away as the crowd gave the men wide berth.

"I have thought on it long and hard," Varro said, luxuriating in the weight of the cleaver. He grabbed Timarchides by the neck, raising the cleaver high above his head in victory.

"I am a free man," Timarchides choked as Varro pulled his head back. "And you, a slave. Take my life, and you take your own as surely as if you had slit your own throat."

Varro hesitated, only for an instant, before a wooden club descended upon his head. His vision exploded in a cloud of pinpricks of light, whirls of darkness encroaching from the edges of his sight, the sharp pain registering only briefly, as unconsciousness came over him, and he slumped to the ground.

"Gratitude," Timarchides said to the butcher who had struck the blow.

"No slave shall strike a freeman," the butcher said, holding out his arm, partly in a gesture of camaraderie, but also with the palm upturned, in hope of reward. But Timarchides had already turned, running for the next set of stone steps toward the harbor, leaving Varro at the feet of an inquisitive crowd.

Varro moaned, softly, stirring from his sudden slumber. He made to get up, but slumped once more, weary beyond words.

The bearers were sweating hard now, their feet stumbling as they tried to keep up the pace. The Sardinian boy at the back was dragging his feet. The old man at the front was flagging, causing the litter to lean dangerously along the axis.

Verres frowned with irritation, and prepared to rebuke them, only for something to come charging out of nowhere, speeding from a staircase between two houses, straight into the side of the litter.

The litter pitched to the side and then crashed to the ground, upending Verres and his cushions.

"Fools!" he shouted, clambering to his feet. But as his head poked through the curtains, he saw the agents of his demise, Spartacus and the Getae witch, chained together by manacles at their wrists, and already locked in combat with the bearers.

Verres gazed momentarily on the scene, and then caught sight of Timarchides dashing into the street a block further up at the next set of steps.

"To the harbor, Timarchides!" he shouted. "We sail with tide, with all who reach docks in time." With that, Verres darted for the alleyway between two houses that concealed the next staircase toward the harbor, the masts of the ships already looming above the rooftops nearby, the cry of gulls already rising above the voices of the streets.

Spartacus and Medea faced four, all bearing knives. As one, he and Medea snatched up broken pieces of the carrying poles, now readied as makeshift clubs.

The first bearer lunged at Spartacus. The gladiator dodged instinctively, unwittingly dragging Medea into the blade's path. She batted it away with her own club, smacking down on the man's arm and causing him to drop the knife. Spartacus punched the surprised attacker in the face, but was forced to duck beneath an attack from a second assailant.

Medea snatched up the knife with her left hand, sweeping it up and into the chin of the man who had dropped it, driving its blade through his mouth and into his skull. He tried to scream, but the deluge of blood already choked his throat, causing him instead to cough bright red liquid over the chained fighters. Medea kicked him away, twisting his ruined face from the knife, and leaving him on the ground to die.

Three yet remained, the brands of the House of Pelorus visible on their arms.

"You are betrayed!" Spartacus cried. "Your masters desert you. Surrender and see them brought to justice."

"Justice already awaits us," the older man said, whom Varro had called Charon. "Execution is our fate."

He lunged at Spartacus with the knife. Spartacus leapt backward, dragging an unwilling Medea with him.

"Run!" the old man shouted at the other two.

"But, doctore…" the boy said.

"Run!"

They hesitated long enough for Medea to stab at one, tearing a gaping wound through his ribs to a ruined heart. The man tumbled to the ground, grunting in final agony, leaving but the old man and the boy.

The old man threw himself at Spartacus and Medea, barging them to the ground amid the wreckage of the litter.

The boy saw his chance and fled, pelting down the

steps as Spartacus and Medea flailed in the dust. The old man punched and kicked with fierce precision, seemingly knowing all the points where nerves stood close to skin, or muscle gave way to bone.

Medea howled in pain as one well-placed jab found her shin. She rolled away, but was halted by the chain that bound her to Spartacus.

The old man struggled to his feet, only to be tripped by the chain itself as Spartacus and Medea tugged it round his ankles. He landed badly, close to a fallen knife.

"Wait!" Spartacus said. "Do not!"

But the old man drove the dagger deep into his own throat, and crumpled before them, his blood pooling and swelling in puddles, reaching over the edge of the topmost step, and beginning a slow, viscous cascade toward the harbor.

"The boy yet remains!" Medea said.

Spartacus waited not a moment, deserting the still-twitching corpse of the man who once played Charon, and dragging Medea down the last set of steps that terminated in the harbor itself, amid a thrumming bustle of sailors and merchants, whores and slaves.

Spartacus and Medea charged with locked steps, their paces matched as if a single man of twice their weight pounded along the dockside jetty. Their arms pumped in unison, unencumbered by the chains that truly bound them, and steadily, achingly, they began to draw near to the fleeing Sardinian boy.

He leapt over boxes on the jetty. He darted past sailors at their tasks. But then, he tripped.

His flight was halted for mere moments, but it was long enough for his twinned pursuers to reach him.

Spartacus grabbed at the boy, bringing all three of

them down hard onto the wood with the thump of bodies and the rattle of chains. The boy twisted and wriggled, straining against Spartacus's firm hold, his free hand reaching for his fallen knife.

"Let me go," the boy pleaded, "and I shall live free. Hold on to me, and I shall be broken in pursuit of futile truth."

Spartacus looked into the boy's eyes, and saw for the briefest instant what some slaver might have once seen in the eyes of a forgotten Thracian—a plea poised on the brink between chains and liberty, a moment when a man might yet be free, if only he could make one final sprint for sanctuary.

"I have my orders," Spartacus said, with reluctance.

"If you are victorious," the boy said, "then I will die, merely for being present in the house of a murdered master. That is all you will achieve."

Spartacus let his grip slacken, suddenly prepared to disobey Batiatus in the pursuit of a greater victory.

It was then that the boy struck out with his knife.

Medea had time for but a single syllable of denial, grabbing at the knife with her own hand. It tore through the soft webbing of her fingers, and cut deep into the flesh of her palm. Even as she screamed, the boy's knife descended again, rending a deep, savage gash across her chest and into her abdomen.

Spartacus clutched at her, failing to staunch the flow of blood, as the Sardinian boy pelted away from them, sprinting like a deer for the jetty and the departing ship.

Medea clutched at the gaping wound, her mouth quivering in involuntary shivers.

"At last," she said, forcing a smile, "I have my desire, and died to a purpose: preserving you."

"We shall find a medicus," Spartacus said desperately,

looking in anguish at the thick river of blood pouring from her, soaking him and the wooden slats of the jetty, dripping in long streams into the waters below.

"It is too late," she said. "Do not lie to me now, Thracian, after we have been so true. The enemy of my enemy is my friend," she wheezed, her hand reaching out to rest on his cheek.

"A... medicus..." Spartacus repeated, his words catching in his throat, as he looked about him and saw no chance of aid.

"Do not concern yourself with Verres and Timarchides," she said, with a smile that belied the pain. "They will come to no good end."

"How do you know?"

"I see posterities, Thracian," she coughed. "Do you not yet believe me?"

"Apologies."

"And I see yours, Thracian. Such wonders lie before you."

"My wife? Do you see my wife?"

"Your Sura? Your beloved Sura? Yes, Thracian, I see her. I see you reunited, but..." She coughed again, black blood erupting from her mouth and running down her cheek. "Apologies."

Spartacus had held dying warriors before. He felt the twitching in her body that spelled the end, as internal organs gave up their unity and each began to fight in solitary panic.

"I see my forests," she breathed. "Forests in snow at sunset..."

"Apologies," he said to her. "I should have protected you."

"You did," she said. "I had but one message."

"Did the bitch say *message*?" Batiatus demanded, stumbling along the dockside toward them. "Did she say message?"

"Batiatus?" Medea wheezed. "Your name will be known throughout... the Republic... You will be famous... as dominus to... Spartacus..."

"Yes, yes," Batiatus said dismissively, finally reaching the place where they lay. "Tell me not what I want to hear, woman. I will not fall for such tricks. Give me words for Cicero. Give me something for the Books Sibylline!"

"She dies." Spartacus whispered hoarsely.

"And it is costing me a fucking fortune!" Batiatus shouted.

Medea's eyes turned glassy, staring but unseeing. Her voice croaked, as if not her own, choked with errant blood.

"*Unto your beasts of burden*," she choked, "*Thracian manumission*."

"What?" Batiatus said. "What the fuck does that—?"

"*And as a legion hell-bound, violent expedition*."

"Cicero!" Batiatus called. "Come quickly!"

"*Across great Greece's heel and toe, the fires shall spread*."

Cicero began to run across the docks, a flurry of linen as his toga bloomed outward. He pushed aside porters, leaping ropes and boxes. Spartacus glanced up momentarily to see the quaestor's approach, but kept his eyes on Medea as she struggled to speak her dying words.

"*A final Saturnalia*," she said, "*to seven hills imperiled dread*."

Medea's hand fell, still, causing her chains to rattle to the dirt. Spartacus held her gently, uncaring of the blood that soaked him.

Dockside slaves pushed the ship away from the quay with long gaffes, setting its prow pointed toward the sea, ushering it into deeper water so that its journey could begin.

"The Afer Ventus will blow tomorrow," Verres said frowning. "We will do well to clear port before it, else we must tack far away from Italia, if we are even to creep closer to Silicia."

"I hurry not," Timarchides said. "Though I yet wish I could have witnessed the death of the Getae witch for myself."

"Pelorus is avenged. In this life or the next. Do not trouble yourself with petty grievances."

"Petty?" Timarchides said. "I lied concerning our intimacy, following your suggestion. But he was still trusted friend, and the best of masters."

"Cruel Fortuna caused his death, and that of his gladiators."

"I tried to save them," Timarchides said quietly, almost to himself. "I tried to save as many as I could. Nobody would have missed the undertakers whose place they stole. It could have worked. *Eight* might have lived, had not the sicarii failed. Or even the four that carried us to the harbor. That would have been *something*."

Verres turned back to look at Neapolis and the black mountain that hung above it like a shadow, and caught the sight of a lone figure sprinting down the jetty.

"They were loyal to me," Timarchides said. "They died for me as they might have died in the arena. But voluntarily so."

"Timarchides!" called a boy's voice. "Timarchides!"

"One of the 'dice' yet lives," Verres said, pointing to the approaching figure, blood-stained but whole, darting along the outer harbor wall.

"We should wait for him!"

"And miss wind and tide? They wait for no man."

The lone surviving slave of the House of Pelorus, seeing the ship receding, hurled off his clothes as he ran toward the sea. Wearing nothing but a loincloth, he cast aside his knife and plunged into the water, swimming after the ship in a powerful crawl.

"Fortuna smiles," Timarchides noted. "It is the Sardinian boy!"

"A strong swimmer, then," Verres noted, as the boy drew closer. His arms began to flag, but he was almost upon the ship, his hands reaching up, flailing for a rope to grab.

"What news of the others?" Verres called to the boy.

"Dead, dominus, all dead," came the reply from amid the waves.

"You are all that survives?"

"I am," the boy answered, returning to his diligent, steady crawl through the water, edging ever closer.

Verres looked dolefully at Timarchides.

"He is the last," Verres said. "He is the last survivor that may yet, on some future day, relate truth of our machinations to a quaestor in hope of mercy or manumission. He is the last of the House of Pelorus that might reveal the depths of your deception, and consign you once more to the slavery whence you came. What would you do?"

Timarchides stared at Verres for a moment, and then snatched up a rope, throwing one end into the water. He hung tightly onto the hawser as the boy clambered up, gasping with the effort, his lungs heaving with great exertion.

"You did well," Timarchides said, as the boy reached the gunwhales.

The Sardinian boy smiled, panting, with relief and elation.

Then Timarchides snatched up a knife, and slashed the boy slave's throat in one sweeping deadly movement. A wounded, pleading look came into the boy's eyes as he tumbled from the ship, splashing red into the waters of the bay of Neapolis.

Timarchides watched the body as it floated face-down, a branded "P" on its right forearm, matching the faded one that yet persisted on his own. The ship began to leave it behind, sailing ever farther out to sea, leaving the body where it fell, drifting on the waters.

Verres laid a conciliatory hand on the freedman's shoulder.

"Death comes to us all, Timarchides, but not freedom. Think on that as we sail to Sicilia."

Timarchides shook off his hand, and stared at the churning waters of a bruised sea.

"The story of Rome is the story of us," Verres said. "Of you and me. The story is of the freemen of Rome. There is no space for slaves. They are invisible. No one has care for thoughts of a slave. His hopes. His dreams. His desires. No more worthy of our consideration than the dreams of an insect. You are free. Be free."

As the ship's prow turned to face the harbor mouth, her sails filled with a strong breeze, propelling the ship forward, firstly at a crawl, and then with the increasing wash of broken waves against the hull.

XVIII

RECONCILIATUM

HE LAY ON THE FIRM WOODEN TABLE, AS HE HAD LAIN FOR days, his chest barely moving in halting breaths. The early signs of a beard poked through the clammy skin of his face. His hair, usually cropped close like a Roman warrior, had begun to grow out toward its original Gaulish mane. His eyes stared ahead, at the ceiling, unseeing. His hands were folded gently on his stomach, pressing on the sodden bandages, sticky with blood and pus.

When the door opened, he made no sign of noticing it. He stayed on the table, almost as still as Pelorus had been on the bier.

The footsteps that approached were light, dainty, unaccompanied by the clack of hobnails or the slap of hardened sole leather. They were the steps of feet shod in mouseskin or deerskin, supporting a frame far lighter than the average inmate of the ludus. The newly arrived figure halted, its passage marked by the continued waft of draping silken sleeves, and the unmistakeable scent of Egyptian musks.

"Crixus," she said.

On the table, his lips twitched. His eyes showed no emotion or reaction, but his mouth moved the tiniest degree.

"Crixus," she whispered.

There was no further movement from him, save the faintest sigh in the slowly moving chest.

"The medicus will return presently. I do not have long."

She rested her hand on his shoulder, thought better of it, and returned with a damp cloth, dabbing fitfully at the grime on his torso.

"It gladdens my heart to see that you yet live."

There was another shudder, but still no reaction from his eyes. She waved her hand experimentally in front of his face, but got nothing save the faintest touch of his labored breath.

"The gods will see you well," she said.

The door opened.

"Domina!" the medicus exclaimed.

"Medicus," she said half-laughing, half-gasping. "I only thought to—"

"It does you credit that you take such eager interest in your chattels!" the medicus said, oblivious.

Lucretia drew herself to her full height, the cloth forgotten, her softened features hardening into a businesslike demeanour.

"Crixus is valuable investment," she said, coldly. "If he cannot fight again, the House of Batiatus will have lost substantial sum."

"Further calculated by your presence here," the medicus said, "following long journey from Neapolis."

"Calculations made greater with the cost of your life if Crixus falls," Lucretia spat.

And with that she was gone.

On the table, the still form of Crixus seemed to twitch in his open-eyed sleep.

"I only hope," the medicus said, "the gods watch over you as closely as your mistress." He lifted the bandage on the stomach, wincing at the sight of the festering wound.

"Ashur," Varro called. "Ashur!"

The nervy Syrian ducked into an alcove in fear, peering behind him to determine the identity of the man that sought him.

"Cease tongue," he hissed. "Barca seeks me out, eager for winnings from the last game in Capua."

"I care not," Varro said. "I seek you, too, not to take coin but to give it."

"To what end?" Ashur said, straightening himself and dusting off his robe.

"I seek the company of a woman," Varro said. "The finest woman you can in the flesh markets, and bring her to the ludus for my enjoyment."

"I shall see it done," Ashur said. "And welcome the opportunity to be absent the ludus a few moments longer."

He made as if to leave, only for Varro to stay his hand.

"And Ashur," Varro said, "make her a Greek."

"I have kept them well," Pietros said.

"So I see," Barca said, gently caressing the head of a white bird. He placed it back into its cage and securely fastened the door.

"And you, have you kept well?" Pietros said scowling, his gaze fixed on Barca's bandage.

"It is but scratch," Barca said with a shrug.

Pietros flung himself into Barca's arms, his head nestling against the gladiator's chest.

"I had a dream while you were away."

"A dream is a dream, gone by morning."

"I saw you gutted and still, lying in water, your blood seeped away. I feared that I would never see you again."

"I am here, Pietros. Safely returned."

"I gave Naevia coin for offering. To hasten your safe return."

"Mercury is no god of mine," Barca said gruffly.

"He is the god of all travelers, whether they believe in him or not."

Barca tightened his arms around Pietros and stroked the boy's curly hair.

"I, too, had a dream, Pietros," he said. "You were happy. You and I stood as freemen near where Carthage once stood. Rome's new colony close by. We were out in fields, wringing crops from red dust."

"Both of us?"

"Yes. My arena battles having bought freedom for us both. Our toil and sweat turned us into farmers."

"It is a long way from the ludus and the arena."

"It is not a long way," Barca said. "It is but days away. Ashur owes me the balance of the coin I require. We have but another day in chains, but perhaps years of labor."

"But labor as freemen."

"As freemen. Now, is that a better dream?"

"It is."

✦

The rains pelted down, as they had done for days. But Batiatus breathed deeply and smiled.

"The festering odors of Neapolis," he said, "replaced by the land of my fathers."

He looked at Spartacus for acknowledgment, and saw only a Thracian deep in thought.

"Put the fate of the Getae witch from your mind, Spartacus. She died as she wanted, costing a good Roman precious coin. Costing *me* precious coin!"

"I think only of her portents of posterity."

"Pay it no heed. She was a charlatan. A barbarian mumbling of futures yet unseen to earn her keep."

"She offered a future for Rome, to replace that lost in the Capitoline fire."

"Tailored no doubt to her audience, as any good conjuror does. Mention of Thrace purely because you were at her side. Mention of greater Greece simply because that was where we found ourselves, close to the heel and toe of Italia."

"And what kind of legion is 'hell-bound'?"

"Any legion in Neapolis, considering the Vulcan caves of its surroundings."

"A Saturnalia?"

"A *final* Saturnalia! Slaves and masters changing places. What better incitement for an audience in chains to pay to hear more?"

"But she was dying. There was nothing for her to gain."

"Nothing save seeds of discord sown from the afterlife. 'Seven hills' in peril! Indeed! She speaks of the seven hills of Rome knowing that it will affright good citizens as dogs bark at horses. It surprises me, Spartacus, that you dwell on such artifice and contradictions."

"Apologies, dominus."

"Ah, but now I see. She told you something *else*, did she not?"

"She said that I would see my wife again."

"And if that prophecy is to be believed, then you must accord unwarranted credence to her other utterings. Peace, Spartacus, you shall see your wife again because I, Batiatus, have willed it so. Not the Fates. And not a dying savage. Now, prepare yourself. I predict that I shall proclaim you as the Champion of Capua. And *that* is a prophecy that shall surely come to pass."

Sailors called it the Afer Ventus, the wind out of Africa. Sometimes it brought dry dust that stung the throat and clung to the clothes. Sometimes it brought blustery days and clouds that sped across the sky like sheep fleeing Apollo. Sometimes it brought ships.

Household slaves cursed it for the dirt it brought to laundry drying on lines. Sailors from the east welcomed it for the opportunity it offered, even as it grew stormy. Sail past the toe of Italia, into Sicilian waters, and you were sure to meet the Afer Ventus blowing toward the north-east. Even if it rained, even if the waters rose and swelled like Neptune in anger, you could point your ship at the coast of Italia and ride ahead of the storm.

No ships were leaving Neapolis. The storms were too dangerous, the risk too great. One might, if one were religiously inclined, burn incense and make offerings at temples of Neptune and Mercury, but the priests were always disconcertingly vague about the amount required to guarantee safe passage. Better to ride it out in the harbor, or send goods along the soggy land routes.

But some ships still dared to arrive. Some ships, caught at sea as the storms rose, chose to forge on ahead to their destination, heedless of the rain, fearless, or at least apparently fearless, of the danger to life and limb.

This was one such ship. This was the last ship likely to arrive for at least a week. She had been a dot on the horizon, but her sails swiftly grew in size. When they were visible through the pitching waters—and they frequently were not—they bobbed on the horizon, but grew ever closer to the safe haven of Neapolis.

Her sailors drew in her sailcloths. They threw lines to the slave-rowed cutters that towed her in. They steered her to the best of their abilities as the rope-ringed hull thumped noisily against the similarly wrapped dockside. On land and on deck, the sailors heaved on ropes, lashing the ship against the shore, lest Neptune have one final laugh by dashing the vessel against the land.

She was safe. She had reached a sanctuary harbor. She was almost on Italian soil.

They began unloading their cargoes. Syrian silks and Greek wines, Egyptian incense and perfumes, olive oil and crocodile skins. The scribes tallied the manifest, making marks on their wax boards, so that the harbormaster knew the correct tariffs.

The unloading was slow. But the captain himself soon edged ashore along the gangplank, dragging one other cargo in transit: a woman.

Her hands were chained. Her face was hidden beneath a man's rain cloak, bestowed upon her by some kindly mariner. She was barefoot, her feet etched in patterns by raindrops falling on earlier filth.

The dockside scribe stopped the captain as his feet touched the flagstones of the quay.

"There is no slave on your manifest," the scribe said. "You registered no living cargo."

"This slave is not mine," the captain said. "She is registered as the possession of her receiver."

The scribe frowned, his eyes scanning over his wax tablet.

"I see no record of her."

"She was a late arrival. A trans-shipment taken as a favor. Bound for the House of Pelorus."

"What is her destination now?"

"Absent Pelorus, we must send her on to his heir in Capua. Mark her for the House of Batiatus."

"Her name?"

"Sura."

ACKNOWLEDGMENTS

NEARLY THIRTY YEARS AGO, TED READ WOULD FLY OFF ON WILD tangents about Roman folklore when he was supposed to be teaching a Latin class. He would laugh to see his name here. At Titan Books, Adam Newell noted my enthusiasm for *Spartacus*, and Cath Trechman bought me at the auction block. I was then inspected by Jo Boylett… what a thought. At Starz Entertainment, Allison Miller meticulously knifed anything that did not sound like it came from the show. This book owes much to the cast and crew of *Spartacus: Blood and Sand*—knowingly obscene, carefully vulgar, garishly hued, conscientiously Latinate—who created such a memorable and distinctive look, feel and sound for the show. I heard their voices while I worked, even that one that is now silent. Gratitude.

ABOUT THE AUTHOR

J. M. CLEMENTS IS THE AUTHOR OF OVER THIRTY BOOKS, including *Pirate King*, *Marco Polo* and *A Brief History of the Vikings*. He has also written a dozen audio books and radio plays, including *Robin Hood: The Deer Hunters*, *Highlander: The Secret of the Sword* and *Doctor Who: The Destroyer of Delights*.

SPARTACUS

MORITURI

PAUL KEARNEY

Batiatus and Solonius vie with each other for the favor
of one Marcus Licinius Crassus, a nobleman who aims
at the Praetorship. Grieving for his wife, Spartacus,
the Champion of Capua, shows a fearsome level of
aggression in these combats, taking each bout closer
and closer to a violent death—only Varro stops him
from committing murder.

Thrilled by the bloody violence of the fights, Crassus
decides to set up his own gladiatorial school. He ships
in suitable candidates from all over the Republic, and
so harsh is their training that they become known as the
'Morituri'—those who are about to die.

In the arena, the Batiati are ground down by injury and
death, while the Morituri's numbers never seem to shrink.
Can the ludus survive against such odds?